Abbott's Reach

Abbott's Reach

by Ardeana Hamlin

ISLANDPORT PRESS
YARMOUTH • MAINE

Islandport Press
P.O. Box 10
Yarmouth, Maine 04096
www.islandportpress.com
books@islandportpress.com

First Islandport Press Edition, February 2011

ISBN: 978-1-934031-42-1
Library of Congress Card Number: 2010937802

Book jacket design by Karen F. Hoots / Hoots Design
Book design by Michelle A. Lunt / Islandport Press
Publisher Dean L. Lunt

For my parents,
Ruth Herrick Hamlin and Floyd Hamlin,
who taught me how to speak in stories.

Table of Contents

Prologue
page ix

Part 1
Alongshore
page 1

Part 2
At Sea
page 115

Part 3
Hawaii
page 155

Part 4
At Sea Again
page 217

Part 5
Alongshore Again
page 239

Epilogue
page 277

About the Author
page 281

Prologue

We pass this way but once in the world—or so it is said. But it can be argued that in our wake we leave hints and clues, rumors that define our paths long after we are gone from this Earth. The byways of the past echo with the stories of long ago, seeking hearts open enough to hear them.

Those vibrations haunt the shores of the Penobscot River from Bangor to Searsport, Maine, emanating from names etched on the gravestones in shady cemeteries, contained in the brittle pages of leather-bound diaries, folded into yellowed envelopes addressed in copperplate script, and limned in the graceful architectural details of old houses lining the streets of villages situated along the river.

Stand on the riverbank on a sweet spring day, or when a spell of deep cold has hardened the river to ice. Listen. The voices of the past speak in the rustle of the leaves, the glitter of sun on snow, the breath of the wind.

And so it was with the notorious house in Bangor known as Pink Chimneys and the characters that came to inhabit it. The story began in 1814 in Bangor, when the British invaded the Penobscot region. Maude Richmond, the teenage daughter of Dr. Eli Richmond, feared for her father's safety when he traveled to Hampden, where a battle was to take place against the British. Her father had instructed her to answer any calls for medical help that came in his absence. And when a call came, Maude walked into Bangor to do what was required, little knowing that she would find herself in direct confrontation with the British and the only female around to assist at the birth of a baby.

When she and her father were reunited after the British left, Maude told him that she wanted to follow in his doctoring footsteps. But women were not allowed to study medicine in those days, so Eli arranged for her to apprentice with the midwife Sally Cobb Robinson, who lived across the river in Orrington.

The story shifts to Fort Point in 1832 when Fanny Abbott ran away with a no-good sailor, Robert Snow. Soon, she found herself pregnant and alone in Portland, until she crossed paths with Joshua Stetson, who would become both her savior and her ruin. She also met Maude, now married to Sam Webber. Maude assisted Fanny when she gave birth to a daughter, Elizabeth. And Maude and Fanny, unlikely as it seems, became friends.

Then, the story is carried upriver to Bangor, to the icy rogue Joshua Stetson and the infamous house he had established, Pink Chimneys, where he installed Fanny, now calling herself Fanny Hogan to avoid embarrassment to her family back home, as its mistress. It was at Pink Chimneys that Maude, Fanny, and Elizabeth were caught up in an eddy of incidents that cemented Fanny's friendship with Maude. It was there that Elizabeth's fate was cast to the sea as the wife of Abner Giddings. It was also the place where a new story drew breath—the story of Mercy Maude Giddings, Elizabeth's daughter, known as M, a child conceived in violence.

The events at Pink Chimneys sent out ripples of rumor and invention, of gossip and allegations that reverberated through time, carried on the wind—or, perhaps, by the current of the Penobscot River itself. Those ripples washed ashore on a tiny beach at Fort Point in 1871, where M lived with her grandmother, Fanny, and where Maude often visited—the invisible stuff of which history is composed.

This is their continuing story. This is what happened after Fanny left Pink Chimneys, after Elizabeth went to sea with her husband, after Maude and her husband began to grow old. This is what happened after Fanny returned to Fort Point, her relatives long gone, and opened another house, the respectable boarding-house known as Abbott's Reach.

This is what happened to M as she grew up, fell in love, and went to sea on her wedding voyage.

Part 1
Alongshore

1.

Mercy Maude Giddings pointed her chin resolutely into the wind blowing up the channel of Maine's Penobscot Bay, where it flowed around Verona Island and narrowed to become the river. The breeze pulled her dark auburn hair, free of its pins, away from her fine, freckled face. She held her faded blue cotton skirt out of the water that lapped at her bare toes. She had wrapped an old gray shawl hastily around her shoulders. It was her sister Grace's birthday, and she had come to the water, as she always did on that day, to commune with the past.

The tide was running out fast. Tangled as it was in the hard, swift current of the Penobscot River flowing toward the Atlantic, the water's surface showed crinkles and creases, signs of a treacherous undertow. The action of those currents, river and tide, created the thin spit of sandbar shaped like a ship's anchor where Mercy—always called M—stood looking out across the water.

Behind her, the small, sandy beach sloped gradually upward to a rim of sparse vegetation—apple trees and tall grass interspersed with late-summer asters and goldenrod. Then the land sloped upward more steeply before it leveled off to the grassy expanse where her grandmother's boardinghouse, Abbott's Reach, stood solid and predictable, not far from the ruins of the old fort, built a hundred years ago in the days of the American Revolution.

M had lived with her grandmother in the big, airy house for ten years. She had been eight when her stepfather Abner Giddings's ship, the *Fairmount*, foundered in a tropical storm off Cape Hatteras. Her younger sister, Grace, a child of five, had been lost that terrible day. After that, Abner and her mother, Elizabeth, would not take M with them on their voyages, as had been their habit since M was an infant. They decided M would live with her grandmother, Fanny Abbott.

M knew that her grandmother had once called herself Fanny
Hogan, and had been the mistress of a notorious house in Bangor
known as Pink Chimneys. All that was ancient history, of course,
but sometimes M filled in the details, imagining what her grandmother and her friends, Sam and Maude Webber, had either
glossed over or omitted when they talked about those long-ago
days before the War Between the States. Of course, M had eaves-
dropped and learned a great deal more, and to their credit, whenever she asked questions, they always gave truthful answers.

But on this day—Grace's birthday—M walked on the beach,
eager to give in to an overwhelming urge to stand knee-deep,
thigh-deep, waist-deep in the dark, billowing water. It was in
water that the bones of her sister lay. In the water, she felt close to
Grace, as if the water itself had the power to renew her fading
memories of her sister.

That M had not been aboard the *Fairmount* on that terrible
day in 1860 was purely a matter of fate. She had been recovering
from a fever, so her parents had left her in the care of Maude and
Sam Webber, whom M called Mrs. Maude and Dr. Sam. Abner
and Elizabeth had intended to make a voyage to Baton Rouge
with a cargo of Maine lumber before heading home again with a
load of cotton for Boston—perhaps the last such cargo, for the
war between North and South was imminent. It was on the
return leg of the voyage that they had encountered the tempest.

M remembered how Mrs. Maude and Dr. Sam had told her of
the tragedy with great care and gentleness. Grace had been playing
with her dolls on deck under the awning. Elizabeth had gone
below to fetch a sunbonnet. A fierce wind had bored down on
them suddenly and churned the water until great waves washed
across the deck. Terrified, Grace had attempted to run for the
hatch doorway to safety, but in an instant, a wave had swept her
away. At almost the same moment, the top of a mast let go and a

spar fell, strewing the deck with splinters of wood, shredding a sail and snapping ropes. In the ensuing confusion, no one was able to rescue Grace—even if it had been possible. It was terrible and tragic, but it was no one's fault, though Elizabeth would always blame herself.

The *Fairmount* was repaired at Charleston while M's parents recovered from their shock. Abner wrote that they would not come home; they would continue carrying cargoes up and down the eastern seaboard until Christmas, then come home to stay for several months. Work would help assuage their grief, he said.

M remembered how anxious she had felt, how bereft, how abandoned—how terrified that the sea would take her parents, too. She withdrew into herself more and more, unable to express her grief and her fears. Letters passed back and forth, and it was decided that M would go and stay with her grandmother. Maude Webber felt that the air at Abbott's Reach would be beneficial.

As M walked the beach, thinking about Grace, and her own life with her grandmother, she thought about the times when she, her parents, and sister had spent long weeks visiting at Abbott's Reach. Those had been good times for the most part, but M, always sensitive to unspoken emotion, sometimes sensed an oddly constrained mood, tinged with a sense of loss, of sadness and regret, a mélange of feelings she did not comprehend, emanating from her mother and her grandmother.

When she was sixteen, her grandmother had told her how her mother had been born out of wedlock, and how the roads of life had taken them both to Pink Chimneys in Bangor. Maude added other details to the story, and gradually M came to understand that her mother, Elizabeth, was Fanny's child by a seaman named Snow. She knew that her grandmother's sister, Mercy, at Fort Point, had raised her mother, and that after Mercy's death, Elizabeth had traveled upriver to Bangor aboard a ship commanded by Abner

Giddings. She knew Elizabeth had taken a job as a seamstress at Pink Chimneys, and that her mother had been attacked by a drunken man. As a result, she had given birth to M. She knew that her mother and Abner Giddings had fallen in love and married, giving M a name and two parents, instead of one, to love her.

M knew that many things had been left unsaid—things she was certain no one would ever tell her—not even Mrs. Maude.

On this day, if she could not be on the water in the *Fairmount*, then she would be in the water—like the *Fairmount*, she would be a creature of the waves. For a few moments, until the cold temperature sent M back to shore, her skirts dragging heavy and wet around her legs, the wind chilling her to the bone, she took a perverse kind of pleasure in being as cold as her sister, asleep in her watery grave.

And yet, even as all of these memories rose and fell in her mind, what outshone them all was the overwhelming pulse of her feelings for Madras Mitchell. She smiled as an image of his face surfaced in her mind—his black hair falling onto his brow, his dark eyes looking at her with amusement and tenderness, his big hand clasped around hers.

M glanced toward the house. She knew they were up there watching, peering at her through the spyglass, Mrs. Maude and her grandmother, whom she called Grand Fan. But she did not care. Let them fret. Let them wonder if she was about to have a fit of melancholy. At this moment she only wanted to be alone, immersed in the water of the bay, tossed and blown by the currents of her emotions.

M's Log—August 1871

They think I do not know they are watching, but I see the glint of the spyglass up there on the piazza. Behind it the two old ladies are squinting, taking turns—my grandmother, Mary Frances Abbott (my dear Grand Fan), and her old friend Maude Webber, for whom I am named. Mercy Maude Giddings, that's who I am— daughter of Abner and Elizabeth Giddings, big sister of Grace, who always called me M.

I know why Grand Fan and Mrs. Maude watch me. They think I am having another of the fits of melancholy that have afflicted me ever since my sister was lost at sea. They have watched me closely for years. They do not want me to be sad or lonely. But mostly, they do not want me to go upon the water—and for several years after I came to live at Abbott's Reach, I did not. That's what made me so terribly angry and sad, to become so suddenly a land-lubber. They watch me, those two old women; they watch from the piazza of the house, moving along its length as I move along the sandy beach at low tide, speaking perhaps in their quiet voices of the heat of the day, this long spell without rain. But their eyes always say so much more than their lips.

They are wise in the ways of the world. They believe in the power of women. They have taught me to think for myself.

But now that I can, they wish they hadn't, for I will marry Madras Mitchell no matter what they say.

2.

"We can't stop her, you know," Maude Webber said quietly as she pushed the ends of the spyglass together, collapsing it into a short brass tube. Maude was still spry at seventy-one, her figure still harboring something akin to girlishness, Fanny thought. Maude's hair was white now, pulled back into an untidy knot that slipped its pins and straggled about her ears. She threatened to cut her hair short from time to time, but never followed through, even though Fanny had dared her to do it more than once. Maude wore a brown cotton skirt and plain white blouse with a high collar. She looked well enough if one discounted the uneven hem of her skirt and the lack of ruffles or furbelows on her clothing, details Fanny no longer urged on her after years of having had her fashion advice ignored. Maude had never cared a fig about fashion or the state of her clothing; none of Fanny's hints or suggestions had ever made the slightest impression on her.

"She's nineteen, Fanny—old enough to know her own mind. She's in love with Madras Mitchell," Maude said. Maude had delivered Fanny's daughter, Elizabeth, in Portland, when Maude had practiced midwifery back in the 1830s. She also had been present at M's birth in 1852. She had helped Elizabeth open a dressmaker's shop in Bangor after M was born, before Elizabeth had married Abner Giddings.

In spite of the difference in their ages—Fanny was just fifty-seven—and the fact that they ought not to have anything in common, Fanny and Maude had become lifelong friends.

"What in heaven's name can she know about love?" Fanny demanded, her blue eyes filled with anxiety. "She's a child!" Fanny was still a handsome woman; no gray showed in her abundant auburn hair, the result, Maude suspected, of henna rinses. As usual, Fanny's hair was coiled beautifully atop her head in an intricate lattice of narrow braids and escaping curls. Her dress of fine white cotton lawn was delicately embroidered, the skirt fitting at the hip and flaring into fullness at the knee, elegant enough to put any other woman in the shade. Despite her own indifference to fashion, Maude had always admired Fanny's flair for style.

"She's three years older than you were when Elizabeth was born," Maude said complacently. She recalled that day vividly, the two of them in the small rented room of the rooming house near the waterfront, Fanny's fear, then the business of bearing down, and the child, at last, arriving into the world. She had worried then about what would become of Fanny, never dreaming that Fanny already was tangled up with Joshua Stetson, and that she would find her way to Bangor to become the madam of Pink Chimneys.

Now here they were, two women of a certain age, peering down at the shore, all aflutter about their darling M. You never knew about life and where it would take you, what it would bring to you.

Maude moved away from the piazza railing and sat down in a wicker rocking chair.

"That's precisely my point, Maude. I knew nothing of life at that age, and neither does M. She's led a sheltered life. I've given her every comfort . . ."

"But it's not comfort she wants, Fanny. It's the sea. It's what she was bred to."

"The next thing you'll tell me is that she has seawater in her veins," Fanny scoffed. She stayed at the railing, gazing down at the beach, watching. Her heart felt numb in her chest. She could not bear to think of Abbott's Reach without M's quiet presence, without the sound of her light step on the stairs, without her sudden laughter.

"She does have the sea in her veins, Fanny. She was still a baby when she first went to sea with Elizabeth and Abner." Maude paused, choosing her words carefully. "I know that raising M these last few years has given you the experience of motherhood you never had with Elizabeth, but you can't keep M with you forever. You know you can't."

"No, I can't keep her with me forever. I don't want to," Fanny said. "But I do want to keep her safe. Why can't she take an interest in one of those nice boys from the Bangor seminary who come here every summer?"

Maude laughed as she remembered how the local clergy had railed against Fanny when she was known as Bangor's most notorious lady. It was so like Fanny to ignore the fact that she had been—and in some ways, still was—a social outcast. Nevertheless, over the years, Fanny had made a life for herself at Fort Point. She had been accepted by the ladies of Stockton Springs, the nearest village. And to the credit of those same ladies, they had not branded M, by extension, with the stain of Fanny's shady past. Maude thought that this was remarkable, attributing it to the fact that many of the Stockton Springs ladies had followed their husbands to sea, had traveled the world in ships, and had a somewhat broader perspective. Or perhaps, because they had so seldom been alongshore, they had fewer social grudges to hone.

"Really, Fanny. The role of mother hen does not become you. You know exactly why M is in love with Madras Mitchell—for precisely the same reasons you were in love with Joshua Stetson. Madras is dashing and handsome. He possesses that odd streak of ruthlessness, tempered by a desire toward kindness that so many successful sea captains often have. Not to mention the fact that he comes from a good family—the very qualities that attracted you to Joshua. Or need I remind you?"

Joshua Stetson had rescued Fanny when she was alone, penniless, and pregnant, abandoned in Portland by sailor Robert Snow. After Elizabeth's birth, Fanny had followed Stetson to Bangor. He had installed her in the grand house he had dubbed Pink Chimneys. He had been her lover, her nemesis, her beloved, her ruin.

"That is not fair, Maude. Madras Mitchell is nothing like Joshua Stetson. Joshua had a streak of cruelty in him . . ." She faltered, and Maude knew she was remembering Joshua's terrible fate—how all traces of him and that part of her life had been reduced to ash along with Pink Chimneys, destroyed in a fire that marked the end of Fanny's days as a notorious woman.

"Yes, perhaps it is unfair of me. But you'll have to concede that Madras Mitchell is steady and hardworking, and in some

ways, very like Abner Giddings. And that is another point I'd like
to make. M has fallen in love with a man of her own kind, a man
whose work and life she understands."

"I thought you were on my side, Maude." Fanny tried, but
failed, to keep a note of accusation out of her voice.

"I am, Fanny. I don't want to see her go either. But go she
will, with or without our blessings. I'd rather let her go with my
hand open than force her to break the clutching grasp of my fingers. I advise you to do the same. Madras Mitchell will be here in
a few days to ask your permission to marry M. If you say no,
you'll lose her anyway. The melancholia . . ."

Since coming to live with her grandmother, M had suffered
periodic bouts of depression. They were always alert to the signs of
M's dark moods; hence, their need to train a spyglass on her. There
had been times in the past when M had become so melancholy
she refused to eat or would not get out of bed. Sometimes she
cried for hours, giving no reason. And each year on Grace's birthday, when she insisted on wading in the water, they worried she
would wander too far and be caught by the undertow—worried
that this is what she wanted—even though M had never behaved
in a way that suggested she wanted to bring harm to herself.
Rather, she wanted to behave in a way that summoned the past so
that she could dwell in it, if only for a moment—to be, for that
moment, in control of all that was not and never had been hers to
command.

"Yes, the melancholia. And if I say yes, I lose her, too. Damned
if I do, damned if I don't."

"But if you say yes, she'll always come home to you," Maude
said gently.

"Providing the damn ship stays afloat."

"We all sail in ships, Fanny, literally and figuratively. We are
always in danger of going down with all hands lost."

Fanny made a wry face at Maude and returned to her vigil at the piazza railing.

M's Log—August 1871

Grand Fan and Mrs. Maude came down to the beach to get me, although they pretended, as they always do, that they had not. Trailing in the wake of their skirts was Grand Fan's coon cat, Tennyson, the tortoise-colored plume of his tail carried in a delicate question mark above his back. Even he seemed solicitous of my welfare.

Mrs. Maude wrapped me in a blanket. They led me back to the house and Grand Fan fussed. She made me drink hot tea laced with brandy. Everything they did for me showed me how dear I am to them, and I felt like such a traitor—to want to leave them to go upon the sea with Madras. But Mrs. Maude, whom I swear can sometimes read my mind, said, "We are your past, M, not your future." She and Grand Fan exchanged meaningful glances, as if they were reading one another's minds, as well as mine. I think what Mrs. Maude said was meant to give me permission to choose Madras over them. When I understood that, my mood lifted. Maude noticed, of course, and it allayed her worries about me.

Later, after they had put me to bed and Mrs. Maude had gone downstairs, Grand Fan said, "I agree with Maude, M. We are not your future. I don't want to let you go, but I don't want to hold you back either. I want you happy."

I knew then that she had made up her mind about Madras and me, and when she bent down to kiss me good-night, I hugged her extra hard. I do love her so.

3.

Madras Mitchell felt no trepidation about asking Fanny
Abbott for permission to marry M, even though M had warned
him that her grandmother was cool to the idea. He had met
Fanny a few times and had been impressed by her quiet self-assurance and her strength of character.

He stepped out of the small sailboat he had piloted from
Searsport and tied it fast. As he walked up the path from the beach
to Abbott's Reach, he wondered if M was watching from a window.
He liked the look of the house, with its wide piazza wrapped around
three sides of the dwelling, facing the bay. It appeared solid and
respectable with its white paint, newly applied just that summer.

Madras noticed flower and herb gardens fenced in by white
pickets. The rocking chairs on the piazza were empty of paying
guests who usually sat there. He noted these things only vaguely, as
a way to divert himself, for his thoughts centered on M and his
impatience to see her. He was eager to be done with the formality
of his errand. He was confident that his powers of persuasion would
carry the day, though he much preferred commanding over per-
suading, an approach he knew was not called for on this occasion.

For the most part, Madras had courted M when she was in
Searsport visiting the Griffin girls, Lily and Lucia. Or he had called
on her in Bangor when she was staying with Maude and Sam
Webber. M had not wanted him to visit her at Abbott's Reach,
pleading that her grandmother would be unsettled by his presence,
and, perhaps, forbid her to see him at all. They also had written
volumes of letters to one another over the last few months.

Madras and Fanny had met a number of times in the village at
public social occasions and had had a cordial speaking acquaintance.
His impression of her was always favorable.

Well, the tide always turned. Fanny Abbott had come about and had summoned him. Madras was just back from a coasting run to New York—a load of hay and lumber out and fruit and bales of cotton fabric back. He had been away six weeks, and in that time he had received two letters from M, the first full of despair because her grandmother kept coming up with long lists of reasons why she was too young to marry. Each letter reflected M's spirited determination to defy her grandmother should that become necessary.

Madras did not like being caught in the middle. He was accustomed to command, having served as master of his father's ship, the *Boreas*, for nearly ten years, since the age of eighteen. Nonetheless, he was not certain how one commanded a woman like Fanny Abbott, who ran her own ship, as it were, and according to all he'd heard, ran it well and profitably.

Madras had heard of her past; everyone had. Women whispered about it, while men mentioned it more crudely. But that had nothing to do with M. He didn't give a damn what they said about her grandmother, as long as they kept their mouths shut about M. It was wrong to visit the sins of the grandmother on the granddaughter, a fear that bobbed around in the back of his mind because his own grandmother, Augusta Mitchell, also was opposed to the match. But slaying that dragon would have to wait until this skirmish was over—not that it would be easy to defy his grandmother once she had dug her heels in.

Madras did not relish a confrontation with Fanny Abbott, but if it came down to that, he guessed he'd do just about anything for M's sake, which already included telling his parents he intended to marry her. His mother, Zulema, had objected at first, but his father, Isaiah, had persuaded her to allow Madras to choose his wife without interference from them. Zulema favored a match with a distant cousin who disliked the sea. His mother had, of course, heard the talk about Fanny Abbott. But she was a fair-minded woman and refused to base her opinion of M solely on what she had heard about the grandmother. In fact, when she had met M for the first time, at a party given by the Griffin girls, she had been impressed by M's intelligence and pleasant manners.

Maude Webber answered when Madras knocked on the door, ushering him into a sunny parlor with large windows overlooking the bay. She looked Madras over somewhat pointedly as she took his cap and gloves. Then she grinned at him, and he knew she was on his side—always good to know that one had allies.

The room Maude left him in surprised Madras. No drapes or curtains impeded the full, strong light. The interior was simply, almost sparsely, decorated. In one corner stood a beautiful French desk from some previous era, before furniture became heavy, square, and upholstered in dark, heavy fabrics. The simple white mantel held a collection of seashells. Rows of books with dark leather bindings—Shakespeare, Dickens, and Thackeray among them—arranged on floor-to-ceiling shelves drew his attention. It was clear these books had been read; they were not just for show. Several oil paintings, one of roses and lupine, another of Turk's cap lilies and pale pink peonies, hung on the walls. He recognized the paintings as the work of Eliza Hardy, daughter of painter Jeremiah Hardy, the much-respected artist who lived upriver at Hampden.

A carpet in a floral design in shades of blue and buff covered the floor. A fainting couch done up in pale gold brocade occupied a place by the windows. A comfortable sofa and two matching wing chairs were drawn up to the fireplace. Large cushions made of rose-print chintz softened the lines of all three pieces of furniture. The overall effect of the room was warm and inviting—some would have said charming. A coon cat curled up in one of the chairs lifted its head and said *Mur-row?*

All at once, Madras felt disarmed, off balance. He had not expected to feel at home. He had expected a stiff, formal parlor like

the ones favored by his aunts, female cousins, and grandmother—
rooms where voices were never raised and where one almost tripped
over civility as if it were a well-padded footstool, poorly placed.

Madras noticed a piece of embroidery, still in the frame, set
casually aside on the sofa. He saw a knitting bag, and escaping
from it the beginnings of a gray sock on three needles. A small
table with a plain wooden chair drawn up to it held Chinese puz-
zles, a cribbage board, and a bowl of dark red dahlias.

He felt Fanny's presence before he turned to see her standing
in the doorway. She was dressed in a gown of black decorated
with cobwebby gray lace at the neck and wrists. Her hair was simply done, drawn back from her face and pinned into a loose knot
at the back. Here, then, was the enemy.

Fanny liked what she saw in Madras Mitchell in that moment,
had liked the cut of his jib every time their paths had crossed in
Stockton Springs or Searsport. Madras Mitchell, she thought, had
something of a Byronic air about him, as if he belonged to an earlier time. His linen was white and well starched. His navy blue
jacket fit his lean frame well. His black leather boots gleamed from
the polishing he had given them—as shipshape a man as she had
ever seen, and one who most certainly wished to impress her.

She noted that his nose was long and finely made, his chin
strong and well shaped. His dark hair fell forward onto his forehead,
giving him an air of boyish romance; quite poetic, really. He had,
Fanny thought, the kind of face that would grow more handsome as
he grew older. Creases of age would become lines of character. His
shoulders would stay broad and capable. His hips would stay lean and
flexible. His confidence and self-assurance would grow and become
imbedded in the lines of his body. He did, indeed, put her in mind
of Abner Giddings and Joshua Stetson. It quite took her breath away.

"How do you do, Mr. Mitchell? Won't you sit down?" Fanny stepped into the room, and Madras made a small half-bow as she seated herself in one of the wing chairs by the fireplace.

"Yes, thank you, Miss Abbott." Madras headed for the other chair and hesitated, as the cat occupied it.

"Do take the sofa, Mr. Mitchell, and excuse Tennyson's bad manners. He thinks he owns that chair, and I tend to encourage him."

"Thank you," Madras said, smiling as he sat down. She was being extremely formal, hiding behind it, giving nothing away, as if intent on making his task more difficult. Well, he had expected that. For a moment he did not know what else to say, except to comment on the weather. "Lovely day," he said. It was not how he wanted to begin, but he knew she would pilot their conversational ship.

"Mr. Mitchell, you didn't come here to discuss the weather. I believe you want to discuss certain matters pertaining to my granddaughter, Miss Mercy Maude Giddings."

No, she was not going to make it easy for him.

He faced her and looked directly into her lovely blue eyes. She was a fine figure of a woman. He liked what he saw—her gently fading beauty, her quiet grace, her perfect dignity, her resolute will. Had she been a man, he thought, she'd have made a formidable sea captain. Perhaps even a pirate. He felt a smile turn up the corners of his mouth ever so slightly.

Fanny's expression did not change, though she noted the smile and it charmed her.

"I have come to ask your permission to make M, ah, Miss Giddings, my wife." He smiled as he thought of M. Fanny noted the smile and the way his eyes grew tender as he said M's name. He was obviously besotted, and the knowledge pleased her.

"And what, Mr. Mitchell, recommends you to me as a prospective husband for my granddaughter?"

He did not know what to say for a moment. He was not accustomed to praising himself. He knew his own worth, but he depended on his deeds as a man, a ship's master and businessman—as his father's well-raised son—to define him, not on words. He gathered his thoughts and remembered what M had said: *Don't leave anything out; she'll keep you dangling until she's satisfied that I am as safe with you as I am with her.*

"First, Miss Abbott, let me say that my regard for M is so strong . . . It does not matter to me . . . "

"Ah, I see. It does not matter to you that she is the granddaughter of a woman with a somewhat irregular past?"

"Not at all, ma'am." He refrained from saying aloud what immediately came to his mind: *Nor does it matter what you think of me, good or ill, for I will have M as my wife.* He did not intend to throw down the gauntlet quite so quickly.

"Then surely, Mr. Mitchell, you can recite those qualities and attributes in yourself that will recommend you to me." Fanny spoke coolly and did not take her eyes from his face. She watched him regain his composure and was pleased to see that his self-confidence was in no way affected by her direct reference to things in her past that were not spoken of in polite company.

Madras saw that Fanny Abbott had a will of iron, not unlike his own grandmother. What she required of him was simple and straightforward. He'd give her the facts.

"I am the master of the *Boreas*, ma'am. She is owned by my father's firm, Mitchell and Curtis, and I have shares in her. For that reason, I can contemplate marriage and the happy choice of taking my bride to sea with me. As I am sure you know, Miss Abbott, my family is of some significance in Searsport, and we are known in ports all over the world. It is within my power to establish an excellent home for Miss Giddings and myself in Searsport, when and if she wishes it. It is also within my power, when and if I wish it, to leave off going to sea and take up shore duties in my father's shipping business."

"I have heard, sir, that you are indeed well-known in ports all over the world, especially those in Hawaii." Fanny watched him carefully, gauging his reaction to her pointed comment.

"People often discuss things they know nothing about, and make judgments that are harsh and ill-conceived. Surely, ma'am, you know that to be true." Madras looked Fanny in the eye, daring her to be more frank.

Touché, Fanny thought. She noted that he did not look away when he mentioned Hawaii. The whispers she had heard involved his bad behavior with a Hawaiian girl. She did not know the details, but, given her own past history, she could easily imagine them. Still, she wanted to give him the benefit of the doubt as he, clearly, had done for her. She decided on a different tack.

"Do I understand correctly, Mr. Mitchell, that you propose to carry my granddaughter to the ends of the earth, exposing her to the dangers of the sea? That you plan to deprive me of her company, and to bear and raise my great-grandchildren on the ocean, so I will rarely see them? Why, sir, would I want to give you permission to do that?"

"You paint a bleak picture, Miss Abbott. While I do intend to carry Miss Giddings to the far ports of the world, I also intend that there shall be long periods between journeys so that she can come home—to her own house, to yours, or to my mother's house. In fact, it is quite likely you will see as much of her, or more, than if she married a seminarian and went with him to live at some remote mission in New Zealand."

Fanny laughed out loud at this, a sound so infectious that Madras laughed, too, at the absurdity of the statement. He knew then that she would not refuse his request.

When Fanny's mirth had passed, her face became quiet, as if a shadow were passing over it. "You know, of course, about M's tendency toward melancholy?" she asked.

"She has mentioned it to me," Madras replied. "It is my understanding that it stems from her grief at losing her sister, and from her great desire to go to sea again."

"There is also the possibility that it stems from a fear of death by drowning which will seize her when she is, indeed, upon the deep water, a fear which may cause her irreparable harm." That had been the opinion of the specialist in Boston Fanny had consulted. Maude did not share that opinion. She had her own theories, believing that because water had been the source of M's suffering, it also would be the cure.

"But isn't it possible, Miss Abbott, that Miss Giddings merely fears death, as we all do, and that what she fears most is being denied the opportunity to do what she wants—to travel the world in a ship with the man she loves, a life she used to know well?"

"You are very wise for one so young, Mr. Mitchell."

"I have an old soul, Miss Abbott, or so my parents were told by the Chinese cook aboard the ship *Courageous* on the day I was born—in a storm as we came into the harbor at Madras, India."

Fanny drew a long breath and regarded him thoughtfully. Well, it was out of her hands now. What would be, would be. M could do worse than Madras Mitchell—far, far worse, as she knew so very well.

"You will find M in the summerhouse on the beach, Mr. Mitchell. You may tell her that you have my blessing. But I should say this: You must wait until spring to marry. I won't have M ill-equipped for her venture into matrimony." Fanny stood up and extended her hand. Madras rose quickly to his feet and grasped Fanny's hand. He held it for a moment and looked deeply into her eyes. He felt himself drawn in and made welcome, caught in the charming aura of her personality.

"Thank you, ma'am. All voyages require preparation and provisioning."

"Well said, Mr. Mitchell. Follow the path beside the fence. It will take you to M."

Maude stepped into the room as Madras was leaving. "Victory is yours, I see," Maude said to him.

Madras grinned and lifted his hand in salute. "Aye, and neither of us the worse for it."

When he was gone, Maude said to Fanny, "Apparently he survived the inquisition. That can only be in his favor."

"Not only survived, Maude, but did not grovel, did not flatter me outrageously—for which I may never forgive him—and did not let me bully him. I believe he will be a devoted and loving husband. But the rumors about that business in Hawaii still trouble me."

"Pots, Fanny, should not call the kettles black," Maude said complacently, her eyes merry with mischief. "Besides, whatever did or did not happen in Hawaii was years ago, when he was hardly more than a boy. He leads an upstanding life. Everyone says so."

"You are getting to be a dreadful old woman, Maude, always so practical. I can't think why I let you stay around here," Fanny declared, with good humor.

"You keep me around, Fanny Abbott, because I know you so well, and because the common history we share is a rare and precious thing."

M's Log—August 1871

I knew from the set of Madras's shoulders as he came running down the beach that Grand Fan had said yes. No doubt Grand Fan imagined me waiting in the summerhouse, cool and dignified, with maidenly blushes tingeing my cheeks to a becoming pink. But she was quite, quite wrong. The moment I saw Madras I raced to meet him—barefoot (Grand Fan does not approve!), with flying hair and shouts of joy.

Madras caught me to him, lifted me off my feet, and whirled me around until I was dizzy and mad with laughter. Our kisses were not a chaste meeting of respectful lips, as Grand Fan must have imagined.

"If they are spying on us," I said, "they will get more than they bargained for."

Madras grinned at me, such beautiful teeth, such pleasing eyes, and he kissed me more deeply. "You give them too much credit, M," he said. "They imagine nothing of the kind. They know how ardently I love you . . ." And he kissed me again.

"I never thought Grand Fan would give in so easily."

"She didn't give in easily, M. She knows the repairs to the Boreas *won't be completed until spring."*

"She's going to make us wait until spring! I won't wait! I won't!" I clung to him, shaken by sudden anger.

Madras looked into my eyes. "M, where is your good sense? The Boreas *is in for repairs. I have a great deal to do before I sail again—provisioning, a cargo to arrange out and back, a crew to assemble. We need these months of working together, M."*

I saw then that he was right, and what could have resulted in a drift toward melancholy changed course for the better.

4.

Several days later, Ellis Harding saw Madras Mitchell stride down the road toward the Stockton Springs town wharf. He knew just by looking at Madras that he had the answer he'd been hoping for: Fanny had given her permission. It was as plain as day in the wide smile Madras turned on everyone he passed.

Ellis stepped away from the window and turned his ear to the room off the parlor where his wife, Bethiah, lay. Bethiah had been ill for many years, suffering from a wasting disease that gradually compromised her ability to move and speak. He listened for the faint sounds she sometimes made when she was restless. He heard nothing. He had fed her, tended her. Cassie Eaton, an elderly cousin who looked after Bethiah in return for room and board, had gone out for her evening walk. When Cassie returned, Ellis would go out, and that excursion would take him to Abbott's Reach.

Ellis first saw Fanny in the early 1850s, when she still called herself Fanny Hogan. He had been a river driver then, one of the hell-raising, dare-anything bunch known as the Bangor Tigers. Like all lumbermen, he'd heard stories about Fanny Hogan's fabulous house. One day, he wandered over to Oak Street to stare at the place with the pink chimneys, just to say he'd done it.

When the log-drive season ended, he spent most of his time in the Hell's Half-Acre grog shops on the Bangor waterfront, places he remembered with a rough kind of fondness. He'd been a brawler then, no getting around that. When he went home to Bethiah, as he always did, he was restless and always glad when it was time to head back into the woods. He liked the life of danger, the falling trees and the evil rush of roaring water, challenges he confronted with just a pickpole, an ax, and his caulk boots.

Ellis knew the way he lived and worked was hard on Bethiah and their three children. She urged him, in her gentle way, to come home for good, to try another line of work. He told her he'd give it up when he was damn good and ready. He'd see the hurt in her eyes and curse himself for being such a selfish bastard, but he had a mean streak then.

Ellis had been one of the crowd, an odd mix of the curious
and righteous, when the Reverend Comfort Drummond preached
against Fanny Hogan and demon rum that day in 1852. But unlike
the others, Ellis had not come to hoot and jeer. He was curious in
a very different sort of way. He had seen Fanny, quite by chance, a
few days before, as she drove down State Street in Bangor. Her
carriage passed by him so closely that he could have reached out
and touched it. She had turned her head as she passed and looked
right into his eyes, and he had seen there a pain he'd never
thought to feel in his own life. It reminded him of the pain he'd
seen in Bethiah's eyes, pain he'd put there. Who, he wondered, had
put such pain in Fanny Hogan's eyes? Could such pain, in her eyes
or Bethiah's, be replaced by gleams of contentment and happiness?
It was a sobering moment, one he would not forget. For the first
time in many years he remembered something his mother had said
often to him: "There are deep things inside you, Ellis Harding.
Fish for them and let them see the light of day."

As the crowd gathered in front of Pink Chimneys, he was
drawn there, too, although he couldn't for the life of him figure
out precisely why. Joshua Stetson's fancy woman was nothing to
him. Who was she but a kept woman of common origin who
thumbed her nose at the likes of him and those in the crowd? As
for himself, who was he but a common man fleeing home and
hearth, who left his wife to cry alone while he drifted north in
the fall and rode the long logs south on the river every spring? It
rattled him to have such alien questions rise in his mind like
strange fish out of the dark waters of a swiftly moving river. Was
this what his mother had meant?

He was there when Pink Chimneys billowed with smoke and
roared into flame. He watched with growing dread as women in
the crowd screamed and men ran to organize a bucket brigade. He
thought Fanny Hogan had gone up in smoke, too, and he felt his

heart grow smudgy with a new awareness of how quickly life flared into being and how, just as quickly, it could be extinguished.

He thought of Bethiah and the loneliness and worry she endured because of him. It was a crazy kind of thinking, and he blamed it on too much rum the night before, or not enough the morning after. But Fanny Hogan's face, the bruised look in her eyes, and Bethiah's face with that forlorn expression every time he left, would not leave his mind. He drifted back to the taverns on the waterfront and resolved to look for another kind of work, something to keep him closer to home and Bethiah, something that would bring her happiness and contentment. It was a pleasing thought, one that washed him with warmth and a sense of purpose.

That summer, Ellis went home to Stockton Springs for good. He fished, did odd jobs, cut wood for local farmers in winter, worked in the shipyards at Searsport. He took pride in his adaptability. When Bethiah's mother died, he moved his family into the old house on the Fort Point road. He saw that Bethiah was content. They were happy together, and the laughter of their children filled the house. He began to tend the family graves at the village cemetery, and people in town took notice of him with respect.

In 1858, Bethiah began to stumble and fall. She broke an arm, then an ankle, and it became clear that something was terribly wrong. Her health failed in increments over the years, and she spent most of her time in bed. Their daughters, Nancy and Damaris, did the best they could to take care of their mother, and Ellis was grateful for it, but he saw that their devotion to their mother could interfere with their chances for lives of their own. He did not want them to be old maids stranded at home, dutiful daughters shouldering the family burdens until they were too old to marry.

Ellis arranged for Cassie Eaton to come to stay and take care of Bethiah. It was from Cassie that Ellis heard about the woman who lived in the big old house at the Point.

One fine spring day shortly after Cassie had come to stay, Ellis walked out to the Point to see if the woman in the old place might need someone to do odd jobs. The house, built fifty or more years previously, occupied a rise of land giving panoramic views of the Penobscot River, both up and down. A sign hanging from the wide wraparound piazza said ABBOTT'S REACH BOARDINGHOUSE.

Ellis saw at once that things needed attention. Slats were missing from the picket fence, a screen door sagged off its hinges, the garden spot was full of weeds. It was spring and the season for summer visitors was not far away. He knocked at the door and a small woman with gray hair answered, no one he knew by sight or name. He stated his business and the woman told him politely that Mrs. Abbott was not at home. He thanked her and went away.

A year went by. His daughter, Nancy, married Abel Davis, a missionary, and went over the seas to Hawaii to live. Damaris went to teach school in New Hampshire and soon found a husband there. His son, Benjamin, went to sea in the *Golden Bough* with Captain Curtis and rarely came home.

In the meantime, Ellis heard the Misses Merrithew, the town's dressmakers, whisper about the woman who owned Abbott's Reach. They said despite a shady past, she now lived a quiet and upright life, earning her living by taking in summer boarders. They did sewing for the lady and could find no fault with her manners or the way she dressed. She always paid her bills on time.

Ellis decided to call again at Abbott's Reach in search of work. This time, he noticed that the gate was newly repaired. It seemed like an ill omen. Obviously, someone else was doing the odd jobs around the place. As he turned to leave, a slender woman in her fifties, he judged, stepped out to the piazza. He recognized her at once. Fanny Hogan. The years had not dimmed her beauty or the air of mystery hovering about her like a smoky veil. He gazed at her in awe, as if she had risen from the dead.

She saw that he recognized her, and for an instant, fear and uncertainty shadowed her face. It still held traces of the emotionally bruised look he remembered. She came down the steps cautiously, with a slow kind of grace that made him draw a sharp breath. She moved toward him, her eyes on his face, her manner quietly contained yet full of authority, as if she might dispatch him with a word or a look. She stopped a few feet from the gate, the bright points of red leather shoes visible beneath the dark blue hem of her skirt. She held her hands at her waist, clasped lightly together, a slightly defensive gesture and oddly endearing.

"My friend Mrs. Webber says that you are Ellis Harding from the Springs," she said without preamble.

"I am," he replied, never taking his eyes from hers.

"Do you know how to fix a screen door so it doesn't bind?" she asked.

"I do."

"I have six. Five bind, the other squeals."

And that was how it began.

Now, several days after the interview with Madras Mitchell, Fanny waited for Ellis in the summerhouse on the low cliff above the shore. It was where they met in the summer and early autumn months. Other times of the year, she waited for him on the piazza or in the kitchen. Most often he came to her as the hired man who did odd jobs around the place. Then, they merely smiled at one another as she discussed with him the work she wanted him to do. She respected the fact that he had other work to do, and serious responsibilities at home.

And she, too, had responsibilities and other concerns to attend to, not the least of which was M. She and Ellis respected one another's private parameters. But after the busy summer months of taking in boarders, Ellis called on Fanny one evening each week, and he came to her then as the man she loved.

Fanny watched Ellis move slowly down the path. She could not see his face clearly, but his wavy white hair shone in the moonlight. She knew the shape of his square face intimately, the deep-set blue of his eyes, his thin mouth that settled into a wide grin, the strong modeling of his jaw and cheekbones, the rough white stubble of his beard on those days when he had not shaved. Everything about him stirred in her a quiet, barely restrained delight.

She watched him come toward her with the easy, sure-footed confidence of a man on a familiar path, one who knows the woman he loves is waiting to receive him fully and unconditionally. She felt her heart catch with a queer sort of love only slightly tinged with sadness for what had never been and could never be between them. She had made her peace with that, and she felt little guilt. Ellis was a man of deep passion—a passion that matched her own. He needed her in an intensely physical way, and she loved that in him. She did not believe that their relationship took anything from anyone—not herself, not him, and certainly not Bethiah. Much, she thought, was given. The love they felt for one another was not selfish.

When Ellis left her side, Fanny knew he left renewed and replenished, with greater resolve to shoulder his burdens, to carry out his duties. His passion for her in no way diluted his devotion to Bethiah or his family. It was a fact so paradoxical and so at odds with everything Fanny had ever believed, it made her wonder if she had invented it all.

For years, after Pink Chimneys burned, after Joshua died, Fanny shunned those terrible memories of her life within those extravagant walls. She had hidden herself away at Abbott's Reach, rarely going to the village. She saw only Maude and Sam Webber, and they had not urged on her any behavior to the contrary.

"It takes time," Maude said every so often, not elaborating further. Her remark was a kind of blessing. It gave Fanny the right to hurt, to despair and cry, to find a way out of herself and into a new life, a new way of being. In those years, she often walked to the farm where she had grown up, now owned by a family with young children. She would think about her sister, Mercy, her mother who had died so young, the charming wiles of Robert Snow, who had compromised her and left her to her fate. She had cried many tears and reached a point where she saw herself as a broken rail fence—something that could be mended if you were willing to work at it—though perhaps, not a perfect fix. Nothing was ever perfect.

Fanny remembered the day Ellis came to the house seeking odd jobs. It had been a Tuesday, gray and lowery. M had not yet come to live with her. She had felt in herself, all the preceding winter, a quiet yearning welling inside her—for growth, for a change of direction, a need to move out of the past and into the present. That winter she had read Hawthorne's novels and the writings of Ralph Waldo Emerson. She had read Shakespeare's tragic plays. And the more she read, the more she felt herself mended and improved by literature. As Maude said, it took time; although, more important than time, it took thought and reflection.

When Ellis stood at the gate that first day, he had regarded Fanny with an intensity of interest she had come to expect as her due from men. It came as a shock to realize that she had been longing for that very thing. Her fingers had trembled with her need to reach out and touch him.

For a moment, when she realized that he knew her by reputation, she had wanted to run back into the house, slam the door, and retreat to the dim safety of her bedroom at the top of the stairs. But something in his sweet blue eyes stopped her. It was as if he had shone a warm light upon her. At once, she was intensely aware of his height, the turn of his ankle in those scuffed leather boots, the size of his hands, the length of his fingers. She sensed in him something lost, something given up on, something regretted, something kindred.

The sound of his voice, light and confident, had filled her with an astonishing sense of calm and safety. And with no thought for past or future, she asked him to fix the screen doors. She had known in that moment that Ellis Harding would return again and again, and that slowly their hearts would merge and fuse until it seemed they had always been together.

Months later, she told Maude it was all Shakespeare's fault.

After a discreet inquiry of the Misses Merrithew and a pointed conversation with Maude, Fanny learned many details about Ellis: He gave good care to his wife, he worked hard and well, and he was respected. They said he was not a layabout or a womanizer. He did not frequent the tavern or gamble his money away at cards. He seemed almost too good, too respectable. He was the antithesis of Joshua Stetson.

As they became better acquainted, she asked for the details of his life. Ellis gave them freely, leaving nothing out. And she had done the same.

Now, a steady breeze blew up the Penobscot and Fanny drew her shawl more closely around her shoulders. "Ellis," she said, as he joined her, all the delight she felt at being in his company contained in that single word. He pulled her to him and kissed her, a kiss full of his innate calm and confidence. Fanny leaned against him, wishing she had on fewer layers of clothing, the better to feel his body curved and warm around her.

"For a grandmother about to give up her only grandchild to wedlock," he said, teasing, "you seem uncommonly happy to see me." She stepped away from him and sat down on the wicker sofa. Ellis sat beside her, his thigh warm against hers, their hands clasped together.

"I'm not losing M, Ellis. I'm gaining a sea captain," Fanny said, a note of sarcasm in her voice. "He loves her deeply—I can see that. And heaven knows M adores him. But I can't help worrying.

What about that business in Hawaii that's whispered about? What if there is truth in that?"

"You can't protect her forever, Fanny. She'll sit on some thorns in her life, and maybe young Mitchell will even be so foolish as to leave a few on her chair. But M is no fool. A bit headstrong, at times, maybe, but she's got a good head on her shoulders. You and Maude have seen to that."

"It's not her head I'm worried about, Ellis. It's her heart. I won't have it broken."

"It's not *her* heart in danger of being broken, Fanny. It's yours." Ellis drew her to him and she laid her head against his shoulder and let the tears slide down her face. The familiar feel of his arms around her, the scent of freshly split wood on his clothing and the fainter scent of shaving soap on his skin made her cry harder for a moment. The tide, the tide, she thought wildly, it runs out so fast. But she wasn't the kind of woman who would let herself be swept helplessly out to sea in a flood tide. Tears, she knew, were essential to beginnings and endings. All change—birth, the seasons, death, leaving home, coming home, working—contained water: Sweat, tears, milk, blood. She did not cry long, and soon dried her cheeks with the backs of her hands.

"Walk with me," she said softly, rising and holding out her hand. He took it and pressed it to his lips.

The beach in moonlight was silvery with long patches of dense shadow, no color but rich shades of gray from light to dark. The sky glittered with a strange kind of energy that always made Fanny think of the desires of the flesh, of warm smiles, and the many kinds of love men and women fashion for themselves. She said so and Ellis laughed softly.

"It makes me think of a hundred million candles lighting a grand ballroom, and you, my dear, the brightest light in the room." She was lovely in a pale yellow dress, the skirt swishing softly with each step she took. Her hair was down, but pulled back and tied with a narrow black ribbon. In the moonlight, as slim as she was, she looked like a girl. He felt himself fall in love with her all over again. He reached for her, swung her into his arms, and, humming a tune in a pleasant tenor, stepped out into a waltz. Fanny added her competent alto and they dipped and twirled and swayed along the edge of the beach, sand seeping into their shoes, until they were out of breath.

"Stay, Ellis," Fanny whispered, gazing intently into his face, dazed by her passion for him. She knew he'd reach for her again and again, and each time he did so, she would love him more.

"For a little while, Fanny, my darling," he murmured as they turned back toward the house.

Off the summer kitchen was a small room Fanny called "the back bedroom." She had furnished it with a four-poster bed covered with a crazy quilt, a tall pine bureau, a marble-topped commode, hooked rag rugs, and several comfortable chairs. It was their room, the one place where they might shed not only their clothes, but also their responsibilities and worries, their cares, the very denominations of their lives. It was where they might be together as man and woman . . . nothing more, nothing less.

M's Log—August 1871

I am the happiest woman in the world! I am to be Madras Mitchell's wife, and I am to go upon the sea with him as I was born to do. I have written Mother and Father. They are somewhere on the Atlantic bound for Spain. By the time they receive my letter it will be only a few months until my wedding. I told them that it's very unfair of Grand Fan to make me wait until spring to marry. Not that it will make a dent with Mother or Father; they always side with Grand Fan.

I have resolved to spend the time wisely as I wait for my wedding day. I will not let melancholy darken the very great happiness I feel. Still, I cannot help but think of Grace, and how I will have no sister to help me put on my wedding dress and weave flowers in my hair. Mother and Father will try to be here for the wedding, I know. I will pray for fair winds to send them to me.

Grand Fan is in the summerhouse where I feel certain she is crying on Ellis Harding's shoulder. I have seen their eyes when they look at one another. It is a look of the greatest tenderness and the deepest understanding. It is how Mrs. Maude and Dr. Sam look at one another. It is how my parents look at one another. It is how Madras and I look at one another. "After Maude and Sam," Grand Fan said once, "Mr. Harding is my dearest friend." But they are much more than friends. I find it oddly touching that as old as they are, they dote so on one another. Mrs. Harding is very ill and barely sensible; it is probably unwise of Grand Fan and Mr. Harding to love one another in that way. But I do not believe it is wrong. I believe it is a mystery, just as life is a mystery—just as the fact that I live, and Grace does not, is a mystery.

5.

M's arm lay confidently around the tiller, her sun-browned hand resting lightly on the wood. A nondescript bonnet, faded from much use, shielded her face from sunburn. The *Zephyr* was not much more than a large rowboat fixed with a mast and a sail, but her bow cut through the light waves on the bay smoothly and gracefully. The water slipping away under her keel sounded like fine cloth being torn.

Sam Webber sat in the bow, the breeze snarling his white hair, one hand resting on the gunwale. He grinned at M and she thought how he never seemed to age—how even though the grooves around his mouth grew deeper each year, the light in his dark blue eyes seemed to stay always young. They had spent many a summer and autumn day cruising Penobscot Bay in the *Zephyr*. It was a bit beyond seven years since that June day in 1864 when he had taken her to the wharf to show her the little boat.

"It's yours," he had said, and she had climbed into the *Zephyr* with no word of thanks, with nothing but a wildly beating heart and a sudden gush of tears dripping down her twelve-year-old cheeks. She had pushed off, hauled the sail up, and within minutes was skimming across the bay off Abbott's Reach, the breeze making a hash of her hair, the sun hot and friendly on her skin. That day as the Fort Point shoreline receded and the edges of Verona Island drew near, she felt something in herself shift from the girl she was to the young lady she was becoming. She felt the old power of the sea surge through her heart. She sailed all that day, up and down and around the bay, never going out of sight of the spyglass she knew Mrs. Maude, Dr. Sam, and Grand Fan had trained upon her. And when she returned to the wharf at twilight, Dr. Sam was waiting to hand her out of the boat and help her tie it up.

"I never thanked you that day," M said now to Sam.

"The look on your face was thanks enough," Sam said. He recalled how M had been listless and rebellious after she had come to live at Abbott's Reach with her grandmother. He had given M the little boat against Fanny's and Maude's wishes. They felt that M would grow more sad and impatient, and that having the boat would give her only a momentary joy that would gradually give way, once again, to melancholia.

"I guess I was quite a handful before that. Poor Grand Fan! How I cried and carried on!"

M had done much more than cry and carry on, Sam remembered. He had, more than once, been obliged to organize a party to search for her when she had packed her things and run away. Once, he had found her at the Searsport docks dressed in boy's clothing, her hair tucked into a watch cap, about to sign on as cabin boy. Another few minutes and it would have been too late. Eventually, the dockhands and mariners who frequented the area came to know her and where she belonged. The danger of her getting aboard as a stowaway, which she also had attempted twice, ceased to worry them. When she understood, at last, that all avenues of escape had been blocked, she kept to her room, day after day, week after week, until Sam could stand it no longer. It was then that he had given her the *Zephyr*. And it had made all the difference in the world.

"Of course, if I had known this little tub was going to be the catalyst for finding you a husband who would take you so far away from us, M, I might have thought twice about the whole thing."

M grinned as she thought about the day her maritime path had crossed that of Madras Mitchell's. She had gone upriver that day, past Sandy Point. She had started out at mid-morning on a sunny early June day with a picnic lunch and a spyglass in her basket. She knew a place on Verona Island where bald eagles made their nests and she looked forward to watching them. By early afternoon, the sky had lowered and mist was creeping rapidly up the channel. It had been one of those days when, in a defiant mood, she had not been precise about her destination and had simply gone off without explanation.

Fog did not disturb her; she knew how to navigate well enough by compass. But she knew Grand Fan, Maude, and Dr. Sam would worry, especially since they had no idea where she had gone, except upriver.

"I lost my foghorn overboard that day, Dr. Sam," M said, as if she hadn't told him the story many times. As a small-craft sailor, when fog rolled in she was obliged to alert other vessels of her presence by frequently blowing her foghorn. All had gone well until she was halfway across the channel. Then, a sudden high swell, impossible to see coming, lifted the *Zephyr* unexpectedly, jerking the tiller out of her grip. Her quick and sudden reaction to regain control of the boat had cost her the foghorn.

"That was when I started to get scared," she said to Sam. "I was no longer certain of my direction; the wind had died, so I reefed sail, thinking I'd drift on the current, which was more or less going south, until I regained my sense of direction. And that was my second mistake." Almost immediately the *Zephyr* had slammed into a very large moving object, which turned out to be the *Boreas*. The blow pitched M into the water, and she remembered gasping for breath and clawing to the surface, seeking anything to hold on to. Somehow—and later, she had no clear memory of it—she managed to grab the gunwale of the *Zephyr*. The waterlogged weight of her dress and petticoats made it impossible to do more. She did not know how to swim. It was not a skill girls and women, or even sailors, ever learned.

Above her head, she had heard male voices cursing, and one, particularly emphatic, wanted to know where in hell a rock square in the middle of the channel had come from when the damn thing sure hadn't been there on the way upriver.

"I wish you could have seen Madras's face when I started yelling for help and he looked over the side and saw me," M said, laughing at the memory. "He looked as if he'd seen a sea serpent or a ghost."

"When, in fact, he'd seen a mermaid," Sam said, laughing with her.

"Well, yes, but that didn't dawn on him until somewhat later."

The sailors on the *Boreas* had grabbed the *Zephyr* with a boat hook. They threw M a loop of rope, which she managed to slip over her head and under her arms. They hauled her aboard, dripping gallons of water. The *Zephyr* had, by some miracle, escaped serious damage.

"The first thing Madras Mitchell ever said to me was 'If you don't look like a half-dead mackerel, I don't know what does.' He threw me a blanket and left me to the attentions of the cook, who took me below and set me by the stove." She knew it was not the time or place for the captain of the vessel to introduce himself or see to her comfort. His concern was for the safety of the situation, and only his presence on deck would ensure that. She understood that implicitly and accepted it as natural. She had learned at an early age aboard the *Fairmount* to take orders—as well as to give them.

She began to tremble from chill and the shock of realizing how close she had come to drowning, how very close she had come to duplicating the fate of her sister, Grace. But even as her teeth chattered and she was frighteningly aware of her own mortality, she felt rage grow hot inside her. How dare that man compare her to a mackerel! She threw off the blanket and before the cook could stop her, stomped up the companionway ladder and onto the deck where she confronted Captain Whoever-he-was.

"I don't know who you are, sir, and I don't want to. I'd be greatly obliged if you'd give the order to have me lowered back to my own boat. I can find my way across this bay in the dark and would have—"

"And would have if you had the sense God gave a goose to blow your own damn foghorn."

"Which I had done repeatedly, sir, until a swell jolted it from my hand . . ." She trembled suddenly, and saw the annoyance on the captain's face soften for an instant as he reached to steady her.

"I'm Madras Mitchell of the *Boreas*. And you are?"

"Miss M Giddings, the daughter of Captain Abner and Mrs. Giddings."

A look of cautious interest came into Madras's eyes; she saw that clearly.

"Of Abbott's Reach, I believe."

"Quite. Now that we have that settled, I'd like to go back to my boat and return to my grandmother, who will be wondering what's keeping me from supper."

"Worried as hell, more likely, that you've gone and drowned yourself." She remembered how the rough tone of his voice gave her an irrational urge to kick him right square in the shins. "Well, I'm not going to let you set foot off this deck. We'll dock at Searsport in another hour, fog or no, and I'll lay odds that some-one will be there looking for you. Which, as I understand it, won't be the first time."

"You, Captain Mitchell, don't understand a damn thing!" She turned on her heel and made her way forward, each step severely hampered by the wet folds of her skirts clinging like tentacles to her legs.

"What a snit I was in, Dr. Sam," M said. "I don't think I ever disliked anyone so much as I disliked Madras Mitchell that day."

"And sure enough, when the *Boreas* docked at Searsport, your grandmother, Maude, and I were right there, organizing a search party. They were convinced you'd finally carried out your plan to ship as a common seaman. But I knew you better than that. I fig-ured you'd gone aground or decided to wait somewhere until the fog lifted. I knew you'd turn up."

"Once I had the *Zephyr*, the need to run away left me. It's because I had the sea back. I finally understood that Mother and Father did the right thing for me by leaving me alongshore. Eventually, I saw how much Grand Fan wanted me with her, and I saw that while my first years were shaped by the sea, my present years were to be shaped by land. And when I was grown, I would know them both and be the better for it."

M's Log—August 1871

*Today, when we were out on the bay, I told Dr. Sam why I
had left off running away, and how I began to understand that I
might be freer to choose if I accepted my landlubber fate. But what I
did not tell him is this: that I had planned when I reached my
twentieth birthday to sail away on my own, to find the Havener sisters—China, India, and Persia—and sail with them, a vessel filled
with women, with never a thought for husbands or fathers.*

*I saw the sisters once, from a distance, when I was a little girl.
Mother pointed them out to me, and their ship, the* Empress, *when
we came to anchor off Ireland. "They are maiden ladies," Mother
said, as if that explained everything. Dr. Sam says they sail their
ship because their father, who is always aboard, is indisposed from
over-fondness for rum. Father told me the Havener sisters have
made a great deal of money and built a large house at the edge of
the sea somewhere on the Maine coast, between Mount Desert
Island and Machias, but no one knows for sure.*

*Fate, however, decreed that I would not run away, and has
given me Madras instead, who is of the sea, bred upon and born to
it, just as I am.*

*Grand Fan has begun to cluck about lace wedding veils and prac-
tical cotton or wool dresses for my trousseau. I, of course, will have to let
her dress me as a bride, which she never was, and will never be as long
as Ellis Harding is not hers to have. I said as much to Mrs. Maude
and she said I must not be cheeky, nor should I concern myself with
matters about which I know nothing. It was a mild reproof and I did
not take it to heart. Generally, Mrs. Maude will speak to me of anything, but when it comes to Grand Fan, she is capable of closing up
tighter than a clam at high tide. And when I said as much, Mrs.
Maude merely fixed me with that look of superior complacency I
always find so amusing; it's as impenetrable as a burdock bramble.*

6.

"I don't like this new custom of public weddings in churches," Fanny said. She shook out a fold of silk ivory satin and held it to the light. "But every bride ought to have an extravagant dress, something out of the ordinary to wear again on special occasions." She had not said so, but she wished M's wedding was to take place at Abbott's Reach in the sunny parlor, or outside under the arbor when the roses bloomed in June.

"Don't fret, Grand Fan; Madras and I will be married aboard the *Boreas*," M said quietly. "The ceremony will take place the morning of the day we sail, most likely May Day. We'll have the wedding dinner on the deck if the weather is fair, or below if it's not. As for a fancy dress, you know I'll have no use for one. There are no special occasions at sea. There's only the wind, the sky, and the water."

Fanny nodded in agreement, knowing that M's choice of a neutral place for the wedding would suit everyone.

Isaiah and Zulema Mitchell, Madras's parents, had accepted M as their son's choice, Fanny knew. She also knew that Augusta Mitchell, Madras's grandmother, was not enthusiastic, and she knew why. While Augusta Mitchell had perfectly good reasons to dislike and distrust Fanny, M knew nothing of that, and never would. Fanny would see to it.

Fanny neither wanted nor expected to be included in the village society of Searsport where the Mitchells lived. It was enough that the people of Stockton Springs tolerated her, exchanging polite nods with her whenever she went into the village, some even engaging her in conversation. That small favor had been granted her almost from the moment M had come to live with her. She had seen, then, that for M to get on in the world, she must not be hindered by the unavoidable fact of her family connections. What mattered was how things looked, and Fanny had become adept at keeping up appearances. It helped that she had been raised at the Point and that her parents had been known and respected in Stockton Springs village.

Fanny draped the lovely ivory fabric around M's shoulders and picked up a piece of fine blond lace fabric several yards long. She fixed it to M's head with hairpins and stood back to assess the result. "Yes, that's quite lovely," she said. Fanny turned M gently toward the gilt-framed mirror hanging over the mantel. "See?"

M regarded her reflection with quiet detachment, trying to see herself as her grandmother did . . . as Madras did. She saw a young woman of nineteen with good features—a pretty mouth, lustrous blue eyes, and auburn hair inclined to wave, especially on damp days. She saw in her face all the melancholy, guarded thoughts she rarely voiced aloud, thoughts she confided only to her log. She saw a quick, spontaneous spirit never quite free of something vaguely sad and wary hovering beneath the gentle smile. She saw little in herself that was remarkable, and marveled that someone as vigorous and handsome as Madras Mitchell wanted her for his wife. A little rill of panic surfaced. How could Madras love her? Why was he not enamored of one of the Miss Griffins—Lily or Lucia—or Atlanta Sears, whose beautiful figure and flashing dimples made her the object of many a young man's hopes? But those young ladies did not go to sea. It was she—M—who was a creature of the deep. Madras loved her because the sea was in her veins. For a moment, M imagined a starfish stitched to the blond lace veil and seaweed braided into her hair. She imagined herself with a mermaid's tail. She smiled suddenly, liking the whimsical image of herself.

"I sent a note to the Misses Merrithew, M. You are to stop by their dress shop for measurements."

Fanny picked up the latest issue of *Peterson's* magazine and leafed through the pages. "What do you think of this model?" She showed M a color sketch of a dress lavishly bustled, flounced, and draped.

"Very beautiful, but much too fussy, Grand Fan. I want something simple: no bustle, no ruching, no rosettes. Something to
wear ashore in tropical latitudes. Perhaps in lightweight linen, a
simple white dress with a sweet little fitted jacket in velvet." She
knew velvet would go a long way to offset her grandmother's dis-
appointment about the lack of satin. "The satin is lovely, Grand
Fan, but it's just not me."

"Very well . . . but I insist on a lace veil. You can lay it away
against the day you have a daughter of your own. Or if you don't
care to put it away, you can wear it as a shawl."

"Very well, then, the lace veil, but not the satin." M did not
mind conceding on that point. It was a small enough thing to do
to please her grandmother.

"The linen for your dress must be as fine as can be had. I will
send to Bangor for it."

M removed the lace veil and handed it to her grandmother.
"And I will go to see the Misses Merrithew."

The Misses Merrithew, always referred to collectively, kept a
dressmaking shop in the front room of their little Cape Cod house
located on a street just off the main road in Stockton Springs village. No one in town knew their given names because they called
one another "Sister," and that only. They were maiden ladies, said to
be twins, but no one knew for sure. No one knew how old they
were, either, but it was supposed they were in their seventies. They,
like many in the village, had been born and raised entirely at sea. In
their youth they had perfected their sewing skills on numerous voyages to seaports all over the world. People said that if anyone could
make a silk purse out of a sow's ear, it was the Misses Merrithew.

A little bell jingled delicately when M opened the door to their
shop later that week. The odor of freshly baked gingerbread scented
the air, and beneath that lovely smell, M detected the scent of lavender and rose petals. The shop was empty, but presently a door at the

rear opened and the Misses Merrithew fluttered in, their sweet blue eyes alight, beautiful but reserved smiles on their finely wrinkled faces. They were dressed alike in dove-gray gowns with white collars embroidered with cutwork roses. They wore their hair in identical fashion, too: a fringe of curls at the forehead, the rest drawn back into a loose knot and held in place with ivory hairpins, carved, it was said, by rough-and-tumble sailors who loved them from afar.

"Oh, Sister, it's Miss M Giddings," one Miss Merrithew declared.

"Yes, yes, she's to be married in the spring, Sister," the other Miss Merrithew said, "to Mr. Madras Mitchell of the *Boreas.*"

The sisters exchanged quick glances before they fixed their expert gaze on M, measuring her proportions, M was certain, merely by looking at her.

"I brought some linen I want made up into a dress suitable to be married in," M said.

"Linen! Oh, dear me, Miss Giddings. It's not at all the fashion for a bride. Satin. It must be satin and white. It's all the mode. All the great beauties of Bangor are wearing satin at their weddings. Surely not linen."

M smiled politely as she laid her parcel on the counter where the Misses Merrithew displayed ribbons, white kid gloves, and cards of glass buttons. "It's the very best linen, Miss Merrithew," M said. "Very finely woven. I will have no use for satin at sea . . . but I will need a little white velvet jacket to set off the linen dress."

The sisters' eyes lit up. "Velvet!" said one sister. "Yes, it's just the thing to guard against the chilly breezes of May." That Miss Merrithew went to a cupboard. "Here's the very thing, Miss Giddings." She held out some fabric for M to touch.

"It's lovely. Is it silk velvet?" M asked, stroking the fabric and admiring its lovely texture.

"Oh, yes, more than twenty yards, and we've saved it for many a year. Mama bought it in China on Papa's last voyage there. For our wedding dresses, she always said. Satin was not the fashion then. Poor Mama! How could she have known that we would never marry? Such a bitter pill for her to swallow. I swear she never got over it."

"But we might have married, Sister, if only we had found brothers we liked well enough to take."

"No, we never found any brothers we liked well enough to make us want to part from one another . . ."

Miss Merrithew cradled the carefully folded yardage as if it were the embodiment of all their lost and hopeful youth.

"I've brought a sketch of what I want," M said. "Very simple, as you see."

A look of quiet horror descended upon the faces of the Misses Merrithew. They returned the yardage to the cupboard, their hands smoothing and patting, before they looked at the sketch again.

"Why, it is much too plain, Miss Giddings! Not a ruffle or a bow!"

"But it's what I want, Miss Merrithew. My tastes are plain, and you know as well as I do that fancy dresses at sea are more of a hindrance than a help."

The Misses Merrithew nodded to one another, understanding, in spite of their disapproval. "Well, then, we must find other ways to make it elegant," one Miss Merrithew said. "We will make the wrists pointed. And the basque will have pink glass buttons shaped like roses down the front. And at the neck, a collar band edged in a fine lace ruffle so narrow you'll hardly know it's there. But quite elegant, I assure you. We will gather the fullness of the skirt toward the back. In that way you will have the modern silhouette, but not the aggravation of a bustle," she finished with a smile.

The other sister chimed in: "And the jacket sleeves shall come just to the elbow, slightly full at the shoulder, in a bit of a bell shape.

The front edges of the jacket must be scalloped—with delicate pink roses embroidered on them—in a bullion stitch. And the front must close with a single silver clasp." That Miss Merrithew made rapid sketches on the back of an envelope. She held it up for M to see.

"Yes!" M exclaimed, smiling. "That's exactly it!" In fact, she thought the embroidered roses went a bit too far, but she saw that the Misses Merrithew had their hearts set on this detail.

The other Miss Merrithew reached for the tape measure and yardstick.

"Come along, Miss Giddings, we must take your measure, although I feel I have already got it—you are so very slender." They led M into a smaller room, which had once served as the borning room back in 1795 when the house was built. They helped M remove her dress and petticoats. They undid buttons and untied petticoat strings with gentle fingers until M stood in her shift and stays.

One of the sisters wielded the tape measure and the other jotted down measurements on a slip of paper. "Her waist is still twenty-four inches, Sister. But you have grown a bit taller, Miss Giddings, since the last time we made you a dress."

They helped her dress again and led her out to the shop.

"Will you be needing other things for your trousseau, Miss Giddings? Bed gowns, perhaps? Or several day dresses?"

"Yes, I think so, but I still haven't decided exactly," said M.

"Oh, it's all so exciting, isn't it, Sister? M Giddings going off to see the world. Why, I remember the day you came to live here, my dear. Such a sad and unhappy child you were. But I said to Sister—Sister, that one will be a beauty, and one day we'll make her wedding dress."

"What will your wedding voyage destination be, Miss Giddings?" the other Miss Merrithew asked.

"Hawaii. And then California."

The Misses Merrithew glanced at one another, their smiles suddenly replaced by expressions of concern.

"Surely you are not going to Hawaii! Surely Mr. Mitchell would not take you there!"

"I believe, Sister, you don't need to say more . . . we must not tell tales or get involved in business that does not concern us . . ."

"But I haven't finished, Sister. I have much more to say. Surely someone ought to tell Miss Giddings what has been said . . ."

M looked at them, mystified. "What do you mean? What has been said?"

"Nothing, Miss Giddings, nothing at all, merely a rumor, an old rumor, one that has been told about every young man who has ever gone to the Pacific . . . Why, the very same rumor was said about our very own brothers . . ."

"What rumor?"

The Misses Merrithew, their mouths settled into prim, identical lines, as if holding pins in them, propelled M, one on either side of her, gently toward the door.

"The one about wild oats, dear," one Miss Merrithew whispered. "Sowing wild oats."

"Yes, wild oats," the other Miss Merrithew echoed. "All young men, whether they go to sea or not, sow wild oats—or so we have heard."

M's Log—October 1871

Madras has gone to Boston on business, but if he were here I would not be sitting by the window in my room, watching it grow dark—and wondering. I would ask him if he has "sowed his wild oats." I believe he would say that he has.

I know what it means for young men to sow wild oats. I asked Mrs. Maude about it a few months ago. She told me it meant a young man had enjoyed physical intimacy with a woman. I do not like to think that Madras has lain in arms other than my own, but if I love him truly, as I know I do, then I must overlook it, for I did not know him then.

He has, after all, chosen me for his wife. I write this and I am content with it. Yet, I am furious with the Misses Merrithew and their stupid old-lady gossip, hinting so carelessly of things they most likely have not experienced. I do not believe they meant any harm—and yet, what they said has caused me much anguish these last few hours.

I will not let their loose tongues spoil my happiness. Nor will I let what they say color my perception of Madras. He is ardent and spirited and full of an energy I cannot name—an energy I both long for and fear. I fear it because I do not know if I have the same energy, and because what is nameless is always frightening. I fear disappointing him in the intimacies husband and wife share; more so now, because if he has sown his wild oats (as no doubt he has), it gives him a basis for comparison—one I do not have. Perhaps he will find me wanting in that way. Yet, how can it be to my disadvantage to have a husband with experience of such matters?

I will put it out of my mind and think only of the intoxicating joy I feel whenever Madras touches me.

7.

M thrust the trowel into the damp soil to unearth the dahlia tubers. She gathered a few more and tossed them into a willow basket. The dahlias had bloomed in a gaudy profusion of dark red, vivid yellow, and fiery orange. Although she loved the brightly colored dahlias, she did not like digging up the tubers, and she had grumbled about it.

"This is more trouble than it's worth," she said again, as if she had not said it several times already. "I won't miss digging dahlia tubers when I am at sea." At sea, she would have geraniums, herbs, and ivy in pots hanging from the transom in quarters she'd share with Madras. Yet, even plants in pots presented at least one basic problem: They required freshwater, not salt, so if the casks ran low, as they sometimes did, only people—not plants—would be allowed a precious ration of water.

Ignoring M's grumbles, Maude said, "I've always thought that a garden is the perfect metaphor for life." She was on her knees, her hands stained dark with dirt, her head bare, her cheeks pink from exertion and the cool breeze. Her sleeves were rolled up and she had tucked the bottom hem of her faded blue cotton gown into her front waistband, creating pantaloons of a sort, which gave her more freedom of movement. As a child and in the early days of her adolescence, M had cheerfully fixed her skirt that way, too, for work, but now she shunned it, thinking it old-fashioned and not the least refined. She feared that Madras would arrive unexpectedly, as he sometimes did, and find her with her skirts all awry in a makeshift way.

"How do you mean?" M asked, hitching herself toward the next clump of dahlias. Her petticoats dragged and tangled at her knees. She yanked the fabric free with a savage jerk.

"Birthing, blooming, and dying. Constant and predictable cycles of renewal and transformation. Gardens have their sweet, shady places just as life does. And noxious weeds and rocks where you don't want them; rocks and weeds . . . you can't get rid of the cussed things." Maude pried a stone out of the dirt with her trowel and flung it away into the woods bordering the grass. "It's impossible, when I'm in the garden, not to think of roots, hidden, and going down deep into the earth. Anchoring there. I think of the edges of things, too, how they shift and change no matter how many bricks I line up to keep it all straight and contained. Then there are the unexpected pleasures—something grows and blooms and you didn't even plant it. It volunteers. Or insects arrive and chew up and make ugly all you've tried to make beautiful and fair. I think gardens are a vain human attempt to impose a benign kind of order on what essentially is governed by pure chaos." She wiped her forehead with the back of her hand, leaving a streak of dirt on her face.

M laughed and threw another handful of tubers into the basket. Maude liked watching things grow and she had nurtured that enjoyment in M. In spite of M's dislike of the work, she loved being outside in the garden with Maude.

Maude, M knew, liked the physical pleasure of digging in the dirt and the exercise it gave her mind as she thought about how to take care of what she grew. She was best at growing herbs and medicinal plants, an art she had perfected with long years of practice and study. Because her midwifery skills were wanted less and less (as more women preferred to be attended by doctors), she had fallen back on selling herbal remedies. She also sold bunches of dried sea lavender and potpourris of rose petals for scenting trunks and bureau drawers. She put up small brown paper bags of rose hips, mint, and chamomile for tea. M helped her with picking, drying, and packaging the "simples," as Maude called them.

But now it was mid-October, and herbs and dahlias had long gone by. Leaves fell from maples and oaks, rustling and shifting in the intermittent breeze. Change was in the air—change, M felt, that would set her on her course upon the great waters of life. For Maude, the garden served as metaphor, but for M it was the sea.

Out on the bay the water's surface glistened in the sun, and M spotted several ships, some headed upriver to Bangor, some headed downriver to the open ocean and Boston, or to cities along the Atlantic coast and to ports all over the world. A sudden restlessness came over her. She dropped the trowel into the basket and wiped her hands on the coarse cotton apron tied around her waist. "That's enough for today, don't you think, Mrs. Maude? Let's go inside and see what Grand Fan is doing."

She knew perfectly well what her grandmother was doing. Fanny was cleaning her house in anticipation of a gathering planned for later that week, to celebrate M's engagement. The party was to take place in a few days' time.

"I don't know, M. We might be better off staying out of your grandmother's way." Maude's grin held a hint of mischief. The fine wrinkles around her mouth and in her cheeks deepened in an oddly becoming way. As usual, her gray hair was slipping its pins. Dirt streaked her face and her knees were muddy.

"I fear, Mrs. Maude, that Grand Fan will take one look at you caked with garden dirt and chase you out with a broom," M said, laughing.

"In that case, we'd better sneak up the back stairs." Maude banged her trowel on a rock to rid it of clods of dirt. She picked up the basket and headed for the barn where she and M stored the dahlia tubers in a barrel of sawdust. They washed the worst of the dirt off their hands at the outdoor pump in the yard.

Fanny accosted M and Maude as they were halfway up the back stairs. She raised her eyebrows and looked pointedly at their muddy shoes and grimy dress hems. The furrows lightly etched into her face gave her demeanor a certain indisputable air of authority. Caught, Maude and M glanced at one another and shrugged. Obediently, they sat down on the stairs and removed their shoes.

"Are we free to go, or are we prisoners of Zenda?" Maude asked.

Fanny fixed her with an annoyed look.

"You are free to go so long as you put on clean but old gowns. When you have done that, please come downstairs. M, I will expect you to dust everything in the front parlor. And Maude,

I need you in the kitchen to mix up some of your salt and lemon solution for cleaning the silver candlesticks."

M made a wry face. She disliked dusting the bric-a-brac—the seashells, the jars of beach glass, the books, all the little porcelain figurines and treasures and portraits and photographs and tintypes her grandmother had collected over the years.

"See," Maude said to M. "I told you we should have stayed outside longer—a lot longer. In fact, we probably should have run away to sea."

M giggled as she and Maude went up the stairs, shoes in hand, holding filthy skirt hems up to their knees.

M's Log—October 1871

I wish Grand Fan was not so set on the gathering she has planned so carefully. At first she said she would invite only a few people, and I agreed to that—Dr. Sam and Mrs. Maude, Ellis Harding, the Misses Merrithew, several young ladies of my acquaintance, and several young gentlemen of Madras's acquaintance. But last week she told me she had invited Mr. and Mrs. Mitchell. It was, she said, the proper thing to do, and if they sent regrets, she guessed she'd bear up under the snub. Grand Fan wants them to accept her invitation—it matters greatly to her, although she pretends otherwise. I see no reason for them to be here, even if they are my future in-laws. I fear their presence will cause us to feel awkward and strange. Grand Fan has spent her life on the edges of things; she is not a tame flower, as they are, in one of Mrs. Maude's metaphorical gardens.

Today, however, their acceptance arrived in the mail, and not only for Mr. and Mrs. Mitchell. They also will bring Madras's sister, Pacifica, who is a year older than I, and his brother, Gordon, just fifteen, and Mrs. Augusta Mitchell, his grandmother, and Miss

*Honoria Cobb, his grandmother's sister, a maiden lady. I have met
them all before, and they have treated me kindly because Madras
has chosen me. They know they cannot dissuade him, for he is fierce
in his love for me. It is my belief that they are not hasty in their
judgment, so perhaps all will go well and I worry for nothing.
Pacifica has been especially friendly and I like her very much. But
Mrs. Augusta Mitchell and Miss Honoria Cobb are cool and intim-
idating. They are ladies of a long-forgotten world of rigid manners
and perfect formality, not the least bit modern in their ideas or
thinking, and being in their presence is like facing dragons.*

*Grand Fan, I fear, is quite bowled over by this news; she had
convinced herself that they would not come. No wonder she has been
cross and has no time to talk to me these past few days. All she
thinks of is what kind of impression she will make, if her dress is
suitable, the house clean enough, the food elegant enough. She says
she wants this party for me, but I think she wants it for her. She
wants, perhaps for the first time in her life, to feel as if she is just
another ordinary woman preparing for her granddaughter's wedding.*

*What she does not understand is that she is not ordinary, nor
am I. Fate, the stars, some strange quirk of destiny has decreed it so,
and we are flung about by it, flimsy crafts upon the rough sea, the
weather ahead uncertain.*

8.

It stormed the afternoon of Fanny's gathering and the guests
arrived cold, wet, and buffeted by the wind. A fire crackled in the
parlor fireplace and oil lamps glowed softly in all corners of the
room. It was the sort of day, the daylight hours grown short and
hinting of winter, that pushed people instinctively toward warmth,
light, food, and talk.

Maude had encouraged Fanny to invite the Mitchells. "The worst they can do is say no," Maude had said. "But they won't. They are as curious about you as you are about them. They are not unkind people—with the possible exception of old Mrs. Mitchell. But even she will give in to curiosity. Mark my words."

"Which does not strike me as a promising beginning," Fanny replied acidly as she took up her pen and wrote the invitation. She said nothing about the fact that her path had crossed Augusta Mitchell's many years ago. Maude was not privy to all of Fanny's secrets.

The evening of the party, the Mitchell family entered Abbott's Reach clumped together like a phalanx of Roman foot soldiers intent upon defending some poorly defined territory. They filled the front hall in a tight knot of rustling black and gray silk skirts and sober black wool trousers and cloaks. Safety in numbers, Fanny thought, a small rill of amusement playing in her mind. For a moment, she was not quite certain how to greet them, but her innate sense of sociability asserted itself, and she murmured all the proper civilities and made the proper gestures of welcome, just as she had all those years ago when she had reigned so confidently as the hostess at Pink Chimneys. Joshua Stetson had trained her well in the ways of polite society. The phrases came to her lips and her manner was gracious. In response, she saw the Mitchells relax as they removed their capes and cloaks and jackets.

Maude and Sam stood by Fanny's side, solid and natural as granite. Maude was well turned out in a pretty wool gown of China blue, its only ornament a cameo brooch set in silver which had belonged to her mother. Her hair was coiled into a neat knot atop her head, over which lay a band of white lace. Sam was dapper in a navy blue seaman's jacket and a white satin brocade waistcoat. His old-fashioned cravat was as white as his hair. Fanny had chosen to wear a dark green velvet gown sporting a fall of white lace at the throat and wrists. Her only jewelry was a pair of garnet earrings, a gift from Abner and Elizabeth. In her hair she had placed the ivory comb Sam had given her for her fiftieth birthday.

Madras emerged from the group.

"Please, let me introduce you to everyone. Miss Abbott, my parents, Mr. and Mrs. Mitchell."

Zulema Mitchell, tall, dark, and elegant in a plum silk dress trimmed with a beautiful black lace collar, smiled with friendly reserve. Isaiah Mitchell, slightly taller than his wife, his face thin and handsome, bowed slightly. His white silk waistcoat under his black wool jacket was embroidered with a Chinese design of red and pink peonies.

"Miss Abbott—how very kind of you to host this party for M and Madras," Zulema said in her light, pleasing voice. She glanced around quickly and Fanny saw surprise in her eyes, as if she had expected evidence of vulgarity or a room decorated in poor taste. Seeing the glance, Fanny felt her confidence slip, but Maude made a slightly wry face as if to say, "So what?" Fanny's mood brightened. Zulema indicated the two elderly ladies in the party. "This is Mrs. Augusta Mitchell, my husband's mother, and her sister, Miss Honoria Cobb."

Augusta Mitchell, statuesque in a rust-colored dress, fixed Fanny with a cold eye and a vague smile. She acknowledged the introduction with a curt nod of her head, the gesture of a woman accustomed to obedience. Honoria, a faded and much less robust version of her older sister, wore a dress of navy blue trimmed with ecru lace. She nodded with distant politeness, as if she did not quite know what to think or say unless prompted by Augusta.

Isaiah offered his hand, and when Fanny took it, she felt in his clasp a cautious friendliness and kindness. He drew Pacifica and Gordon, his other two children, forward and introduced them. Pacifica was tall and lovely. She had her mother's dark good looks, and she cut an elegant figure. She wore a sapphire-blue dress, which highlighted her pretty blue eyes, so startling with her dark hair. She curtsied prettily and Fanny inclined her head in return.

Gordon stared openly at Fanny, full of curiosity, but respectful. He made a polite bow, but his blue eyes twinkled with laughter and good humor, a sharp contrast to the correct and sober politeness of his relatives. His parents, M had told Fanny, found the boy to be a handful. But, she said, he was good-hearted in his high spirits.

The introductions were barely over when the Misses Merrithew arrived, escorted by Ellis Harding, who helped them alight from a hired carriage. He held a huge black umbrella over their heads as they made their way into the house.

"Happy is the bride it rains upon," chirped one of the Misses Merrithew as she divested herself of a voluminous Kinsale cloak lined in dark purple satin.

Later, Fanny did not quite remember how she managed to usher everyone into the front parlor, but once there, they fell naturally into conversation, grouped according to age.

Soon, Lily and Lucia Griffin and Atlanta Sears arrived. They had been friends with M since their schooldays in Stockton Springs village. Their mothers were quietly accepting of M's irregular family circumstances and had, over the years, allowed their daughters to visit M at Abbott's Reach.

Close behind the young ladies were Mindoro Matthews and Hugh Chapman, friends of Madras. They, too, were sons of the sea. Mindoro had been born off the coast of Japan and Hugh had been born off the coast of Ireland, their given names reflecting the geography of their places of birth. They were not mariners, however. Mindoro worked in his father's shipyard and Hugh in his father's ship chandlery business.

M, at Fanny's insistence, stayed upstairs until all the guests had arrived. She entered the parlor quietly and stood in the doorway, her eyes seeking Madras. Her mauve velvet dress, created by the Misses Merrithew, fit tightly in the bodice and sleeves. The skirt fell from a pointed waist in slender lines down the front, with fullness at the back. It gave her an air of romantic loveliness. Mindoro and Hugh saw her first. Their conversation stopped and admiration filled their eyes.

"You see, Sister," one of the Misses Merrithew whispered into the lull. "I told you that color on M would be one of our greatest successes." The other Miss Merrithew shushed her with a gentle touch of her hand.

Madras moved to M's side with the leisurely haste she loved so much. He took her hand, tucked it into his elbow, and led her, as if she were precious cargo, to sit on the sofa beside Pacifica and Zulema.

"Well, Miss Abbott," Ellis whispered to Fanny, "I'd say you've pulled the whole thing off pretty well."

"That remains to be seen, Mr. Harding. Much yet depends on your skill with the fiddle and the Misses Merrithew at the piano."

With that cue, Ellis took up his fiddle and the Misses Merrithew went to the piano, where they launched into a series of pleasant tunes.

"Do you or your daughter sing, Mrs. Mitchell?" Fanny asked Zulema during a pause in the music. Zulema laughed and glanced affectionately at her husband. "Not at all, Miss Abbott. Neither Patsy—Pacifica—nor I can carry a tune. But Madras, Gordon, and Mr. Mitchell have the best of voices, if only we can persuade them to sing. What do you say, my dears? Won't you favor us with a ballad or two?"

The others in the room broke into spontaneous applause.

Madras kissed M's hand and joined his father and brother, singing "Beautiful Dreamer" and "Annie Laurie."

"All my family is musical," Augusta Mitchell confided, with authority.

"All," Honoria Cobb echoed gravely, her thin hands folded into her thin lap.

M listened intently with eyes only for Madras. How handsome he is, she thought, with his dark hair falling across his brow. The three men sang easily and naturally, Gordon taking the tenor part. Ellis added his fine baritone to the choruses.

M longed, suddenly, for her parents, but they were far away at sea. Why were they not here to share her happiness? Why had they been so cruel as to leave her alongshore? Why had Grace died? She felt her lips tremble and tears prick her eyes.

"Are you unwell?" Patsy whispered, taking M's hand.

The men finished singing and Ellis laid aside his fiddle. The Misses Merrithew continued to play a soft, plaintive melody. Zulema, sensing a sudden change in M's mood, leaned toward Fanny. "Can it be, Miss Abbott," she said quietly, "that M has been too excited to remember to eat properly today?"

Fanny, with Zulema following, went to the table and put several sandwiches on plates. She handed them to M and Patsy. Zulema dipped glasses of punch for the two girls.

Maude moved quickly to M's side, sliding her arm around M's waist, checking to see if she had laced her stays too tightly. "It's not that," M said crossly, sensing Maude's concern and resenting it. "I don't need to be fussed over. I'm quite all right." She took a deep breath and felt the dark mood ease its grip.

"The sea is no place for a girl with thin blood," Augusta Mitchell remarked to the room at large. "The women in my family do not have thin blood. Except, of course, for Honoria."

"Except, of course," Honoria murmured.

M fixed old Mrs. Mitchell with a cold look. "Is that your way of implying I have inherited bad blood?" she asked, a note of shrill anger in her voice. She saw her grandmother's face flush a deep pink as she comprehended M's meaning. Augusta Mitchell's mouth settled into an offended line as her eyes opened wide in shocked surprise at such cheekiness.

An expression of patient concern came over Zulema's face. She slipped her arm through Augusta Mitchell's.

"I'm sure Mother Mitchell only meant that she is concerned for your health, M. Mother, won't you step over here with me and try some of this lovely lemon pound cake?" And with infinite grace and diplomacy, she maneuvered Augusta toward the table.

Maude turned to Patsy.

"Perhaps, Miss Mitchell, you can persuade M to take you and the other young ladies upstairs to refresh yourselves," she said. "And, M, while you are there, would you be so kind as to fetch my paisley shawl? I believe I left it draped over the banister."

"Oh, yes," Lucia Griffin said, "show us your room." She turned to her sister. "Lily, I do believe your hair needs re-pinning."

M nodded in agreement and allowed herself to be led from the room and up the stairs.

"A short rest will do M a world of good, I expect," Fanny said.

Hugh, Madras, Mindoro, and Gordon relaxed and settled into a circle near the fire. Soon, they were talking and laughing as if nothing had been amiss. Ellis, Sam, and Isaiah occupied a corner of the room where they, too, began to talk of shipping, farming, and business.

The Misses Merrithew left off playing the piano and went to sit by Honoria Cobb. Maude ushered Fanny, Zulema, and Augusta to a sofa and chairs near the big window overlooking the river. "Please accept my apologies, Mrs. Mitchell. Sometimes M forgets her manners," Fanny said.

"I have heard of your granddaughter's high spirits, Miss Abbott, and I feel that I must warn you: Nothing good ever

comes from it. High spirits in a female can only lead to willful-
ness, which in turn will only bring unhappiness to her and those
around her. I have raised five daughters of my own. I know what I
am talking about," Augusta said.

Maude reached for Fanny's hand, a tacit way of saying, *Take no
notice of what is being said, and be silent.*

"Experience is always the best teacher. Don't you agree, Fanny?"
Fanny nodded stiffly in agreement.

"Mother Mitchell and I are most interested to hear about M's
trousseau, Miss Abbott. Perhaps you'd tell us about it," Zulema
said. That was not precisely true. Augusta had pointedly avoided
any discussion of anything pertaining to the impending marriage.
Nonetheless, soon the conversation was all about linen sheets, crocheted pillowslip edgings, and needlepoint slipper patterns.

When M and the other girls returned, all was peaceful and
civil. M, contrite and knowing her duty, went immediately to
Augusta Mitchell. "Please forgive my lapse of manners, Mrs.
Mitchell," she said. "I can't think what came over me."

"High spirits, my girl—that's what came over you. High spirits. You must learn not to carry so much sail."

"Thank you, Mrs. Mitchell, I'll remember what you say," M
said. Her mother had given her similar advice many times, but no
matter how she tried to heed it, she always ended up speaking out
of turn.

"Then you may sit here beside me and we'll say no more of
it." Despite her softer tone, the polite, fragile edges of Augusta
Mitchell's tolerance had been severely frayed, and everyone in the
room knew it.

What they did not know was that Augusta Mitchell had swallowed a great deal of pride even to set foot in Fanny Abbott's
house. Augusta always wanted to have the upper hand, and she
believed the only way to get it was to face the enemy. She did not

want Madras to marry M Giddings, and she had a weapon or two at her disposal she felt sure would prevent the marriage. She was certain that by going into enemy territory, she could greatly improve her advantage, for surely she would find vulgar evidence of Fanny Abbott's checkered past.

Unfortunately, Augusta had been disappointed. Fanny Abbott kept a decent, respectable house, and she had raised a decent, respectable granddaughter. Well, Augusta thought, it's a long road that doesn't bend.

M's Log—October 1871

Sometimes I would like to shake Grand Fan until her teeth rattle. How she could stand there and let old Mrs. Mitchell insult us is more than I can understand. When we were upstairs, Patsy said her grandmother would most certainly accuse me of being high-spirited. That, she said, is like the pot calling the kettle black, for it is a fact that no one was more high-spirited in her day than Mrs. Augusta Mitchell! How we all laughed at that. Lucia and Lily did perfect impressions of the incident, right down to the look of confusion on Miss Cobb's face. Atlanta said she had nothing but the strongest admiration for me. After that I felt better and quite able to return to the room with an apology ready.

What I want to know is—why is it all right for young men, like Gordon, to be high-spirited, but not young women? When I asked Grand Fan, she said high spirits in a young woman hint at the lack of a proper moral character and imply that one is not a lady. Grand Fan knows all too well, although she has never said so to me, the price one pays for being viewed as lacking in moral character. What other people think, apparently, is the most important factor when it comes to how one is perceived in the world, which hardly

seems fair to me. I am not the sum total of what others think I am;
I am who I believe I am.

It falls upon a young lady, Grand Fan said, to temper the high
spirits of a young man by restraining her own, and in that way, the
danger of flouting social convention or being drawn into behavior
one will later regret is greatly reduced. That is the most unfair thing
I have ever heard! And I told her so. She replied that life is not fair,
and the sooner I understood that, the happier I would be.

Mrs. Maude said I cannot expect to change what old Mrs.
Mitchell thinks—not at this late date. It is always wiser, she said, to
wait and see than to speak rashly and regret.

But I don't regret my attempt to defend my grandmother's
honor, and by extension, my own, even though Madras was quite
cool toward me afterward. Later, he told me his grandmother holds
controlling shares in the Boreas, and it is within her power to give
the ship's command to someone else. And if she did, it would not be
possible for us to marry.

You need to learn to eat humble pie gracefully, he said. Then,
he called me his lovely mermaid and kissed me.

9.

The morning after the gathering at Abbott's Reach, Augusta
Mitchell summoned her daughter-in-law. Zulema, dreading the
interview, and busy with the morning's baking, begged off until
late afternoon. Augusta knew a delaying tactic when she saw one,
and was not pleased.

When Zulema arrived in the late afternoon, Augusta sat, with
an air of pomp and circumstance about her, in the front parlor of
her large house on the upper end of Main Street. Plush maroon
draperies muted the light in the room. The furniture loomed like

dangerous rocks off the Down East coast. Augusta was not accustomed to disobedience of any kind. She had learned a great deal about command in the twenty years she'd spent at sea with her husband aboard his ship. She knew from long experience that if unpleasant incidents were not dealt with swiftly and directly, mutiny was the likely outcome.

"The way you indulge Madras in his ridiculous attachment to that unsuitable girl is beyond me, Zulema," she said without preamble. "It simply will not do."

Madras, as it happened, was her favorite grandson; it galled her considerably to see him throwing himself away on M Giddings—galled her even more that he had chosen the girl without consulting her. Zulema, no stranger to the veering storm of Augusta's moods, retained her composure and said nothing.

"I do not like the girl's cheekiness, Zulema," Augusta continued. She poured tea from the blue willow pot she'd acquired on her bridal voyage when she'd gone with her husband to China on a clipper ship. She still remembered how it felt like flying, to stand on the deck when the ship was under full sail. She handed a teacup to Zulema. Honoria emerged like a shadow from the far corner of the room and Augusta handed her a cup, too.

"Cheeky," Honoria murmured. She was dressed in gray, the color she usually wore. The remote, placid expression on her face did not change. She drifted back to her corner.

"M is very young, Mother Mitchell," Zulema said, "and deeply devoted to her grandmother. She is quite sensitive about her family and quick to take offense where none is intended. Surely, you understand that." Zulema, in spite of her quiet gentleness, was not intimidated by Augusta's imperious ways. She had, over the years, worked out her basic differences with her mother-in-law, and if Augusta had any respect for the opinions of any other woman, and this was doubtful, it was Zulema.

"I understand it, but I do not like it. I want Madras to have a
wife who is more pliant, but worthy of the name Mitchell—
someone whose grandmother's name can be mentioned in polite
society without eyebrows being lifted." The tone in Augusta's
voice reflected how deeply offended she believed herself to be.
Zulema knew she favored Lily Griffin as a prospective wife for
Madras, and had made that fact known to him. She had even
made it clear to Lily that Madras was hers for the taking. But
Augusta had not foreseen that Lily was already in love with
Mindoro Matthews. Thus, nothing had come of her embarrassing
efforts to throw Madras and Lily together.

"Yes, the girl can be prickly, but surely, Mother Mitchell, it is
far too late to think of that." Although Zulema had not said so to
Augusta, the thought of being connected by marriage to the former mistress of Pink Chimneys had unsettled her, too, at first.
When she was a young bride, she had listened with horrified fas-
cination, in ports all over the world, to stories about Fanny. But
she had seen, in those same ports, how women were exploited by
men, or by desperate circumstances, and were forced to live lives
not of their choosing. She also had heard many stories of fallen
women who eventually become proper wives to good men. She
knew, too, that the success of those women in transforming their
lives often depended on how adept they were at quieting the
voices of the past. Fanny Abbott could not keep her past quiet or
concealed, no matter how she tried. She had been far too visible
in her day. She had lived loudly. And for that reason and no other,
who she had been and what she had done, like a vague, unpleasant
sound, continued to reverberate around her.

Zulema also knew that such women needed the acceptance of
women like herself. Thus, she had worked through her initial objection to M. It occurred to her that if M had spent her childhood at

sea, known only as "the Giddings girl," Augusta, too, would have welcomed M without reservation.

Zulema had decided that she would not object to the marriage for several reasons. She liked M's edgy spirit, her flashes of temper, and her unswerving devotion to those she loved. She saw her son's happiness whenever he spoke of M. M would make Madras a worthy wife in spite of what Augusta thought—one who would balance his tendency to be overly commanding, like his grandmother. Zulema felt that M's spirit complemented Madras's, and that ultimately, they were good for one another.

Shaking her head, Augusta replied, "No, Zulema—it is only too late after the ship has sailed and gone to sea."

"I hope, Mother Mitchell, that you are not considering giving command of the *Boreas* to someone else." It was always best to be direct with Augusta. "You know it won't stop Madras from marrying M. He comes well recommended, and he'll soon have the offer of another ship."

"But not necessarily one that will allow him to take along a wife. I do not believe M Giddings will marry anyone who will sail away and leave her alongshore. I believe she wants the sea more than she wants Madras." Augusta sniffed in disdain and pinched her lips together firmly to punctuate her statement.

"She wants Madras and the sea, just as you wanted Reuben Mitchell—and the sea. Just as I wanted Isaiah—and the sea. For how else were we to leave the narrow confines of our mothers' kitchens and Searsport village? How else were we to go out into the world to learn of its wonders if not in the company of a husband aboard a ship? Little has changed for women in that respect, Mother Mitchell."

"We are not talking about opportunities for the education of women, Zulema. That is all nonsense. We are talking of what I believe is best for Madras."

"You do not know what is best for Madras, and neither do I. Only he knows that. And he believes it's M Giddings. Surely you do not wish to make his life harder because he dared to fall in love without consulting you." Zulema took care to keep the anger she felt out of her voice. Augusta tended to meet anger with anger and it made her behave in unreasonable and sometimes cruel ways.

"What of that incident in Hawaii . . . you were as quick as the rest of us to make certain he did not bring that girl home to you as your daughter-in-law!"

Zulema felt her face grow hot with shame. Madras had pleaded to be allowed to marry the girl. He had threatened to desert ship, and his uncle, the captain, had treated him like any potential mutineer: He had locked Madras in the hold and sailed away. Gradually, Madras had come to see that they were right. But until M came along, he had not lost his heart to anyone else.

"He was barely eighteen—and she was completely unsuitable!" A look of sly triumph crossed Augusta's face.

"Which brings us, I believe, right back to where we started— if you see what I mean, Zulema."

Zulema stood up quickly and began pacing about the room. Her skirts dragged against the floor with a strange kind of halting sound.

"It is not the same. That girl was . . ."

"You see, Zulema—you can't make an argument for it."

"Have you spoken to Isaiah? Or Madras?" Zulema demanded, trying a different tack.

"They will come this evening. I wanted to speak to you first because I want you to help me make them see what's best. Of course, I will do as I see fit anyway, with or without your help, but if they believe you are as dismayed as I am about this marriage, they are more likely to take my decision with good grace."

"I will not, Mother Mitchell. Nor will Madras or Isaiah bow to your decision. You forget one thing: You hold the controlling shares now, but in a matter of days that can shift right out from under you. In fact, it may already have happened." She glanced at Honoria.

Augusta turned to Honoria, who sat rigidly in a straight chair, her eyes on her teacup.

"Honoria?" Augusta said softly. "What have you done?"

"Signed and sent," she said. "A wedding gift to Madras." The teacup rattled against the saucer sitting on her lap. Her voice was quavery and contrite, with a vague note of triumph.

"You wicked, wicked girl!" Augusta said.

"Yes, wicked," Honoria said, her voice low and breathy.

"I suppose you knew all along," Augusta said to Zulema, "and take great delight in seeing me routed."

"I did not know that Aunt Honoria intended to make her shares over to Madras. I only suspected. And I feel no delight of any kind. I beg you, Mother Mitchell, let Madras and M be happy, as you were happy with Reuben. As I am happy with Isaiah."

"My husband's grandmother, Zulema, was not a fallen woman."

"How do you know?" Zulema said softly. "Didn't Reuben's grandfather find her in Mobile? Did anyone know anything about her? She wasn't from here, was she? Was she who she said she was? And did it matter, one way or the other, when all was said and done?"

Augusta clamped her lips together, too shocked to say anything.

Zulema set her teacup on the table. She kissed Honoria lightly on the cheek and lifted her hand to wave good-bye. Honoria merely blinked in return.

For once, Zulema thought as she walked toward home, I've had the last word. A small smile lit her face.

M's Log—October 1871

There has been a great to-do at the Mitchells'. Old Mrs. Mitchell wanted to take the Boreas away from Madras, but Mrs. Zulema Mitchell stood up to her, and Aunt Honoria Cobb turned the tide. Pacifica wrote me a long letter telling me what her mother told her. She says, in part:

Madras is fit to be tied and says he'll never speak to Grandmother again. He went off with Hugh Chapman hours ago and has not come back. He fears Grandmother will make life miserable for Aunt Honoria, but that is unlikely. For all her vague ways, Auntie is more than a match for Grandmother.

It's all so terribly romantic, don't you think? Just like the Capulets and the Montagues, except you and Madras won't have to do anything desperate. All you have to do is wait a few more months to marry, sail away, and leave all these silly troubles behind.

Grandmother will see reason sooner or later. She always does. She just can't resist an opportunity to play empress and command those around her to bow to her bidding. We will, however, be obliged to tread softly around her these next few weeks. Soon, Aunt Honoria will ask for her shares to be returned and Madras will give them up. Order will be restored. Grandmother will not change her mind about wanting someone else to be wife to Madras, but she will make no more effort to prevent your marriage. We cannot, however, prevent her from treating you coldly, but you must not take that to heart, or even mind it, for Madras's sake.

Mother says that if women like Grandmother were allowed to hold positions of public power, they would not need to domineer over their families!

I showed Pacifica's letter to Grand Fan and Mrs. Maude. They thought it full of sage advice and urged me to heed it. Mrs. Maude said it is not only men who would be tyrants, despite what Mrs. John Adams said to her husband—"Pray remember the ladies"—as he labored to define the rights of men in our American Constitution. Grand Fan said I was not to do anything rash and to calm myself. It was only a tempest in a very grand teapot.

And I? I want to march right up to Old Mrs. Mitchell's door and slap her squarely across the face. Instead, I will go down to the beach where I will draw her effigy in the sand. Then I will stomp it all to h-ll!

10.

Since Augusta's attempt to thwart the marriage, autumn was nearly gone. M missed the sound of birdsong, a sound she had happily taken for granted during the fine days of summer. She did not look forward to the long gray days of winter, the months of waiting for spring and her wedding day to arrive. Autumn was a sad time, the hours of daylight growing shorter, the landscape becoming bare, the days growing colder. Her fits of melancholy became more frequent then. The unrest in the Mitchell family, and the part she played in it, added to her sense of gloom.

Augusta's displeasure unsettled M greatly. Wasn't it her right to become Madras's wife, to be first with him and more beloved than any other member of his family? It was a nagging question, and she wanted the answer to be a resounding *Yes!* But the truth was, when she married Madras, she married his kin, too. She did not want to become a wedge separating him from those he loved. She kept these thoughts to herself despite her grandmother's searching looks and Maude's more direct inquiries as to her well-being.

Now, as they strolled along the dirt road leading from Abbott's Reach, M told Madras what she had been thinking about over the past weeks.

"Perhaps your grandmother is right, Madras. Perhaps I am not suitable and never will be. Nothing can alter the facts of Grand Fan's life. When you introduce me as your wife, no matter where we are, people will look at me and think, 'Her grandmother was a notorious woman.' " She slipped her arm out of the bend of Madras's elbow and stopped to look at him. She felt oddly adrift, as if disengaging her arm from his was the equivalent of slipping a safe mooring.

Madras was handsome in a navy blue jacket and black wool trousers. The breeze ruffled his dark hair. M adored looking at him, loved the feeling it stirred in her.

"You must not worry about such things, M. You can't know what people do or do not think. Your name is Giddings, not Abbott—or Hogan—and never has been. Giddings is an old and respected name on land and sea. A few months from now your name will be Mitchell. It, too, counts for something in seaports all over the world. I believe you will find a great deal of pride in that." Madras took her hand in his, pulled off the brown leather glove she wore, and kissed the tips of her fingers. "Because, my dear, if anyone dares even hint that you are not suitable, I will knock them down." Madras grinned as he spoke, making light of his words, but M knew he meant what he said. She knew the prickly side of him as well as the soft one. He was not a man to back down from a fight if it was warranted. He would stand up for her against anyone, even his own grandmother. He would always be on her side.

"Even the ladies, Madras?" M asked in a teasing tone.

"No. I shall say evil things about them behind their backs and give them a taste of their own medicine." He drew M's hand through his elbow, restoring her delicate sense of ease and safety. She leaned her head against his shoulder in a gesture of gratitude and contentment.

"Could you get another ship?"

"Yes, quite easily, I think. Hugh Chapman took me to see his uncle Seamus, who owns the controlling shares in several vessels. Mr. Chapman said he could accommodate me in a year or so. He knew of another owner who might take me sooner if I consented to leave you alongshore. But that I will not do. I must have you with me."

M nestled closer to his side, happiness flooding her heart. But the feeling did not completely dissipate her sense of uneasiness. She did not want to begin her married life at odds with Augusta Mitchell. She made up her mind in that moment to pay a call on the old lady. She would go, unannounced, without consulting anyone. She would state her case.

M arranged to stay a few days in Searsport with Pacifica while Madras went upriver to Bangor to inquire about potential cargoes and to see to other business. On the afternoon Pacifica and her mother attended the Ladies Literary Society, M pleaded a headache. As soon as their carriage drove out of sight, she walked down the hard-packed dirt road in the opposite direction toward Augusta Mitchell's house.

The house occupied a low rise of ground not too distant from the water's edge. It was an older house, built in the 1830s when Augusta was a bride. In those years she had gone to sea, where all but the last of her eight children were born. By the time of the last child's birth she was past forty and, Madras had said, repeating what Zulema had told him, did not take well to being left alongshore. It was then, according to family lore, that Augusta Mitchell's disposition took a turn for the worse.

Augusta received M in the gloomy parlor recently redecorated according to current fashion with heavy dark-colored draperies, an overabundance of crocheted doilies, and fragile porcelain figurines. The windows looked out on Penobscot Bay, but the aspect did little to relieve the heavy atmosphere and dimness of the room.

Augusta, wearing a dark brown velvet dress, an ecru lace cap, and mitts of the same lace, made an imposing figure in the tall-backed wing chair where she sat as if enthroned. An ebony walking stick with a gold knob lay across her knees. M had never seen her leaning on it. Augusta was not the sort of woman who resorted to using a walking stick.

M stood awkwardly by the door, as she had not been invited to sit. She knew she looked well turned out in a dark blue coat and maroon wool dress. She had no fears for her appearance. Augusta regarded her quietly, her face revealing neither surprise nor outrage. M sensed in the old lady quantities of powerful energy carefully controlled, of a willful woman who feared no one.

"I am not unsuitable for Madras, Mrs. Mitchell," M said all in a rush, forgetting her manners and the common civilities of conversation. "While it is true my grandmother cannot boast of . . . a virtuous past, she can boast of her devotion to those she loves. Virtue requires a rough and stormy passage . . . it may falter . . ." She stammered to a halt, her words sounding, to her own ears, stilted and rehearsed, which in fact they were.

"So you have come to slay the lion in her den with a quotation from Montaigne, have you?" Augusta said, wrapping her plump fingers around the walking stick. M wondered, a bit wildly, if she would raise it against her. A calm resolution overtook her and she took a few steps closer to Augusta, refusing to be intimidated.

Let the old woman strike her. Let her reveal herself as cruel and insensitive.

"I have come to slay no one," M said quietly, her heart hammering. "I have come to ask you to learn more about me before you judge me unworthy. As for Montaigne, when I read that passage, it seemed to fit the present situtation."

"Does it surprise you to learn I know the writings of Montaigne?" Augusta asked, disregarding M's statement. "My husband and I were in the habit of reading to one another on our voyages. And on stormy days when I was confined to my cabin, curled in one corner of the bunk as if it were a life raft, I read nothing but philosophy. It was easier than praying and, I suspect, amounted to pretty much the same thing."

"No, Mrs. Mitchell, I am not surprised by your intelligence."

Augusta raised her eyebrows and said, "Hmmm," very softly. She lifted the stick from her lap and planted it firmly on the floor, using it to rise from her chair. She moved toward M until the distance between them closed. The little jet buttons down the front of her dress glittered in the dim light.

"I don't believe anyone sent you," she said, as if she were talking to herself. "Madras wouldn't put you up to it. Nor Zulema. They don't agree with my ways, but neither do they defy me. You've come to call on me without telling anyone and without enlisting aid. I admire your bravery, Miss Giddings. But bravery has no place where it can avail nothing. You face things squarely. I don't believe you are afraid of me."

"No, I am not afraid of you, Mrs. Mitchell. Nor of Samuel Johnson."

A small, tight smile crept across Augusta's face. She had not expected M to recognize the quotation about bravery.

"But I am afraid of losing Madras," M continued, "afraid of making it necessary for him to choose between me and his family.

I am not brave about that." She hesitated, gathering her thoughts before she went on. "For I love him far more than you do."

Augusta's face flushed an unbecoming red and sudden outrage registered in her eyes. She raised her stick slightly, but M did not flinch. "Cheeky girl! How dare you speak to me like that?" She did not raise her voice, and that made her anger all the more frightening.

"If you loved him more than I, Mrs. Mitchell, you would give us your blessing. You would have only to look at Madras to see his happiness. You would see how he is content with me as his choice . . ."

"Content! How little you know of the world, miss! No man is ever content with merely one woman . . ." She closed her mouth firmly as if she had said more than she had intended.

"It is true, Mrs. Mitchell, I know little of the world. But I know enough to believe I am as essential to Madras's happiness as he is to mine. I have come, not to convince you, or to change your mind, but to ask you not to condemn me without first knowing me. It's not an unreasonable request. And if you find me wanting, I will do as you wish. I will not marry Madras."

The lines in Augusta's face softened for just a moment, and again, she almost smiled.

"It is not you I object to, Miss Giddings. It is your connections. And those, as I am sure you understand, no amount of getting to know you will change."

"But I am not my connections, Mrs. Mitchell. I was born long after the unfortunate incidents that shaped my grandmother's past. I know her only as a kind, loving woman who has cared for me with great devotion."

"And succeeded in instilling in you a far too independent spirit and outspoken manner."

"That may be so, Mrs. Mitchell. But the same might be said of you."

"Sit," Augusta said, an expression of grudging respect coming into her eyes. She pointed to a chair with her stick. M sat down with what she hoped was grace and quiet dignity. Suddenly, the room felt too large, too dim, too airless. The chair was not at all comfortable.

Honoria crept into the room bearing a pierced-tin tea tray decorated with painted roses. She looked like what M imagined Charles Dickens's character Miss Haversham might look like, only without the autocratic manner and tattered wedding finery.

"Tea," Honoria murmured. Augusta acknowledged her sister's presence with a small nod of her head as Honoria set the tray on the mahogany tea table and crept out.

Augusta poured and handed M a cup. "And how do you propose I get to know you, Miss Giddings?" she asked.

"I thought I might call on you from time to time, that we might talk . . ."

"No. I think not. You will come to stay with me. From January to the first of April. I can't abide the winter months. Honoria is no company whatsoever. Zulema and Pacifica visit, but they are much more interested in socializing with the younger set. You do play cribbage, don't you?"

"Yes," M said. "But, Mrs. Mitchell, I cannot come to stay . . . my grandmother needs me . . . and Mrs. Maude . . ."

"Piffle. They will have to do without you soon enough when you sail off into the great world with Madras."

"But that is all the more reason for me to want to spend as much time as possible with them. I cannot come to stay with you." The very thought of spending three months cooped up in the gloomy old house chilled her to the bone. She felt closed in and crushed by some ugly force she had unwittingly unleashed.

"Well, my girl, once you've spliced yourself to Madras you can't divide your loyalty. Your loyalty will be to him. And his family.

For as long as you both shall live. See, now, I give you an opportunity to practice what you preach and here you are fleeing from it. Where is your bravery now?"

It was a challenge, and M knew it. "Very well then," she said, taking a deep breath. "I will come. But I will only come for the first four days of the week. I will spend each Friday, Saturday, and Sunday at Abbott's Reach with my grandmother."

A tiny smile lit the corners of Augusta's mouth, and for a moment an expression of what M thought was delight came into the old lady's eyes. "You bargain well, Miss Giddings. I'll have your hand on it." Augusta extended her right hand. M hesitated, then extended her own. Augusta's handshake was surprisingly firm, yet unexpectedly gentle. "I shall expect you on New Year's Day."

M's Log—November 1871

I have created my own teapot tempest! Grand Fan is furious with me. Maude, for once in her life, is speechless. Dr. Sam shakes his head and says nothing. I have tried to explain, but all they do is walk around in shocked silence.

"I must leave home," I said over and over. "This is how I begin."

"No, it is not the same," Grand Fan said. "I will not allow it."

"You must," I said. "I have given my hand on it."

"You silly child!" Grand Fan said.

She went to her room and has not come down yet. I heard Mr. Harding arrive a short time ago. Perhaps Grand Fan sent for him. Or perhaps he knew without being told, as he always seems to, that Grand Fan's spirits want lifting.

I have written the news to Madras, although I am sure by now his grandmother has informed him of our bargain—and enjoyed every minute of it, too!

*What does Augusta Mitchell hope to accomplish in having me
with her? Surely, we will never be friends. Am I to wait on her hand
and foot, serve as an unpaid companion, simply be there to listen to
her stories, to ally myself with her against the women in her family?
That I cannot and will not do. Yet, I am resolved to show her what
I am made of; it is finer and tougher stuff than she imagines.*

*Why can't I stop crying? Why are we all suddenly so
unhappy? I am to marry Madras. I have got what I want.*

11.

"She's won! That dreadful old harridan has won!" Fanny
stormed up and down the parlor, her skirts snapping, her boot heels
almost stomping against the carpet. It was a sight Ellis rarely had
seen. He sat back in the wing chair, Tennyson in his lap, stroking the
cat's back, and watched with pleasure. He loved Fanny's spirit, but
he did not smile or give any signal of that enjoyment. This situation
required tact and diplomacy, qualities he possessed in abundance.

Weak December sunlight spilled into the room, adding odd,
somber shadows in keeping with Fanny's fury. The fire on the
hearth sizzled sluggishly, threatening to go out. Tennyson pricked
his ears toward Fanny as if to gauge the parameters of her mood.

"Have you talked with M, Fanny?"

"Yes, of course I have talked with M, Ellis. It's as if she has
taken leave of her senses. She won't listen to reason. She insists it's
the only way to make sure Augusta Mitchell does nothing more to
prevent the wedding." Fanny stopped pacing and gazed out the
window at Penobscot Bay. The river, the current, flowing to the
sea, flowing away, always flowing away. From the moment of birth,
so much flowed out and away. Tears pricked Fanny's eyes, but she
blinked them back. It was no time for crying and giving in to

weak-woman vapors. She had to do something, but at that moment she did not know what it might be.

"She may be right."

"She is not right. She and Madras can be married today if that's what they want, and none the wiser . . . but she won't even consider that now. Instead, she's going to spend four days of every week for the next three months with that domineering old lady who dislikes her because of who I . . . was. Who I am . . ." The words caught in Fanny's throat and she could not say them: a fallen woman.

"Fanny, my love, you are no longer that woman. Can't Madras talk her out of it?"

"He likes the idea! He thinks it's the perfect way for M to get to know his grandmother—and vice versa." The thought added another measure of frustration to Fanny's distress.

"It looks like checkmate to me, Fanny." Ellis rose, deposited Tennyson on the sofa, went to Fanny, and took her hand. "Think of it as a rehearsal, my dear. Against May Day when M will leave home for good and be gone for several years at sea."

Fanny closed her eyes and drew a deep, steadying breath.

"I don't want to think of it. I don't want to think of her far away at sea, not knowing where she is, the only woman aboard ship, the storms, the dangers . . ."

"But that is how Elizabeth has lived her life, how M began her life."

"I did not raise Elizabeth. Elizabeth and I are not close, as M and I are . . . and Grace . . . there was so little time to know Grace. M will have children—how will I know M's little ones if she is always at sea? How dare Augusta Mitchell take from me what little time there is left to spend with M!"

Without warning, tears ran down Fanny's flushed cheeks. She let Ellis draw her into his arms, but she did not want to be comforted; he felt that and was not offended. Fanny had her moments, rare, to be sure, and when she did it was like a logjam, a hopeless tangle of rigid thoughts borne along on the high water of emotion. In time, she'd come upon the key logs of insight and reason and all would be well. He held her gently and sorrowed with her, wanting to tell her what he knew about loss, about change. But he said nothing, giving her time to find her own way to her thoughts about those things.

"What do Maude and Sam say?"

"Maude says she cannot talk to me while I am screaming like a banshee, and Sam just sighs and shakes his head like a doctor, bent on prescribing a hefty dose of laudanum to keep me quiet."

"Then you must become quiet, Fanny, and listen to what they say."

"Yes. Yes, I know. We are born with good-byes in our hearts and hands. Maude said that once, shortly after Elizabeth was born. I had no idea what she meant then. I think I do now. And yesterday she said good-byes don't prolong being together, they prolong the pain of parting."

"As many farewells as be stars in heaven," Ellis murmured against her hair.

"Shakespeare! Good God, Ellis, I am in desperate straits when you resort to Shakespeare." She smiled then, almost grudgingly, and her mood lightened. "M won't change her mind; she can be very stubborn. There's only one thing I can do."

"Pay a call on Augusta Mitchell?"

"Yes. Oh, don't look so alarmed, Ellis. I know when I am beaten. But I also know how to take advantage of a bad situation. I have had plenty of experience in that regard. Augusta Mitchell expects me to behave the way a woman 'of my sort,' for want of a better description, behaves: to be uncivil, perhaps vulgar—to behave in a way justifying her idea of what any woman who lives beyond the pale of respectability is like . . . This would be one more weapon she could use to separate Madras and M. But she won't get that from me. Quite the contrary."

Ellis took Fanny's hand, led her to the sofa, and made her sit while he added wood to the fire. The flames blazed up and cast a ruddy light on Fanny's hair. Her beauty made his heart catch. He had said many good-byes to her, would say many more, but each one brought them closer to another hello. He wanted to make her see that it would be the same with M—her coming and going full of as many hellos as good-byes, the distance between them expanding and contracting, their closeness never diminishing. The paradox of human connection: It was both visible and invisible, possessed of a strength that defied time and space. He thought then of Bethiah and felt a deep pang of guilt. His resolve to tend her every need, to take care of her as best he could, had never wavered. What had faded was his need for all those things she was no longer able to give him. He had wept his tears. Delhiah had had no say in what had happened to her. Unlike him, she did not choose her path. But he had chosen his; Fanny needed him, and he needed Fanny. It was enough.

"All will be well, Fanny," Ellis said. He went to the kitchen and came back with a pot of tea, poured Fanny a cup and laced it with a bit of blueberry brandy. "Drink this," he said. "It's what Maude and Sam would suggest if they were here."

Fanny took the cup and sipped. Not since the night she had left Bangor for good had she felt so distraught. Yet, at the same time, she felt safe and content, and utterly sure her decision to call on Augusta Mitchell was the right one.

M's Log—November 1871

Why are they all so aghast? Why is Grand Fan behaving as if it were the end of the world? Old Mrs. Mitchell may have put dragons

*in my path, but I will slay them. I told Grand Fan it would do me
good to live in town during these dark winter months—January,
February, March. A mere three months, twelve small weeks, ninety
days. Such a hurt expression came over her face, I started to cry.*

"M," she said, "it is not necessary for you to do this. Madras—"

*"His people will be my people," I said. I did not know what
else to say.*

*"And your people will be his people," she said after a long
moment. "And that is precisely the problem. Nothing you do or say,
no amount of time you spend with Augusta Mitchell, M, will alter
that fact. There is so much you don't understand."*

*"I understand far more than you think I do, Grand Fan," I
said. "I am not a child." I began to shiver as the dark, melancholy
feelings crept over me. My head began to ache, too. And the next
thing I knew Grand Fan had put me to bed. Mrs. Maude came the
very next day and dosed me with St. John's Wort. I am still abed,
though the melancholy has lifted. This morning I heard Mr.
Harding's voice, so I know Grand Fan has marshaled her forces.
Early this afternoon I heard her go out. I do not know where she
went. But it is late and she has not yet returned.*

Madras has not been to see me, but he sent a note. It said:

M, my love,

I long to see you, but business keeps me here. It will be
heaven to have you in Searsport. We'll go to parties whenever
Grandmother can spare you. We'll dance until dawn. Pacifica is
beside herself with excitement and looking forward to having
you to go about with. Mother sends her warmest regards, as
do I.

Fondly,
Madras

12.

Old Lady Mitchell will keep me waiting, Fanny thought, as she handed her coat to the hired girl who let her in. The girl laid the coat on a side chair. Always before, it had been Fanny who had kept callers waiting. She remembered suddenly what Joshua Stetson had told her once: Never be the supplicant, Fanny; always be the one who dispenses the favors.

But here she was, the tables turned, intent on pleading her case to the autocratic old woman who took perverse pleasure in manipulating the lives of others. *Well,* Fanny thought, *I have my trump card, and I'll play it if it comes to that.*

Fanny glanced in the mirror hanging on the wall at the bottom of the stairs. She looked neat and respectable in a plain black dress set off by a pale-gray lace jabot and matching cuffs. Her color was high, giving her cheeks a healthy glow. She noticed lines she had never seen before between her eyebrows and at the corners of her mouth. But she saw no signs of weakness in her resolve to breach Augusta Mitchell's sanctimonious complacency. Suddenly, Augusta's image appeared in the mirror beside Fanny's reflection. Their gazes intersected. Neither woman moved or spoke as they took the measure of one another in the glass. With quiet deliberation, Fanny adjusted the jabot at her throat before she turned to face Augusta.

"Thank you for seeing me, Mrs. Mitchell," Fanny said with dignity.

"Against my better judgment, I can assure you, Miss Abbott. Or do you prefer Mrs. Hogan?" Augusta, too, wore black, a heavy wool dress with a voluminous skirt, which made her look like Queen Victoria. She wore black lace mitts on her small hands and a matching lace cap done up with wide silk ribbon streamers.

Fanny smiled slightly, amused—not by the pointed reference to her past, but because the remark was so blatantly calculated to humiliate. Fanny drew a breath to steady herself. "The woman who was Mrs. Hogan died when her house burned down many years ago, Mrs. Mitchell. As you know, I have never married. I am, indeed, Miss Abbott." She held out her hand, offering Augusta a clear choice—to ignore it or take it.

Augusta did not hesitate. She took Fanny's hand briefly, an oddly delicate gesture. "Won't you come in and sit down, Miss Abbott?" Augusta said with heavy formality. She led Fanny across the hallway, through double doors into the small parlor, the one she reserved for entertaining the minister and slight acquaintances whose company she wished to be rid of quickly. That fact was not lost on Fanny.

Fanny sat in a brocade lady's chair beside the hearth. Augusta sat down on a sofa opposite, settled herself with dignity and grace, folded her hands in her lap, and primly crossed her ankles. For a long moment, neither woman spoke. Augusta, Fanny thought, was biding her time, giving no hint of her feelings, her face impassive, almost regal, as if deciding whether or not to throw pearls to the swine.

"When I was a girl, it never occurred to me that I'd become a skeleton in anyone's closet, Mrs. Mitchell," Fanny said without preamble. "I never expected to see my daughter again when I left her in the care of my sister back in 1831. I knew perfectly well I had fallen from grace with no hope for redemption in the eyes of people like you. Nor did I foresee M's birth, or any of the events that left her in my care."

Augusta stirred irritably. A look of annoyance crossed her face. "Pray, do get to the point, Miss Abbott. The afternoon grows short."

"My point is this, Mrs. Mitchell: We all have skeletons rattling about in our closets . . . even you."

The color drained from Augusta's face. Abruptly, she stood, her fierce dark eyes glaring at Fanny. Her thoughts darted here and there, refusing to stay in the old, hurtful place she never allowed her thoughts to roam. "How dare you insult me! I might have known you would stoop to this!" Her color had returned; her cheeks were now red with anger.

"Yet you insult me, Mrs. Mitchell, when you dare to manipulate my grandchild into choosing between the two things she loves and needs most in her life—your grandson's love and the acceptance of his family, of which you are a very large part, and her love for her own family, of which I am a very large part."

"I knew you'd come here to torment me!" Augusta moved toward the door, a clear signal that she expected Fanny to follow and leave. Fanny remained where she was.

"Torment you? Quite the contrary, Mrs. Mitchell. The fact is, it is possible to imagine skeletons in one's closet where in fact they do not exist."

Augusta stopped and set her hand upon the doorframe, leaning on it a moment for support. She righted herself quickly and turned to face Fanny. "I have heard quite enough, Miss Abbott. You have shown your true colors, just as I knew you would. But I will not be blackmailed by the likes of you. I'll have the sheriff on you, make no mistake!"

"Blackmail!" Fanny exclaimed, laughter welling up in spite of her effort to remain calm and serious. "You do overestimate me, Mrs. Mitchell."

"You have lost your mind—I can see it in your eyes," Augusta said. "Quite mad, not fit company for a young girl like M. Someone ought to put a stop to it . . ." She floundered for words, found none, and grew silent.

Fanny let the silence grow a moment before she continued.

"There was a period of time, Mrs. Mitchell, when a Captain Reuben Mitchell, your husband, I believe, found his way to Pink Chimneys. I saw him there many an evening, a tall man, very handsome in his navy blue coat with silver buttons. No longer young, but female heads turned when he entered the room, I assure you. I can see him now, standing quietly in the corner of the room, deep in conversation with Joshua Stetson and a few other sea captains. He was a sensible man, and good-hearted, I believe. His manners were impeccable, and I never saw him drink too much or conduct himself in an unseemly manner, as so many others did."

Augusta opened her mouth to speak, compressed her lips into a furious line, then recovered her composure and said in a low voice, "I will not hear this. I will not." Eyes blazing with anger, she took a few steps toward Fanny.

"I think you will, Mrs. Mitchell, because not knowing the truth has poisoned your outlook on life to such a degree that you impose your will on everyone—perhaps to make sure no one ever catches you unaware again, as you were when Captain Mitchell spent so much time enjoying my hospitality."

"Get out, I tell you! Get out!" Augusta's voice broke under the force of her anger.

"No, Mrs. Mitchell, I will not leave until I have told you what I have come to say. In your case, you see skeletons where there are none. Where I'm concerned, you see skeletons that are none of your business because you have not troubled yourself to try to understand how they came to reside in my closet. You assume that Captain Mitchell broke faith with you by going to Pink Chimneys night after night."

Augusta's lips trembled slightly, but she regained control and made her way to the sofa. She sat down carefully, as if she feared sitting on something breakable, or worse, unyielding.

"Those were strange months, Mrs. Mitchell, the beginning of a very bad end to the dishonorable life I had led. At that time, Joshua Stetson had a stranglehold on shipping on the Penobscot. He had a share in every cargo that went downriver. He sat on the boards of most of the banks, and he made and broke men's fortunes. No one dared cross him, not even I, though a few tried to talk to him. Your husband was one of those—he and a few other Searsport men, some who had first gone to sea on Stetson family ships out of Portland, as your husband once did. So night after night, Captain Mitchell came to Pink Chimneys and talked. Yes, talked. Nothing more. And each time, in the early hours of the morning, he went away having gained nothing.

"One evening, the debate between him and Joshua grew heated. And a few days later I heard that Captain Mitchell was to leave the coasting trade and go back to the deepwater journeys. But Joshua couldn't leave it at that. The next day he arranged for one of the . . . ladies who lived at Pink Chimneys to go to your husband's room at The Bangor House." Fanny paused as she recalled how Flora had laughed when she had returned from her mission, regaling everyone with her story, and how they had laughed when she described the look on Augusta Mitchell's face when she opened the door to find her husband wrapped in Flora's seductive arms. Mrs. Mitchell, Flora had said, had turned tail and stalked off down the corridor as if the whole damn place was afire.

"Captain Mitchell was completely blameless," Fannie continued. "He had met the lady in question only once before, long enough to be introduced, nothing more. Your husband had countered all Joshua's attempts to arrange, shall we say, a closer acquaintance."

A stricken look crossed Augusta's face as her thoughts hammered in her mind, flying like crazed birds crashing into a pane of glass. Reuben had tried to explain, had sworn that he had done nothing, but she had not believed him. She immediately threw up a barrier of injured pride and hurt feelings that she refused to allow him to breach. She stayed alongshore the rest of that year, nursing her outrage, honing it into a fine, sharp weapon. When she went back to sea with him the following year, they lived as polite strangers, a state of affairs that endured until he was lost overboard, several years later, during a storm at sea. An accident, or had he jumped? She had wondered at the time, and wondered still. Now, it seemed, here was proof that her unbending ways had contributed to his untimely death. She could not grasp it entire. The very weight of it pressed her down, and suddenly she thought of the early days of their love when she had believed it would deepen with the years and become a fortress to protect them from the perils of human frailty.

"What do you want?" Augusta whispered, her face tight with emotion she could not release.

"Very little. A mere reversal of your plans for M. She may come to you any two days of the week you wish to have her. The rest of the time, until she marries Madras, she lives at home with me. That you cease to paint her with the same tar brush with which you have painted me. That you withdraw your objections to her marriage to Madras. That is all."

"You ask a great deal, Miss Abbott, and give little in return."

"I give a great deal, Mrs. Mitchell. Neither M nor Madras nor anyone else will hear how you unfairly judged your late husband. And, more importantly, I will seek no further connection with you or any members of your family, with one exception: I will dance at M's wedding. After that, I will trouble you no more."

Fanny rose to go. "I thank you for your time. Good day." She found her coat, put it on, and left quickly. Tears spilled down her face as she went down the snowy walk toward the livery stable to hire a sleigh to take her back to Abbott's Reach.

M's Log—November 1871

Grand Fan did not return until early evening. It had grown dark and cold, and I feared her sleigh had overset. She was shivering when she got home and went directly to bed. She was perfectly well this morning and told me Mrs. Mitchell had changed her mind about everything. I will be invited to visit two days each week,

*according to Mrs. Mitchell's wishes. I pressed Grand Fan for details,
but she will tell me nothing. Something of great significance passed
between Grand Fan and Mrs. Mitchell. I know it.*

*Neither will Mrs. Maude tell me anything much. All she said
was, "Your grandmother has great resources at her service, not the
least of which is a remarkable memory. All you need to know is
this: You will marry Madras. Augusta Mitchell will not interfere or
bully either of you again."*

*That's all I know, except that everything has changed. For bet-
ter or worse, I cannot say. But I am relieved to know I am no longer
required to live for the better part of three months at Mrs. Mitchell's
beck and call.*

*I long for spring's arrival, to be carried away on the sea of mat-
rimony, with Madras at the helm.*

13.

Winter closed in heavily on Abbott's Reach soon after Fanny's
visit to Augusta Mitchell. With it came a weighty kind of moodi-
ness Fanny had not experienced in many years. She rose each
morning feeling the cold in her bones and went about the business of the day. She cooked and cleaned and swept snow off the
porch. She spread clean sheets on beds and dusted shelves.
Evenings, she crocheted Irish lace collars and cuffs for M's
trousseau. It was a familiar routine, one she had learned to enjoy,
but now it gave her little comfort. Her thoughts darted and flitted
like chickadees before a big snowstorm, and she found it impossible to concentrate on the small details of everyday life.

Her daily routines remained unchanged, with one curious
exception: When she least expected it, without warning, with no
coherent thought to prompt it, tears ran unchecked down her

face. She hurried from the room, fearing Maude would see her tears and be alarmed. She stayed overlong in the darker corners of the kitchen, brooding, her thoughts indistinct and full of shadows.

At night, she wandered around the house carrying a wavering candle, always arriving in the back bedroom to stand in the doorway, wishing Ellis was there. She needed him in a way that both transcended and encompassed the physical. But he was not there, and standing alone in the empty room where they had been happy together left her feeling even more unsettled. Her longing for him, she knew, was only a small part of the chaos she felt. Yet, when she tried to shape her feelings into thoughts and words, she did not know precisely what she longed for, or why she cried. What roiled inside her seemed to be a stew of foreign ingredients. Sometimes her thoughts were only of her mother and her sister, Mercy. On other days, she thought only of her father. Sometimes, Joshua Stetson entered her dreams and she woke, sweating and fearful.

On this day, morning dawned bright and clear. Fanny stood at the kitchen window to watch the sun rise. Shadows lay blue on drifts of new snow. Another twelve inches had fallen in the night. The black sheen of the Penobscot twinkled with a million facets of sunlight. It made her remember the night she had run away with Robert Snow—the stars reflected in the water had been so bright. She had been so heedless, so eager to seize life and wrest the future from it. It had not occurred to her then that life would grab and mold her into some unexpected shape to suit its own purpose.

"I cannot decide," she said aloud. "Nothing fits together anymore." And that was another annoyance—she had begun to talk to herself.

"The change," Maude said, coming into the kitchen in her usual quiet way. She and Sam had been at Abbott's Reach for several weeks. The long spell of heavy snow had made it impossible for them to return to Bangor. Not that it mattered. They were always content to stay with Fanny.

Fanny did not look up from her teacup. She had slept poorly, and her skull felt too small for her brain. She had not done her hair and it hung down her back in a ragged tangle. She felt no inclination to dress or tidy herself. She wanted to mope and she wanted Maude to know she wanted to mope.

"Maude, please, not this morning." She kept her eyes on her teacup. She did not want to meet Maude's knowing glance. Without comment or ceremony, Maude poured boiling water into a cup, swished it around, stirred it, and handed it to Fanny.

"I think you'd best drink some of this every day for a while, Fanny. It will help."

Fanny wrinkled her nose as she inspected the contents of the cup. "It smells like something the Mitchell family scraped off the bottom of a boat," she said sourly.

"Drink it," Maude said.

Fanny took a sip and made a wry face. "It tastes about as bad as it smells."

Maude pulled a comb from her pocket and set to work on Fanny's hair.

"It's a melancholy time when a woman goes through the change. It's like . . . " She groped for words. "It's like trying to cross a burning bridge. Can't go back because that part's gone—can't go forward because that part's afire." Her hands combed gently and Fanny, soothed, began to relax.

"Fire," Fanny murmured. "We always come to that. Our souls are destined for fire unless we mend our ways and live saintly lives." A touch of bitterness hung in her voice. "Do you believe that?"

"No. Indeed, I do not. You're thinking of Ellis." It was more a statement than a question. Maude braided Fanny's hair and twisted it into a loose knot. She fastened the coil with hairpins. She inspected her work and said, "Better."

"Yes, Ellis is on my mind almost every waking moment. I think of Joshua, too. And of you and Sam, M, Augusta Mitchell, my father. It's as if what I was certain I had straight in my mind isn't straight anymore. I used to think I had found all the answers I'd ever need. Now, all I have is questions. It's as if I'd been reading a story and all of a sudden I discover pages and pages missing."

"M won't be missing, Fanny," Maude said gently. "She'll be out in the world, just as you went out into the world."

A long pause grew between them. Fanny tried to gather her thoughts, but they kept slipping away, changing before she found words to utter them.

"You are quite wrong, Maude. I didn't go out into the world. Quite the contrary. I went into the half-life Joshua Stetson fashioned for me."

"Fanny . . ."

Tears slipped down Fanny's cheeks and she made no attempt to conceal them. "I wasn't," she choked on the word, "anyone."

"You are Elizabeth's mother and M's grandmother, Fanny. That's someone," Maude said firmly. She took Fanny's cold hands into her warm ones. "And you are as dear to me as if you were my daughter."

Fanny managed a small smile.

"What a loss to the world you never had a true daughter, Maude, you and Sam."

"You are a true-enough daughter for any woman, Fanny. And more of a challenge, let me tell you." Fanny smiled as she withdrew her hands.

"What was the change like for you, Maude?" she asked suddenly, as if desperate to grab the question from her mind before it disappeared or transformed itself into something quite different.

"It was about the time you came to Abbott's Reach, those years. I couldn't remember things like where I'd set down my spectacles, or if I'd let the cat out or in, or what errand Sam said he was

going to do. I couldn't cook either. Everything I took out of the
oven was burned, or I'd left out the eggs or the nutmeg. At night, I
dreamed about being with child, of fat little girls and boys hanging
onto my skirt hem. I found myself drawn to young women with
babes in their arms. I wanted to touch them and hold them—in a
way that had nothing to do with midwifery. But mostly, as my
monthly times became fewer and farther between, I mourned the
loss of what I had come to think of as my affinity with the
moon—the lunar cycle had governed my life since I was sixteen."

"Did you cry a lot?"

"No. But I cried sometimes. Usually at night when I couldn't
sleep, when I thought Sam was asleep. But Sam, being Sam, always
knew. He was the one who made me drink the black cohosh bark
infusion I gave you just now. After a few weeks of drinking it, I
began to sleep better and feel, oh, not like myself, my old self, but
like I could go on and figure out how to live the rest of my life
even though I no longer had any idea what it held in store for me."

Tears brimmed again in Fanny's eyes. Maude had Sam beside
her every night, although that had not always been the case in
those years when Sam was away at sea. *No one sleeps beside me,*
Fanny thought. *No one is there when I wake in the night and reach
out my hand.* But she did not say the words. She did not want to
hear herself say them.

"Did you mind knowing you were growing old?"

"Yes, at first. But I am not one to look overlong at the dark
side of things. I looked around me instead, and saw other women
my age with the same unsettled look on their faces. And it dawned
on me that they needed Sam's black cohosh tonic, too. That's when
I decided to make herbals and simples, in quantity to sell."

"Same midwife, different shape," Fanny said in a halfhearted
attempt at humor. *I need to laugh and laugh,* she thought wildly. *I
need someone to laugh with.*

"In more ways than one," Maude laughed, referring to her figure, whose lines had rounded and expanded as she had grown older.

"This too shall pass, then?"

Maude nodded her agreement.

"Come, my dear," she said. "It's time you got dressed. Put on
that pretty blue wool gown and the dark red shawl. It's a perfect
day for sleighing, and I wouldn't be surprised to see Ellis coming
up the path on snowshoes!"

But Ellis did not come up the path that day. Night closed in
and Maude lit the lamps in the front room. Sam lit a fire in the
stove and sat down in a wing chair he placed near it. He had a
recent issue of *The Bangor Commercial* he wanted to read. M settled on the sofa beside Fanny.

"Shall I read to you?" M asked.

"No, I don't think I can concentrate enough tonight to follow
anything Hawthorne says."

M set *The House of the Seven Gables* aside. She glanced at her
grandmother, noted the lack of animation in her face, and worried
about it. Should she delay her wedding? She had not seen Madras
in more than a week and she missed him. A wave of melancholy
washed over her, and with it, a sharp stab of anger. How could her
grandmother be so upset by her leaving? She made herself smile
and speak casually.

"I'll be going to Mrs. Mitchell's as soon as Madras can get
here with the sleigh, Grand Fan. In a few days, I should think."

Fanny turned her face away slightly from M.

"Grand Fan, please don't—"

"You mistake me, M . . ."

"No, I do not mistake you, Grand Fan," M said hotly. "You've
moped around for weeks ever since you called on Mrs. Mitchell.
Don't think I haven't seen you weeping or heard you wandering
around at all hours. First, you refused to see Madras because you

knew he would ask your permission to marry me, and now you act as if the world is coming to an end just because Mrs. Mitchell requests my company!" She kept her voice low and controlled, but there was no mistaking her agitation.

"M, there's no need to unsettle yourself," Maude admonished.

"I'm sorry," M said quickly. "I only want to be happy these last few months before Madras and I marry." She rose and walked to the door. "I'm tired. I'm going to bed. Good-night." She slipped out of the room before either Fanny or Maude could say anything to detain her.

Sam lowered his newspaper with an audible and annoyed rattle.

"January is always a very long month," he said.

M's Log—January, 1872

Mrs. Maude explained "the change" to me and I try to sympathize with Grand Fan. But I find myself impatient with her. She is not nearly as pleasant to keep company with as she once was, and I can't help thinking it's my fault. If I did not love Madras . . . but I do love Madras . . .

It's unworthy of me to look forward to being away from Grand Fan, to be glad I will go to Mrs. Mitchell's as soon as the snow is settled enough for a sleigh to get here. I want lively company and music and dancing. I want to gossip with Patsy about pretty dresses. I want to see Madras every day and spend hours and hours in his company. I do not want to be cooped up here with Grand Fan wandering about at all hours of the night and never knowing when I'll come upon her crying—or getting ready to—and doing her best to pretend to me that she is not.

I had a long letter from Mother and Father. They write in part:

Dearest M,

When you receive this letter your father and I will be well on our way to Liverpool with a cargo of cotton bales from Mobile. We have been hindered by strong gales and much buffeted about. I have spent far too much time confined to the cabin, and your father has spent many a night out in the weather. But that seems to have passed us now, and I am once again able to set down to eat without fear of food sliding off my plate. You are much on my mind, my dear daughter. I am sewing a few things for you—a pair of slippers, several petticoats of a light fabric which you will surely want when you arrive in the tropics. We return from Liverpool directly to Portland, so you can expect us to dance at your wedding. We will visit a few weeks while your father arranges another cargo and be off just in time to avoid the worst of the blackflies.

Your father sends his dearest love and will write you at length in a few days, so you may expect something from him by the middle of April, perhaps. You are constantly in our thoughts. We enclose with this letter the best and warmest love from your loving parents,

Mother and Father

14.

When Augusta Mitchell summoned M, her note was short, its tone formal:

January 14, 1872

Miss Giddings,

I shall require your company tomorrow, though I would have wished it several weeks ago. Thankfully, this long spell of snowy

*weather seems to have lulled. You may expect Madras to call for you
in the afternoon. Please arrive prepared to stay for several days.
Please convey my regards to your grandmother.*
    I remain, yours sincerely,
    Mrs. Reuben Mitchell

As M read the note she experienced two little spikes of emotion. The first was pleasure: She would see Madras and escape the poorly concealed pain she saw daily in her grandmother's eyes. In the space of three heartbeats, she felt the second spike—a quick self-chastisement because she so longed to be with Madras and away from her grandmother's dreary moods. The thought of Madras set her heart racing, and she hurried to the parlor to find her grandmother.

"Will you help me pack, Grand Fan?" Fanny looked up from the letter she was writing to Elizabeth and Abner. She set the pen back in its holder. She took the note M handed her, read it quickly, and handed it back.

"You want to go, I assume?" she asked. It was a rhetorical question. She saw in M's eyes how much she wanted to go. And who could blame her, a young girl shut up in a drafty house with three grumbling old people?

"Of course I want to go. I haven't seen Madras for two weeks." M drew a great breath, willing herself to be patient, to be calm. "Grand Fan, Mrs. Mitchell doesn't want to take me away from you; she just wants to . . . to get to know me better, to let the rest of the Mitchell family get to know me better, too. I am longing to see Pacifica and the other girls."

Other girls. There had been nothing like that in Fanny's youth, no young girls to laugh and make merry with. Quite the contrary. Her "girls" had been her employees, and though she had had good times with them, and had taken care of them, it was business, not friendship. Not lighthearted, innocent gaiety of the kind M looked forward to.

"Forgive me, M. I forget you need to be with people your own age. I have been selfish wanting you all to myself this winter—so much so that I've welcomed all these big snowstorms we've had. So much snow has kept you away from the dragon." Fanny smiled quickly, hoping for an answering smile from M. They had been so gloomy of late.

"So we have you to thank for the dreadful weather, Grand Fan? I might have known." M's smile broadened into a grin as she saw that Fanny was not going to be overcome by yet another fit of weeping.

They found M's valise in the summer kitchen and carried it to her room. They packed her pretty blue gown, several warm wool dresses, petticoats, drawers, and shifts. M folded a shawl, cuffs, collars, and stockings into a bandbox, the very same one Maude had taken with her that day in 1820 when she had gone across the river to apprentice herself to Sally Cobb Robinson, the Orrington midwife.

Around noon when M heard the distinct sound of sleigh bells in the distance, she flung a coat around her shoulders and hurried out to the piazza.

Soon, Madras came into view driving a hired sleigh, and M watched him guide the horse expertly up to the gate. Snow had drifted hard against the fence. A crew of men had rolled the snow only the day before and the road was perfect for good sleighing.

Madras leapt out of the sleigh and hurried to M, swinging her off her feet in a warm, bearish embrace. He set her back down again and they looked around quickly. Neither Fanny nor Maude hovered at the window. They grinned happily at one another, kissed breathlessly, letting their lips linger deliciously, causing in M a sensation that mystified and delighted her, and left her longing for more.

"We mustn't look as if we want to rush off," M murmured. "Grand Fan's feelings are very delicate of late. I try to spare her whenever I can."

"I promise to be the soul of civility and sensitivity," Madras said, putting on a grave face.

Inside, the table was set for dinner. Fanny reverted in the winter months to the farmer's custom of eating in the kitchen—a big meal at noon, and a smaller supper at night. Maude approved; so much better for the digestion, she said. But in the summer months when paying guests arrived to enjoy a few days on the bay, meals were served with quiet formality in the big dining room.

"My mother and sister asked me to bring you their greetings," Madras said to Fanny when they were seated and passing around a bowl of boiled potatoes. "I left newspapers on the table in the hall, Dr. Webber."

"Thanks, my boy," Sam said. "Old news, contrary to popular belief, is better than no news." He liked to keep abreast of what was going on in Washington, D.C. President Grant would be up for reelection next year if he chose to run again.

"And what news do we have of preparations for your next voyage?" Fanny asked.

"We're ahead of things right now, and there's no reason to think that will change. In fact, I'm certain May Day will be the date of our departure."

"Oh, Madras," M said happily. "I was not sure if May Day would be possible! Why, I can carry a mayflower bouquet!" And suddenly, nothing else mattered but the pleasant thought of herself, standing on the quarterdeck, wearing her simple dress and pretty jacket, holding her favorite of all wildflowers while promising to love Madras for the rest of her life. She reached for his hand the same moment he reached for hers.

Maude, Fanny, and Sam fussed as they tucked M into the sleigh under a wool blanket and a buffalo robe. Maude put a hot soap-stone under M's feet. Sam checked the horse's hooves to make sure they were free of ice. Fanny adjusted M's woolen scarf so that it covered her chin and a length was free in case she needed to shield her nose from the cold. They did not call out good-byes as M and Madras drove away. They lifted their hands and waved lightly, silently, as if to say, We have no fear for your safety—we look for-ward to your return—we are always here to love and comfort you.

The sun shone on M's face as they dashed along the road, and even though it held little warmth, she was cozy and content beside Madras. He held the reins with one hand and wrapped his free arm around M's shoulders. She leaned happily against him, safe and free, and so giddy she laughed loudly, sending frosty whoops of joy out into the frigid air.

The road ran along the shore several miles before turning inland toward Stockton Springs. They trotted through the village, waved to the Merrithew sisters as they passed the dress shop, and turned south toward Searsport. They felt no need to talk beyond the occasional comments about the beauty of the day, queries about one another's comfort, and encouraging words to the horse. The sleigh bells set up a cheerfully monotonous chorus. M was acutely aware of the feel of Madras's thigh beside her own under the heavy robes. Every so often he planted soft kisses on her fore-head, her nose, her cheek. She wondered, suddenly, if her grand-mother had ever known such bliss. And she thought she knew the answer—not until Fanny had become acquainted with Ellis Harding. The thought made her cheeks grow warm.

Madras drew in on the reins, stopping to let the horse rest. He took M into his arms and kissed her more deeply than he ever had. All thoughts of home and grandmother flew from her mind and she kissed him back with equal ardor.

"Good God, M . . . ," he said. "If you keep kissing me like that, we'll never make it until May Day."

"I hate waiting," she whispered, kissing him again.

"But we must, my love." Madras tucked the robe around them, spoke to the horse, and they set off again.

They arrived at Augusta Mitchell's just as the sun was setting. The fading light gave the snow a pink glaze. A warm halo of lamplight glowed from the front-room window, welcoming and inviting. M's feet were cold and she had long since wrapped her scarf over her nose. Bits of frozen breath clung to the fibers of Madras's coat, and balls of ice had formed in the horse's fetlocks.

Madras lifted M from the sleigh and carried her into the house.

"Grandmother, Aunt Honoria," he called, "we're here."

Honoria materialized at the foot of the stairs. "Dear, dear," she murmured as she unwrapped M's scarf and unbuttoned her coat. "Cold, my goodness." She drifted away bearing coat, scarf, and mittens, holding them away from her body as if fearful they contained a deeper cold capable of transforming her into a block of ice that might never melt.

"Go into the parlor, M," Madras said. "If Grandmother isn't here, Aunt Honoria will be back directly to make you comfortable. I must see to the horse. He's done a fine day's work for us. I won't be long."

Honoria reappeared almost as soon as Madras left. She carried a painted tin tray set with china teapot and cups—the blue willow pattern, M noted. It was her favorite.

"Sit, you must sit," Honoria said, drawing a chair near the parlor stove. She placed a stool under M's feet, aiming them at the stove's fender. She rattled cups and saucers, poured tea, and handed a cup to M. It was Darjeeling, a light tea with a delicate flavor.

"Thank you," M said. "I'm much warmer now. We had a very pleasant run down here."

"Yes. Pleasant. Snow . . ." Honoria smiled softly as if her thoughts had gone off on some personal tangent.

"And Mrs. Mitchell?"

"Abed." Honoria brought her thin, delicate hand to her forehead and touched it lightly. "Sick headache."

"I'm very sorry to hear it, Miss Cobb."

Honoria clasped her hands together in a gesture of distress, then laid them gently back in her lap. When they heard the front door open, Honoria rose, picked up the tea tray, and vanished soundlessly through the door at the far end of the room. Madras, in his stocking feet and shed of his heavy outer clothing, came in and sat down near M.

"Where's Grandmother?"

"As near as I can make out, she has gone to bed with a sick headache."

"Oh, dear." His expression grew grave. "That doesn't bode well, I'm afraid. She's a tyrant when she's herself, but when she's ill, well, she's . . . let's just say that I've heard Mother refer to Grandmother's headache days as 'typhoon season.' "

M felt alarmed. Suddenly, she wanted to be back at Abbott's Reach with her own grandmother, Maude, and Sam. She did not want to be a frail craft upon the angry, churning sea of Augusta Mitchell's household.

"Perhaps, then, Madras, it would be wiser for me to stay at your mother's house tonight and return tomorrow when, surely, your grandmother will be feeling better."

"Oh, no, M. Grandmother wants you here, and it's not a good idea to upset her right now. Aunt Honoria will see to you. It will be all right. You'll see."

"Madras, I really don't understand . . ."

"There's nothing to understand. Grandmother is an old lady, very spoiled and set in her ways, and we must humor her for now.

Just for now." He reached for her hand, brought it to his lips, and laid a light kiss on it. "Mother and Patsy will call on you tomorrow— although, if Grandmother is still not well, they may wait a day."

"Madras . . ." But before M could frame more questions, Honoria reappeared.

"Your room," she murmured, making a vague gesture, which M assumed meant *Follow me*. Honoria made a shooing gesture toward Madras, making it clear he was to leave.

"I'll stop by in the morning, M," he said hastily as he left the room.

Honoria, carrying a candle, led M to a pleasant room at the far end of the icy upstairs hallway. A fire crackled on the hearth. The bed was turned back and her valise stood open in a corner of the room. She glanced toward the window and saw that no light glimmered from any source—no stars, no lamps from nearby houses, no moon. An annoyed look crossed Honoria's face and she pulled the draperies closed with a quick, energetic snap. The hands on the small clock on the bedside table pointed at the hour—six o'clock.

"We must . . . be quiet . . . very quiet," Honoria said in a whisper as she drifted out of the room. She closed the door so softly, not even the latch clicked. M, bewildered and mystified, sank down onto the bed. *I must be calm and wait*, she thought. Gradually, her breathing returned to normal and her heart stopped hammering.

Honoria came back into the room carrying a tray of food.

"Supper," she whispered, in what sounded like an attempt at cheerfulness. The smell of warm biscuits and fish chowder reminded M that she was hungry. She noted with interest the generous slice of chocolate cake and the lovely red apple.

"But there's only enough for one," M whispered. "Aren't you . . ."

A surprised look crossed Honoria's face and her expression went through a series of odd contortions indicating that she was either not hungry, had already eaten, or never ate at all. M nodded politely, as if she understood, and Honoria's mouth relaxed into a shadowy smile. She patted M's arm quickly, lightly, as if in encouragement, and faded out of the room as she had done before. Once again, the latch made no sound.

M, beyond astonishment or fear of Honoria's strangeness, sat down to eat. She grew aware of the stillness within the house, and only the snap of the fire kept her company. She tested the bed, found it comfortable, and opened the book Sam had loaned her. It was a copy of Bowditch's *The American Practical Navigator*. As a wedding surprise for Madras, she was reacquainting herself with the basics of navigation, which she had learned as a child aboard her father's ship.

M became so deeply absorbed in her reading and in scribbling calculations, she was not immediately aware of the sound that began to permeate the silence. At first, she thought it was the wind making low moans in the trees outside the windows. But there was no wind. Then she thought it sounded like a dog whimpering, but realized the sound did not come from outside. Dressed in her white flannel nightgown and dark blue wool robe, she went out into the hallway, listening intently. She heard nothing. A candle burned in a holder set on a table with slender, turned legs. As she closed the door behind her, she heard the sound again, and this time, there was no mistaking it. It was a human moan, and it came from behind a door up the hallway.

M took the candle, her heart hammering, sure now that Augusta Mitchell was having a stroke of apoplexy and needed aid. She moved quickly and silently, tapped on the door she assumed was Augusta's room, turned the knob, and went in. She held the candle high and the light fell on the deathly white oval of Augusta's suffering face. "No," she moaned, "no, light, no light." M retreated quickly, set the candle on the floor outside the door, but left it open so some small illumination aided her effort to determine what was wrong and how to help.

"Mrs. Mitchell, it's M Giddings. What may I do to help you?"

"No . . . help," Augusta moaned in a barely audible voice. Her bed cap was askew, her nightdress crumpled and soaked with perspiration. The room smelled stale.

"Bad, bad, oh, dear, so very bad," Honoria said as she materialized just behind M. Honoria fluttered about the bed, adjusting bedcovers, attempting to fluff pillows.

"Get away," Augusta hissed, her face contorting into an angry, pain-ridden grimace. Honoria shriveled almost visibly and retreated to the comparative safety of the doorway.

"Mrs. Mitchell," M said gently, softly, "we must ease your pain. You must let us try." Augusta's hand flew up imperiously as if to strike out and M recoiled instinctively. The hand dropped heavily onto the bed and Augusta moaned deeply, gutturally, more like an animal than a human being.

"Miss Cobb," M said, "have you any willow bark?"

"Why, perhaps, but Sister won't . . . oh, dear, oh, dear . . ." Her eyes grew wide and took on an odd echo of wildness.

"Miss Cobb, you must find the willow bark and you must set a kettle to boil. And have you a woolen cloth, or pillow cover? Even a stocking will do. I know what to do to ease Mrs. Mitchell's pain. Mrs. Maude and Dr. Sam have taught me some useful things—but I need your help."

Honoria, her mouth pressed into a bloodless line, looked directly at M for the first time.

"Kettle. Cloth," she said, a note of determination creeping into her voice. She faded away into the gloom of the hallway.

Augusta's moaning had become high-pitched, verging on hysteria.

M felt her way across the room until she encountered the commode with the ewer full of water sitting upon it. She felt the soft fabric of a towel, dipped it into the water, and wrung it out. She moved
to the bed and reached for Augusta's hand. M felt Augusta tense, but
she spoke soothingly and applied the towel to Augusta's wrist.

Honoria returned, hovering in the doorway, looking for all
the world like some strange refugee from the River Styx, her hair
hanging wild and straggly down her spindly back, her rapier-like
fingers clenched tightly around something. She hesitated a
moment, then moved toward M, extending her hand as she did so.
"Wool cloth," she murmured.

"Wait here," M said as she took the cloth. She went down the
stairs quickly, found the pair of mittens in her coat pocket, and
stepped out into the frigid winter night. She scooped up snow
and shaped it into small balls, stuffed them into the mittens,
wrapped the mittens in the wool cloth, and returned to Augusta
and Honoria. She lifted Augusta's head gently and slid the ice pack
under the suffering woman's neck.

"Now, Miss Cobb, if you would go down to the kitchen and
pour the hot water into an invalid feeder and bring it and the willow bark to me."

Honoria returned within minutes and M set the bark to steep
in the hot water. As soon as the liquid had cooled sufficiently, she
held the spout of the invalid feeder to Augusta's mouth. Augusta
rolled her head away, but it was a feeble protest. M pressed her
advantage, turning Augusta's face back toward the invalid feeder
spout. "You must sip this, Mrs. Mitchell. It will ease your pain just
as the snow pack under your head will."

After Augusta drank the willow-bark infusion, M applied a
cool towel to Augusta's brow and began to massage the muscles in
the old lady's arms and neck. Honoria stood a little away from the
bed, a shocked look playing about her eyes every time M laid

hands on Augusta. Gradually, Augusta's moans subsided and in their place came an occasional sigh of relief.

"I'll sit with her, Miss Cobb," M said. "You go back to bed."

"No. You and I . . . we . . ." Honoria pulled a blanket off the foot of the bed and wrapped it around M's shoulders. She settled herself in the rocking chair. "Wait," she breathed. "We wait until morning. Better, I think."

15.

M woke with a start. Her legs were painfully cramped beneath her. She stretched them carefully, wincing slightly with the effort. The sliver of light seeping around the window drapery told her it was morning. The room was cold. She wrapped the blanket more closely around her shoulders and moved softly to Augusta's bedside. The old lady was still asleep, her face peaceful against the pillow. Honoria was not there, but in the far reaches of the house, M heard kitchen sounds. She went out into the hallway and down the stairs. The house seemed empty, but the fire in the kitchen stove had been kindled and coffee was made. She poured a cup and carried it back upstairs.

Augusta's eyes fluttered open at the sound of M's footsteps Her skin looked pale and clearly she was exhausted. Her bed cap had come untied and long, gray tendrils of hair curled against her neck. She closed her eyes wearily and murmured, "A long night."

"Quite so," M replied, thinking of her own long night sleeping fitfully in the chair. "I've brought you a cup of coffee, Mrs. Mitchell. It's very strong. You must drink it. Mrs. Webber says a strong cup of coffee every morning, but only one, will keep the sick headaches from returning as often."

"I never drink coffee." Augusta's voice held a note of its customary imperious tone.

"But you will this morning, Mrs. Mitchell," M said firmly, not smiling, "because you are in my care now and I say you must."

"Cheeky girl," Augusta said in a weak attempt at severity.

M helped Augusta sit up in bed, propped her with pillows, and handed her the steaming cup. "Be careful, it's hot."

Soon, M had a blaze going in the room's small fireplace and the air began to feel less frigid. She moved about the room, smoothing bedcovers, folding articles of clothing that had lain draped over a chair, pulling the curtains aside a bit to let in some light. As she worked, she felt Augusta observing. "Naturally," M said somewhat self-consciously, "I don't do any of this according to your ways, Mrs. Mitchell, but I see what needs doing, and do the best I can."

"Obviously, someone has brought you up to be useful," Augusta said. She seemed to be tolerating the light and M opened the curtains a little more to let the morning fully enter the room.

"Many people have taught me to be useful. My parents, Dr. and Mrs. Webber. And my grandmother—mostly my grandmother. You would do well to remember that." She spoke matter-of-factly, with no impertinence in her tone.

A shadow of a smile crossed Augusta's face. "I am at your mercy. And in your debt."

"You are neither, Mrs. Mitchell." M folded a crocheted blanket and laid it across Augusta's feet. "That is what family is for."

A startled look registered on Augusta's face, and whatever she was going to say next was left unsaid. She took another sip of coffee and lay back against the pillows.

A small tap sounded at the door, and Honoria, bearing a tray set with a plate of toast, a pot of tea, and a dish of custard, slipped into the room. Her eyes were wide with surprise or fright—M wasn't sure which. She glanced at M as if waiting for instructions.

"Your sister is doing quite well this morning, Miss Cobb. Perhaps, while you are here, this would be a good time for me to go and get dressed," M said.

"I will expect you to attend me later this morning," Augusta said, with a peevish tone in her voice.

After M had dressed and eaten breakfast in the kitchen, she cleared the table and washed the dishes. It was still early, not yet past eight o'clock. She thought of Madras, longed to see him, to be at sea with him, far from the complications his family had thrust upon them. Where was he and why had he not come? She stood a few moments in the front parlor, peering out the frosty window, but there was no sight of him, or anyone else. She sighed and made herself think instead of how she might keep Augusta Mitchell entertained for the rest of the day, for clearly, she was not yet well enough to be out of bed.

A quick search around the room yielded a deck of cards, a checkerboard, and a copy of Dickens's *Great Expectations*, the pages uncut. She gathered up those things and went back to Augusta's room. "Shall I read to you?" M asked.

"No, I think not," Augusta said. "I want to talk to you. I have something for you." Color had come back into her face and she seemed stronger. Her hair was combed and braided now, Honoria's handiwork, M surmised. She was sitting up in bed, a dark blue and red paisley shawl wrapped around her shoulders. She looked like a dowager empress, yet somehow, she seemed tamer. Nonetheless, M sensed the old lady's indomitable need to be in command.

"Oh, dear," Honoria murmured, a frightened look moving across her bird-like features. Her hands fluttered to her mouth and she bolted from the room, her skirt hems flying about her slipper heels. "Not . . . that!"

"That woman hasn't the spine God gave a canary," Augusta said. "Sit near me in that chair." M pulled the rocking chair close to the bedside.

"I brought a deck of cards, if you'd care to play a hand of cribbage," she said.

"They scatter, the lot of them," Augusta said, ignoring M's remark, "the minute I take to my bed. Not that I care one whit for their hovering. There's no pity to be had from any of them."

Only because you never allow yourself to show them your weakness, M thought, saying nothing.

"I was a bride of sixteen when I went to sea with Mr. Mitchell the first time. What do you say to that?"

"Were you very homesick?"

"Homesick? Why ever would I be homesick?" A faraway look came into Augusta's eyes. "I saw sights in my day that no white woman had ever seen and none will ever again." She paused, as if gathering the great weight of memory. "Not many women went to sea in those days, back in the 1840s."

"Except for the Havener sisters—China, India, and Persia."

Augusta fixed M with a hard look. "You speak of ghosts and whimsy, child. In all my years at sea, we never once crossed roads with them, nor spoke their ship."

"But the Misses Merrithew say they have made dresses for the Havener sisters."

"The Misses Merrithew have brains no larger than those of kittens. The Havener sisters, indeed!" Augusta slumped down in the bed, clearly intent on being out of temper if M persisted in her talk about the Havener sisters.

"I did not mean to digress, Mrs. Mitchell. I believe you were about to tell me something of your days at sea with Mr. Mitchell."

Augusta stared heavily at M, her dark eyes glinting with unreadable lights. Suddenly, she lifted her hand and pointed to a

sea chest set against the far wall of the room. "Open that," she
commanded. "And bring me the parcel wrapped in muslin."

M did as she was told. She gave the parcel to Augusta, who
unwrapped it slowly to reveal a loosely rolled bundle that
appeared to be fabric of some kind, but like none M had ever
seen before. It was curiously colored, as if it had been dipped in
many baths of strong tea. It was decorated with triangles and leaf
shapes, some golden brown, others almost black. The designs
appeared to have been stamped.

"How very beautiful!" M exclaimed.

"I don't suppose you know what it is?"

M shook her head.

"It's kapa cloth, from Hawaii. Given to me by a woman named
Kamamalu because I once did her a kindness. I watched a woman
make cloth like this once. It's made from mulberry bark that is beaten
into a pulp until fibers are released. Then it is rolled very thin and
dried. The final step is to decorate it. The designs of each family are
unique to them. It's a very sacred thing; they equate it with prayer.

"Honoria can't stand to look at this. To her it's a pagan thing,
tainted with superstition and all manner of evils that come ashore
the minute a common seaman sets foot upon land. She's not far
from the truth, either, but I've kept it to remind myself of the infinite caprices of life in all its varieties. And of my younger days,
before I knew the true nature of the world." She rewrapped the
cloth in the muslin and handed it to M. "You've done me a kindness. I'd like you to have this."

M opened her mouth to protest that she had done nothing,
that she did not need payment for what she had done willingly
But she saw that Augusta had made up her mind and would not
take no for an answer.

"Thank you. It's beautiful. I'll treasure it."

Augusta waved one hand in a gesture of fretful dismissal. "Now you may read to me. But none of that dreary Dickens. There's a copy of *The Innocents Abroad* over there on that shelf. Mark Twain can always be counted on to be amusing."

M's Log—January 1872

When Mrs. Mitchell nodded off, lulled, I suppose, by the sound of my voice and not at all invigorated by Mark Twain's adventures, I slipped downstairs, thinking I would find Miss Cobb and offer to help her with the morning housework. But Miss Cobb, probably tired out from a sleepless night, was nowhere to be found. Thus I was left to rattle around quite alone.

In many ways this is a dreary house: The draperies and wood-work are dark, the walls papered in brooding floral designs, and the furniture too square and ornate for grace or comfort. Mementos of Mrs. Mitchell's days at sea fill the rooms. I was quite taken by a sailor's valentine, made entirely of beautiful seashells, enclosed in a mahogany frame. Delicate Japanese fans with carved ivory ribs embellish a parlor wall and deeply fringed silk Spanish shawls drape the back of a sofa. In the front hallway I noticed a lovely blue-and-white pottery umbrella stand from China. It holds a dozen walking sticks, some carved, some with silver or ivory knobs.

I felt most at home in the kitchen, which is large and sunny and by far the warmest room in the house. I sat down there to think. I had been invited to entertain Mrs. Mitchell. Now, here I was, left to my own devices with no word from Madras and none from his mother and sister, who surely know I am left to fend for myself in an unfamiliar house and situation. My first thought was to dress warmly, walk down to the village to hire a horse, and start for home. But the snow is deep and the cold is deeper. I sat a long time, growing angrier and wanting to give Madras and his entire family a carding out, but then I thought how silly that was, to be angry with him, with them, over something no one had foreseen. It was very vexing.

Then, without warning, I felt the old shadow of melancholy fall over me like some dark curtain closing. I wanted Grand Fan and Mrs. Maude, for I knew they would cosset me and make me see that not all was as grim as I perceived it at that moment.

And that was how Madras found me—my eyes red from weeping, my hair in straggles, my nose a-drip, and a lukewarm cup of tea in my hand. In an instant he folded me into his arms and I knew all would be right. And so it was.

Still, I think I have gotten myself into a very queer family. Zulema (she said I must call her by her proper name) and Pacifica sent a note by Madras saying they would stay away until Mrs. Mitchell was up and about again.

"Grandmother," Madras said, by way of explanation, "can be quite an ogre when she's ill." I didn't contradict him. But I think she is an ogre not because she is ill, but because she is lonely and because no one dares to stand up to her. Being left alone is not at all what she wants. It's what she wants everyone to think she wants in order to keep the upper hand.

When I calmed myself and had all the kisses I wanted, I showed Madras the kapa cloth his grandmother had given me. I am puzzled by his reaction to it. At first he simply stared at it, his mouth set into a hard line the way it does sometimes when he is nettled by something that doesn't quite suit him.

"I can't believe she gave you this," he said. "She's had that for many years. She always said it would be her winding shroud. That's what the Hawaiians use this cloth for, you know, to wrap their dead in."

I did not know that.

"She said the living also wear it."

"*They used to, but when the missionaries brought cotton fabric, the making of kapa cloth nearly ended, and what little was made was used only for important occasions, to bury the royal dead or to drape them when they were born or married.*"

"*I hope she does not intend for us to be wrapped in it when we marry, Madras.*" *Which would be just like her, I thought with annoyance, although I could not imagine why Mrs. Mitchell might want such a thing, unless it was to vex her family.*

Madras fixed me with an odd look. "*No, M, I am quite certain she will not expect that of us.*" *Soon, Madras took me off to his mother's house. Patsy was expecting Hugh Chapman to pay her a call and could not contain her elation. She dragged me upstairs to her room to help her tie blue silk organdy ribbons in her hair. When I told Patsy about the kapa cloth, she stopped her chatter abruptly.*

"*You must give it back,*" *she said.* "*It's a very great prize, so Grandmother always said. I don't know why she would give it away. Grandmother has never told anyone the whole story about the kapa cloth. I believe Mother said it had to do with saving the life of a woman who had been set upon by a drunken sailor. The sailor said the woman was of low moral character, but Grandmother knew other- wise, knew him for the brute he was. M, things happened in Hawaii that I have had hints of, but of course no one will tell me about. Things having to do with Madras, too, when he was much younger, still a boy, really, barely eighteen. He got himself into some disgraceful scrape—although Madras is so good, I can't think what.*"

She stopped her headlong chatter at that point, and I was glad of it. And what did it matter, anyway, if Madras had a small black mark somewhere in his past? It was past and had nothing to do with me.

16.

Gradually, the days settled into a predictable routine. M went back and forth from Fort Point to Searsport each week as the weather allowed. As she did so, everyone at Abbott's Reach began to adjust. Fanny stopped weeping in corners and M stopped feeling guilty for being in love and wanting to leave home.

M's time with Augusta was not the burden she had believed it would be. The old lady, while always maintaining her aura of autocracy, had a well-honed sense of humor. She was also a master at cribbage and M struggled mightily to best her.

But it was Honoria M came to look forward to seeing each week. For it was Honoria who made the house run and provided little unexpected moments of pleasure. She baked special treats when she knew M was coming. She left a dozen linen handkerchiefs, each one edged with the daintiest of tatting, on M's pillow. She showed M her plan for another flowerbed she wanted to put in when spring came. Despite Honoria's natural inclination to be quiet, M had gleaned a few bits of information about her. She had spent her life at home, living first with her parents, then with Augusta after she had come ashore. Honoria had never married, but she had been asked—that poor young man had succumbed to consumption shortly before the wedding was to take place.

One afternoon, when they were sitting in the kitchen, Honoria got up suddenly, disappeared into the far reaches of the house, and came back with something wrapped in a man's silk handkerchief.

"His," she whispered as she unwrapped the cloth to reveal a tintype of a rather plain young man with the most remarkably curly hair. "Frederick. Red hair. Lovely, lovely." Then as quickly as she had shown M the tintype, she wrapped it up and disappeared again.

Tears pricked M's eyes. Now she knew why Honoria, aside from the fact that she loved her great-nephew Madras, had transferred her shares in the *Boreas* to him to prevent Augusta from creating an obstacle that might prevent M and Madras from marrying in the spring. At heart, Honoria was a romantic.

Although she would never say so, it was evident that Augusta looked forward to M's company each week. She only grumbled a little when Patsy and her friends carried M off to go sleighing or to an afternoon tea party. Sometimes, Augusta invited the young ladies to drink tea with her, regaling them with stories of her adventures at sea, pointing out this or that item she had brought home from the far corners of the earth.

Thus, the months passed agreeably and quickly. And before M knew it, it was May.

Part 2
At Sea

Entries from M's Log—1872
Aboard the *Boreas*

May 1, 1872

We departed on the afternoon tide. As we slid past the ships rocking at anchor, I had some very great pangs of regret, a sudden feeling I had never had before. As the men cast off the hawsers connecting us to the dock, I was flooded with memories from my childhood, yearned for my mother, and realized that I had never been to sea without female company. It had always been Mother, Grace, and me, always together, weathering the gales and taking care of Father, who like most shipmasters, was too busy caring for his vessel and crew to take care of himself properly. And what would I do without Grand Fan and Mrs. Maude, without my friends with whom I had spent so many pleasant hours? I wanted to cry then, as the Boreas *swung around and departed the shore and all I hold so dear.*

There is no turning back, although I know that if I became truly, truly so homesick I couldn't bear it, Madras would put me ashore at Boston and I could take the train home.

Home. The word catches in my throat. What is Grand Fan doing? What is old Mrs. Mitchell thinking? Is Honoria Cobb standing by an upstairs window looking out at the river and remembering her young man who loved her so long ago?

Then I think how ridiculous I am to let such thoughts sink me. This is where I want to be.

Earlier on this day, I stood beside Madras, my husband, and together we surveyed what is to be our kingdom for the next several years. Our crew of twelve men and one cabin boy are, Madras said, less scabrous than usual. He went out of his way to find them, thinking of my "finer sensibilities," he said, quite forgetting I have seen, when a child, crews far worse. Not that I care one whit for a crew's quality or lack of it. For I am "the old man's wife" now, and as such command the sailors' respect. If they chance to cross my path as can't be avoided in the usual routine of things, they lower their eyes and spring out of the way to let me pass. I have not yet learned their names, but I shall. Surely, there is at least one Bob or John among them, and no doubt a Paddy or a Sven.

I expect the cook, "Oyster" Duncan, and I will find ourselves drawn together in a conspiracy of food before too many days have passed. Mr. Duncan is a man of middling age, thin as a lath, which may not bode well as a sign of his cooking worth. A really good cook, it seems to me, is always a bit plump from too much tasting. But I must not be hasty in my judgment, for my association with Mr. Duncan must evolve at its own natural pace. For now I must stay aloof from all that pertains to the running of the ship. But I will stay watchful for those times when I may be of use.

Our wedding was everything I had hoped for. Dr. Sam, dressed in his blue mariner's jacket, the silver buttons as shiny as newly minted silver dollars, his cap tipped at a jaunty angle over his twinkling blue eyes, gave me away. Maude surprised us all by appearing in a lovely pale pink dress with a skirt drawn back into a slight train and looped up with white fringes, so very fashionable it astounded us. The Misses Merrithew concocted it for her. Those little ladies flitted about the deck, twittering in phrases so bird-like it made me laugh.

Not a hair on Maude's head was out of place, and even her gloves matched her chip of a hat! But we did not remark much upon it for fear she'd fling her finery into the bay just to prove that her spirit is not girded by the whims of fashion.

Grand Fan looked elegant in pale blue silk, a dear little hat perched atop her pretty hair, which was coiled and braided in a most

intricate way. I made her promise she would not disgrace me with
weeping and she kept her promise. But as the men cast off the bow
and stern lines and we departed Searsport harbor, I saw her clinging
to Mrs. Maude and Dr. Sam as if she were drowning. It was then
that I felt my chest constrict, making breathing almost impossible.
My heart sank, then, and I wondered if I would ever see those dear
faces again. The old melancholy seized me fiercely and I felt my
knees go weak. I wanted to shout, "No, I cannot leave them!" But I
felt Madras's big hand in mine and I leaned against him, knowing
that he was my bulwark, my anchor, my safe harbor, now.

Yet, I see them still—Grand Fan, Mrs. Maude, and Dr. Sam,
receding, receding, waving until the Boreas *rounded the point and I*
saw them no more.

The one blot on my wedding day was that Mother and Father
were not there. They were delayed by heavy seas, which cost them
several spars. They limped to Cuba where they stopped to make
repairs. Knowing they'd never get to Searsport in time for my wed-
ding, they put a letter aboard a steamer bound for Portland. They
said they would go on to New Orleans where it is hoped we will
rendezvous at last. It is more than two years since last I saw them.

All of the Mitchell family turned out for the wedding, and I am
happy to say their manner toward Grand Fan was properly civil
and, indeed, I saw Zulema and Isaiah take special pains to engage
Grand Fan in conversation. I find my new in-laws to be the kindest
of people in their willingness to set aside their judgment of Grand
Fan in order to allow their son his happiness. Augusta Mitchell was
polite, but not inclined to say more than a few words to Grand Fan;
nevertheless, she was civil, and I can ask no more than that.

Grand Fan took everything in stride, I thought, although with
her, it is not always easy to tell. Ellis Harding was not at her side,
and I am sure she felt that keenly, but that is a matter I am not
supposed to know much about, so I was silent on that score. Mr.

Harding's wife was very ill with bronchitis for several months, but recovered, although she continues poorly from another affliction. Mr. Harding sent me a letter introducing me to his daughter, Nancy Davis, who resides at Honolulu. He says she will take me in hand when we arrive in the Islands and show me the sights while Madras is engaged in the business of unloading and taking on a new cargo. I never visited the Islands when I was a child sailing on the Fairmount. *We most often visited South American and European ports, and once we sailed to Egypt with a cargo of ice.*

As for me, I was attired in the simple dress I wanted, a bit more lavishly embellished with beads and embroidery than I preferred, but so very lovely. When Grand Fan presented me, the night before my wedding day, with a lovely veil of beautiful lace, I could not bear to disappoint her by not wearing it. As she said, it will serve a dual purpose—when I get to the tropics, I can wear it as a shawl. I carried mayflowers, of course, and the lace veil was affixed to a wreath made of the same blossoms, which dear Dr. Sam said he had fashioned for me to hang in my cabin, but it was so lovely and so perfect with the veil, I put my little hat aside and set the wreath upon my head. I have no doubt Grand Fan, and probably Mrs. Maude, hatched it all out together, that wreath, but it was done out of love, and I was only too happy to be the object of so endearing a conspiracy.

Madras, of course, wore a new navy blue mariner's coat with silver buttons. His linen cravat, in the old style, was starched within an inch of its life. He did not wear a cap and his new black leather boots were polished to a fine gleam. He looked so handsome and dashing it made my heart burst with pride and joy.

Patsy stood as my bridesmaid and Hugh Chapman stood as best man. I do believe that when next I see Patsy and Hugh, they will be husband and wife. They make a pretty couple, and as Hugh is engaged in the business end of shipping, not the sailing part, they are most likely to stay in Searsport. Patsy wore the loveliest yellow dress, the very color of sunshine, and all the eyes of the crew who witnessed our wedding from the dockside were upon her as she waltzed the deck after Madras and I said our vows.

Evening draws in; soon we will eat supper, and after that, when Madras is convinced all is well above, he will come to me and we will "become one flesh," which I blush to think about, even though Mrs. Maude set me straight on all that the phrase implies.

May 2, 1872

Today, I started housekeeping in our quarters. There was little to set to rights, but I made our bed and watered the geranium hanging from the transom. I polished and dusted the furniture, a job that really did not need doing and which, by rights, belongs to the steward, whose name is, I believe, Lewis. Doing these small chores, however, is the first step in establishing an order to the day, which Mother taught me. It makes the monotony of life at sea easier to endure.

I went to the rail and shook the carpets. This made Madras laugh, and put big grins on the faces of the crew. This was especially true of Oyster Duncan, who emerged from the galley where only moments before he had been punching biscuit dough into fine submission. As I passed by him on my way below, he reached for the carpets, took them from me, and cast a glowering eye on the boy, Lewis.

"The boy'll take care of it, Missus," he mumbled. And I saw then that I will have to tread a bit softly until he and Lewis understand that I am no Queen of Sheba to be waited on hand and foot.

Oyster is a lanky man with graying hair, snaggly teeth, and bleary brown eyes. But he bakes a beautiful "buscuit," as he calls them. His apron is made from what looks like a piece of old canvas, and I have resolved to make him one of unbleached muslin which will be far easier to wash and will wrap more comfortably around him.

Lewis is a thin, shy boy of thirteen or fourteen, with curly blond hair and sad blue eyes. He is the son, so Madras says, of a widow who lives down Rockland way. He seems bright enough, although I have yet to hear him speak. He looks at me with a strange mixture of awe and defiance, as if he expects harsh words, or worse. My heart goes out to him, but I cannot overstep the bounds that must exist between us, and indeed all the crew, lest the authority and dignity of Madras's command be compromised.

I don't have my sea legs yet and I tend to lurch about like, well, a drunken sailor. But that will soon right itself, and I'll ride the waves with the best of them.

Madras inquired several times today if I was suffering from sea-sickness. I teased him about wanting to dose me with something nasty from his medical kit, and that made him laugh. But I am quite well and find the sensation of the constant motion of the ship not at all distressing.

He follows me with his eyes, does Madras, when I move about the deck. He comes to me when he is not at the wheel or giving an order or overseeing the running of the ship. He comes to me to inquire if I am comfortable, if my hat is securely tied, to make certain an awning is shielding me properly from the sun. He comes to touch my hand and I see in his eyes, then, how he looks forward, as I do, to the time when we will be alone together again in our splendid bed, and undressed in one another's arms.

Our first night together as husband and wife, our wedding night, awakened in me sensations I never dreamed of, in spite of what Mrs. Maude had told me. What she did not say, and for this I bless her (for it is the best of gifts to have discovered for myself), is that the love Madras and I make with our bodies bonds us more deeply in mind and spirit. He entered me eagerly, but gently, and I received him eagerly, but fiercely, and his gentleness became fierce and my fierceness became gentle and we rocked together in mutual bliss, the motion of the ship rocking us, too, the entire universe ebbing and flowing beneath, over, and around us until I was flooded with such exquisite pleasure that I wept with the pure joy of it. Now I understand what this phrase means: They took their ease of one another.

That is what I see in my husband's eyes: his longing for that ease, that comfort, that strange exchange of energy which both infuses and diffuses the very core of our beings. It is from this energy, I believe, that the soul of new life is formed. I long to write this to Mrs. Maude, but I will not, for what Madras and I share, though it is surely not unique to us, is the sacred weft uniting us forever.

May 10, 1872

Last evening, while Lancaster Treat, the first mate, was on watch, Madras allowed himself a quiet hour to read the newspapers he had picked up in New York. We are anchored in the harbor there. He lay sprawled on the sofa and I sat on the carpet on a cushion, close by him. We found letters waiting for us, too, and I received a packet containing news of all my best beloveds at home.

Grand Fan writes that boarders are beginning to arrive for short stays and she anticipates a busy season. She says she hasn't a moment, not really a bit of time to feel sorry for herself that I am so far from home. She has hired several local girls to wait on tables and clean rooms during the season, and also has found someone to cook. Of Ellis Harding she says only that he came to fix the fence and will soon set to work replacing cedar shingles on the piazza roof. She admonishes me to wear a wide hat at all times and sends her best love.

Mrs. Maude and Dr. Sam write mostly of the weather, how fine it has been for digging dandelions, the rhubarb shrub they plan to make, and of excursions to little-known places where they gather roots and barks for Mrs. Maude's simples. Dr. Sam has scraped and painted the Zephyr and says he plans to sail Mrs. Maude and

Grand Fan around the bay some fine early June afternoon when the sky is about the color of Grand Fan's eyes.

A note from the Misses Merrithew: "Dear child, Sailing, sailing over the bounding main, oh, yes, you are, and fitted up so nicely in that little white velvet jacket, you were. The lilacs are just budding and Sister says we must find a bit of veiling that very color for it will look so well on Miss Pacifica Mitchell's hat when she walks out with Mr. H.C."

And this from Ellis Harding: "Your grandmother is keeping busy, have no fear she is pining away, for she isn't. My daughter, Nancy, looks forward to seeing you when you get to Honolulu. She wants to show you the sights, as much or as little as you like."

Madras received letters from his mother and from Hugh Chapman. But nothing from his grandmother.

Patsy scribbled a hasty note at the end of her mother's letter: "Dearest M, How dreary the days seem knowing you won't be joining us for a long stay this summer. Yet, gaiety in all its various disguises continues to call. Lily and Lucia Griffin and Atlanta Sears and I made the prettiest belated May baskets filled with wildflowers and pots of jam. We spent an afternoon carrying them to several elderly ladies in town who no longer get out much. Not precisely our brand of excitement, but as Mother says, it kept us diverted to a good and useful purpose. She has, however, promised that I may attend the party to celebrate Atlanta's nineteenth birthday."

Gordon wrote to Madras: "Dear Brother, I still think it's rotten you wouldn't take me as cabin boy at the very least, even though I am a little old for that, but it would be better than nothing. Now I'm doomed to be sent upriver in the fall to Hampden Academy, where Father says I must perfect my mathematics and Mother says I must learn better manners and apply myself to Shakespeare, but it all seems to be Grandmother's doing. She has this notion that I am to be saved from the sea. I wish you could have seen how she carried on and

wrung her hands over it. You must write to her, Madras, and convince
her I haven't an aptitude for books! And if she won't listen to you,
then have M write. She'll listen to M."

Madras will spend the next few days getting our cargo of shin-
gles unloaded and taking on a cargo of textiles. Then we are bound
for New Orleans, where we will meet up with Mother and Father.
Mother's letter said: "My dearest daughter, You cannot imagine the
joy with which I look forward to seeing your dear face before the
month has passed. Your father anticipates that we will have leisure to
go ashore for several weeks, and that we will be as much in your
company as we wish. I have had letters from your grandmother and
the Webbers describing your wedding in great detail, and it gave me
such pleasure to know you had a proper celebration. Your father and
I are well. As I am sure Madras told you, steam vessels are crowd-
ing us old square-riggers out, so it is not always easy to find a cargo
that makes the trip worth the time and effort. Shipping is all about
speed these days, and the hauling of vast quantities in great four-
masted ships. But this is nothing we women need concern ourselves
about. Some things change, but a woman's job of caring for the
needs of her husband and family will never be one of them."

May 25, 1872—New Orleans

I spotted the Fairmount *riding at anchor in the distance as we*
were towed across the Bar and entered the harbor. Even in the midst
of all the other shipping, the coming and going of steamships, tug-
boats, and various other small craft cluttering the waters, I knew the
Fairmount *by the grace of her lines from jib boom to afterdeck. The*
sight of her set my heart a-fluttering like the pennants waving from
her rigging. And suddenly, all the feelings of melancholy that had
plagued me since the day my parents sent me alongshore took flight
and vanished.

"*Madras*," *I said later, when the* Boreas *was properly secured and he was at leisure to join me at the rail, "I have come home at last." Tears started in my eyes then, and the soaring feelings I had had only moments ago ebbed like the tide and something both joyous and melancholic overtook me. My hand trembled in his.*

I saw no movement of human form on the Fairmount, *and for a moment I feared that I was wrong, that I had lost my ability to recognize the ship that had been my home, that small enclosed world where I had lived all the early years of my life, where Grace and I had set out our dolls and little china tea sets on the low table under the canopy rigged beside the hatch to give our fair complexions protection from the relentless sun.*

"Then don't you think it's time we went gamming, M?" Madras asked gently, employing the term used at sea for making social calls. He brought my cold fingers to his lips, then gave the order to Lewis and Lex Nichols, the second mate, to make ready to accompany us. Before I had time to repin my hair, Madras bundled me into the boat. Lewis was at the oars, Mr. Nichols at the tiller. Madras was in the bow and I sat like precious cargo just forward of amidships.

As we drew closer to the Fairmount *I saw them at last—Mother and Father, standing at the rail—and for a moment my heart stopped with unutterable joy.*

"Steady as she goes, M," Madras said gently, sensing my tumult and my propensity to swing on yet another tide of emotion—high, low, and everywhere in between.

"Lean on those oars, boy," Mr. Nichols said, giving the order with perfect authority, which brooked no dissent or disobedience. I felt a surge of haste as the boy put all his effort into delivering me as expediently as possible to those I hold so dear.

We drew closer and closer—Mother and Father were at the rail, waving and smiling! Tears ran down Mother's face, but she was laughing, too, as if all the time that had passed without our seeing

*one another had been some grand prank played on us by forces far
beyond our limited human control, which in a way was perfectly so.*

*I declined the nicety of being hoisted aboard in the bo'sun's
chair, preferring instead to take my chances with the ladder. Lewis
and Mr. Nichols turned their eyes away, lest my modesty be compromised by the sight of my skirts and petticoats failing to conceal the
fact that I have ankles and legs.*

*As I climbed, I heard the unmistakable sound of a bo'sun's
whistle piping me aboard, an honor reserved primarily for admirals
of the navy, Father's humorous way of welcoming me home.*

*Then a swell left in the wake of a passing steamer made the
Fairmount roll unexpectedly and I fell, quite literally, into my parents' arms.*

May 28, 1872

*After introductions, talk of our passage to New Orleans, and
quick exchanges of family news, Mother suggested that we retire to
Madame DeMarche's boardinghouse on Decatur Street, where
Father had booked rooms for all of us. There we found pleasant
accommodations where we could rest before gathering for a fine supper downstairs in the dining room. We were, that night, the only
guests present, which made it feel somewhat like home. After the
long days of being at sea, it seemed odd to be in a room that did
not rock with wind and wave.*

*Mother wore a lovely silk dress in a soft shade of blue that made
her eyes glow. Father had on, under his navy blue jacket, a rather
riotous silk waistcoat embroidered with fire-breathing dragons in
bright shades of orange, yellow, and blue. "Some of your mother's
handiwork," he said proudly when I commented on it. "Little did I
know all those years ago when I brought her upriver to Bangor from
Fort Point, and we had that little set-to over some skeins of silk*

thread, that I would one day wear dragons of her design on my waistcoat." He gazed at Mother lovingly.

"At that time, my dear," Mother said to him, "I had no designs on you whatsoever, nor you on me, for you were most disagreeable, and I was much feistier then, as I am sure you recall." They smiled at one another with complicity and deep affection, something that hinted at the kind of bliss I feel each time Madras touches me. I felt myself blushing. Madras reached under the table, took my hand, and squeezed it. He grinned at me and I could tell he liked Mother and Father very well.

Sitting across the table from them, Madras at my side, I perceived Mother and Father in a new way. The years have changed their outward appearance—Mother's hair is heavily stranded with white, the lines in Father's face have deepened and his hair is completely gray—but everything else about them is as familiar and dear to me as the day they put me alongshore with Grand Fan. We have not grown apart. I have simply grown up, and they have simply grown older. I thought I might feel the old resentment—that they had not wanted me, that they had been too cautious and fearful to take me with them after Grace died. But I saw that they have suffered, too, not only from losing Grace, but from having made the decision to part with me, which they still believe was for my own good. And how can I refute it? Had they not parted with me, I would never have known Madras. Yet, there was something on the tip of my tongue that wanted to sting them, just the tiniest bit. In that moment I understood the meaning of the old saying, "Bite your tongue."

Mother was full of plans to visit the Garden District, a very beautiful section of the city. She was most eager to take me to several shops to fit me for some light cotton dresses she said I would most certainly need when we got below the Line—the Equator—and into Hawaii.

In the ensuing days, Father and Madras spent their time discharging and arranging new cargoes. Thus, Mother and I were on our own to come and go as we pleased. We had many callers, too, for there were others from home who came into port from their various journeys around the world. Captains Blanchard, Ross, and Curtis took us on several excursions and sometimes joined us for supper. We went several times to their ships—Hero, Penobscot, and Challenge—to sing, play cards, and dance. But most evenings we gathered at Madame DeMarche's to eat supper and spend the hours of dusk sitting on the verandah, talking and watching the Southern stars come out.

Father, sitting in a rocker, puffed on a cigar, something he did only rarely. The end glowed in the dark, and fragrant smoke drifted into the night to mingle with the moist scent of the Mississippi River, damp earth, and vegetation. Mother lay in the hammock. Madras and I sat on the steps and sipped glasses of lemonade.

We talked mostly of home. Mother and Father could not get enough talk of home. They wanted to hear every detail of daily life at Abbott's Reach. I was glad to oblige, regaling them with descriptions of old Mrs. Mitchell's house, Patsy's dresses, how Grand Fan looks now, and things that Mrs. Maude and Dr. Sam said.

"I've decided this will be our last voyage," Father said quietly when there was a lull in the talk. "It's time we came alongshore. The day of the square-rigged vessel is petering out, and I can't see myself at the helm of a steamer. But you will, Madras, my boy. You're young enough to make that change, and I advise you to start learning as much as you can about that kind of shipping—those big engines, and not a scrap of canvas to be seen."

"There will always be vessels like the Boreas and the Fairmount, sir," Madras replied, his tone filled with confidence, "as long as there are men like you to sail them."

"Well, that's just the thing, Madras; you see, younger men are all hell-bent for the steamers, so it won't be long before there won't be any like me left who know what it means to ship before the mast. There's no risk, you see. The big companies own the steamships and the captains of those vessels get good pay, or so I am

told. There's no need to buy shares or take any money risks on the part of the captain. The steamships are fast and carry a lot of cargo."

"But not wives and families," Mother said, her voice drifting out from the dark corner of the verandah. "Steamship companies don't want the captain's wife and family along. They say it's too risky." Her voice broke a moment, and I knew she was thinking of Grace. "Steamships will be the ruination of seagoing families like ours, and so many others in Belfast, Searsport, Stockton Springs, and the Point. You mark my words."

"But what will you do?" I asked, not liking what I heard, because it implied that someday Madras and I might have to grapple with events that were beyond our control, and because I could not imagine Father and Mother anywhere else but on the deck of the Fairmount. Nor could I imagine myself anywhere but at Madras's side.

"Why, we will do what people like us have always done, M. We will find a small house, perhaps in Belfast near the water, so we won't be too homesick for it. I will take in sewing to keep me from getting into mischief, and your father will find a position with a chandlery or brokerage firm. Perhaps he will sit on the school board, and I will join a ladies' society where I will recount stories of our adventures at sea."

"It sounds perfectly awful!" I declared, getting up and roaming restlessly about the verandah, my skirts swishing with the sudden anger I felt.

"You have a lot to learn, M," Mother said quietly, a touch of ice in her tone.

"Perhaps you do, too, Mother," I said quickly, thinking of all those long days and nights when I had missed her and Father so fiercely that all I could do was cry and run away.

"That will do, Mercy Maude Giddings," Father said in a stern voice with his "captain look" on his face—impassive, in charge, unyielding—although I knew perfectly well he had not hardened his *heart against me, not even for an instant. For Father was fair in his dealings with me.*

"I'm not a child . . ." I started to say heatedly, then thought better of it, for I was behaving like a child, or worse, a mutinous crew, the one thing Father would not tolerate, especially from his daughter.

"No, M, you are not a child," Mother said. "And for that reason, we are going to talk of other things until we can talk of this more calmly. For it is a very sore subject with your Father and me just now, one that causes us much worry. All we know is the sea. The world has been our home. It will not be easy to give that up and go to live alongshore."

"I understand that quite well, Mother," I said, tears starting in my eyes.

I heard Mother's sharp intake of breath as she perceived my meaning. There was a long pause. Then Mother rose from the hammock and came to stand beside me. She took my hand and looked at me with that see-right-through-you way of hers.

"Sometimes, M, when one stays belowdecks too long, one can't tell which way the wind is blowing. Please forgive me."

It was easy, then, to ask her pardon, which she gave with her usual good grace, and I knew that all was well between us.

Soon afterward, Madras held out his hand to me, we bid them good-night, and went upstairs to bed. Our lovemaking that night was wild and lustful, as it had not been before, as if my anger had fueled something primitive in us both. His desire was urgent and long-lasting and my energy matched his perfectly. That night he was not patient with my laces and cut them with his little pocketknife. That night, for the first time, much to his satisfaction, I left fingernail marks on his back. And when we woke in the morning, we did it again, but more gently, with a passion that had deepened and which left us satiated, but craving more. He did not want to leave me that morning, but he did, and I heard him speak to Father as they went on their way to the docks to see to the new cargoes now being loaded on their ships.

After that, it was as if Mother and I had tacked ship in a new direction. We talked freely of everything, and one afternoon, after we had been to a shop where she bought me a paisley shawl and a new palmetto hat with a wide brim, I showed her the kapa cloth Augusta Mitchell had given me. I had brought it along thinking that I'd ask Nancy Davis about it when we got to Hawaii. Mother touched it, the way women do, to learn about it, to absorb with her hands the nature of its construction, to glean perhaps some iota of those other hands that had in the past created it.

"I know nothing of these things," Mother said. "But I would guess that this is very old, and was a very great treasure to Mrs. Mitchell. That she gave it to you is surely a mark of her esteem for you."

"I don't think so, Mother. Madras is the only one Mrs. Mitchell cares anything about. I don't know why she gave it to me. I have no use for it. It would be far safer left in her husband's old sea chest where she's kept it all these years."

"Did she say what you were to do with it?"

"No. She just insisted I take it. She hinted that it is thought to have sacred powers and to be connected with the royal family of Hawaii. It was given to her because she did a good deed. She saved the life of a young Hawaiian woman who had been attacked by a drunken sailor. But I feel certain there is more to the story. I'm hoping that when I get to Honolulu, Ellis Harding's daughter, Nancy Davis, can tell me more."

"Have a care, M," Mother said. "Some things are best left alone."

"Why do you say that? What harm could it possibly do to find out more about it?"

Mother smoothed the kapa cloth with her hands again, this time more carefully and in a lingering way, as if she were trying to read its past.

"*I don't know, M.*" *She rolled the kapa cloth and returned it to its wrappings. "There's no sense in dwelling on it or conjuring up assumptions that have no basis in fact. You have been given a rare gift, and it's only natural that you want to learn more about it—how it was made, who made it, and the full story of how Mrs. Mitchell received it."*

We had a few more days together before we set sail again. We headed to South America, and Mother and Father, to Liverpool. We were barely out of the harbor when I saw far ahead of us on the horizon a three-masted ship with the distinctive lines of the old tea clipper ships. I hailed Madras and he grabbed the glass to look at it.

"Her name is written in gold on the bow," he said, handing me the glass. "The Empress!" *I exclaimed. "The Havener sisters! They must have been at New Orleans."*

"In the harbor, perhaps, but not likely past the Bar, nor ashore. They say the Havener sisters never go ashore."

"Perhaps we will speak them as we cross the Sargasso Sea," I said with great excitement. I handed the glass to Madras and he folded it into a compact tube.

"No one ever speaks the Empress," *he said.*

June 15, 1872, en route to Rio de Janeiro

And, indeed, we did not speak the Empress. *She stays ahead of us, always on the horizon, her course seemingly identical to ours. She is the first thing I look for in the morning and the last thing I look for at night, not to mention the many times during the day I gaze in her direction.*

The crew takes a lively interest in her, too, especially Oyster Duncan and Lewis, whom Oyster has taken under his wing in a gruff sort of way.

"*I seen them sisters once,*" Oyster said when our paths crossed as I took a turn around the deck. The cook is the one person of the crew I, as the wife of the "Old Man," am allowed to converse with briefly. "*We was wrecked off Borneo. Lashed to what was left of the main mast, I was, and fig'rin' I'd be washed ashore and set upon by cannibals.*" He had never been so talkative. "*Fished me out of the drink, those* Empress *shellbacks did. And that's when I saw them sisters, all three of 'em. Taller than most men and trim as a bowsprit they was, their hair tucked under straw bonnets neat as a galley after supper. Blazin' blue eyes, like nothing I ever seen before nor since. They could look right through a man like they had the second sight.*" He drew a breath and wiped his hands on his apron. "*Never saw the Old Man of the* Empress, *though. Nor never laid eyes on them sisters again, and I was aboard the* Empress *most a month before they set me alongshore in Australia.*" He nodded his head emphatically to underscore the veracity of his story. He ducked back into the galley with a sheepish look on his face, as if he feared he had said too much. Perhaps he did, for he has barely mumbled two words to me since.

June 18, 1872

Oyster's story joggled my imagination and made me wild to hear more.

"Tell me what you know about the Havener sisters," I demanded over and over until my conversations with Madras centered almost exclusively on the subject. Madras does not seem to mind my preoccupation. Indeed, we look forward to those moments in the day or evening when we might let loose our speculation about the three women.

"Grandmother told me once that she had been aboard the Empress," Madras said one night when we were in bed and I lay contentedly in his arms.

"Oh, Madras!" I exclaimed. "And why haven't you mentioned this until now?"

"My, dear, I have far too many concerns to let my thoughts dwell for long on conversations I heard when I was hardly more than a child. I remember Grandmother saying that they were at Lisbon, and one morning they woke to find the Empress *in the roads near them. So Grandmother had herself rowed over to visit them. She said she'd never seen a vessel so shipshape. But she only saw the mate; never saw the sisters or their father, the captain. The mate said they had all gone ashore, and she could get nothing more out of him—if you can believe that of Grandmother. She said she saw signs of women, though, for the main cabin, where the mate took her to drink a cup of tea, was done up with lace tablecloths, pretty bits of embroidery, and a whole array of tintypes and water-color paintings. The tintypes were what interested her, for the largest of the three was of three young girls, very much of an age, each one with white-blonde hair, one holding a model ship, which might have been the* Empress, *one holding a spyglass, and one holding—and this was what astounded Grandmother—a sextant."*

I'm sure my eyes grew wide at hearing this, for Madras laughed out loud.

"Why, Madras," I declared, "just the mere fact that we have seen the Empress *all this time will add weight to the legends. I have already written of it to Grand Fan and the Webbers. And the Misses Merrithew." Madras smiled at me, a very complicit smile.*

"And I have written of it to Mother and Father."

June 20, 1872

Today we spoke the Abnaki. *Captain Pierce is bound for Boston. We gave him our letters to carry homeward, quite gleeful to think we have had a hand in furthering the legend of the Havener sisters.*

And on this very day, the Empress *dropped below the horizon and we see her no more.*

June 25, 1872

Of the members of the crew who shipped with us from Searsport, only four remain with us—Lancaster Treat, the first mate, whose family settled early in Bangor; Lex Nichols, the second mate, who is from a farm in Nova Scotia; Oyster Duncan; and Lewis, whose last name, I learned, is Andrews. The remaining dozen or so seamen are new. Hoku is a Hawaiian, eager to return to the islands. He is often aloft as look-out. Madras knows him, I believe, and I wonder about that, but Madras says nothing of it. Then there is Marcel DuPere, who hails from Aroostook County. He found his way to sea via a log drive on the Penobscot. The remaining sailors are a mix of Swedes, Portuguese, and Irish, whose names I don't know and probably never will. They go about the ship's business without giving any trouble. The Swedes are a stoic, silent lot and do their work well. The Irish always appear discontented, making one think they are up to something. Madras does not like to ship them. The Portuguese are temperamental, Madras says, and prone to mutter secretively among themselves.

Since gold was found in California back in '48, it is impossible to ship a crew entirely of Yankee men, as was the practice in the past. In those years, ships would arrive at San Francisco and the crews would disappear in the direction of the gold fields, abandoning the seafaring life forever, leaving a rougher, less-ambitious element of men available for hire.

Thus, the days aboard the Boreas *settle into a predictable and monotonous routine. I apply myself to the vast store of needlework I brought with me, and never a day passes that I am not hemming an apron, mending Madras's shirts and pants, darning socks, crocheting a bedspread, knitting, or hooking rugs. Madras often joins me in hooking rugs. He is good at cutting wool rags into narrow strips. Using a black crayon, he drew on burlap a fine ship in full sail. Together we set about hooking it. He is accomplished at needlepoint, too, and stitched slipper tops for me. He has no patience for knitting. I am knitting socks and mittens against the day we round the Horn when it will be cold. I have never rounded the Horn, as Father was engaged mostly in the European trade when I was a child. I have heard stories of fearsome weather and many ships lost as they attempt to pass from the Atlantic to the Pacific. I am much worried about it, but Madras says it is useless to worry, and since I was born to the sea, I should not discount the fact I might die at sea. I was not cheered by that statement!*

We crossed the Line somewhere off the coast of Brazil, and since it was my first time over the Equator in a very long time, Madras let the crew engage in a few high jinks for my entertainment. It was Lewis's first time across the Line, too, and the crew dressed him up as Father Neptune. Oyster fashioned him a wig of flour sacking, and the ship's carpenter concocted a makeshift trident. Oyster wrapped Lewis in a sheet I contributed to the occasion. Hoku put a seashell garland around Lewis's neck. One of the Irishmen danced a jig while another played a merry tune on a pennywhistle. The Swedes stood back and watched solemnly. The Portuguese, a bit roughly in my opinion, drenched Lewis with buckets of seawater hauled up over the side. The boy suffered these indignities with good humor.

I was spared such shenanigans, for obvious reasons. But that evening, as I was putting on my nightgown, Madras sneaked up behind me and doused me with a dipper of water. I snatched the dipper from him and chased him about until he collapsed, laughing, upon the sofa in the saloon. I was upon him in mock fury, smacking his shoulders with the dipper, and soon we were making love with joy and abandon, giggling like naughty children.

"Our first time below the Line," he said.

"But not," I replied in a most saucy way, "the last." His reply was a wicked look in his eyes and the most delighted grin on his face.

July 1, 1872

We enjoy fair winds and calm seas, and make good progress daily. I have commenced lessons in navigation, and each noon Madras instructs me in "shooting the sun" with the sextant, and sets me calculating our course and to figuring how many miles we have progressed each day. I seem to have a knack for it. Many evenings I pore over Bowditch to learn more. Madras says if I had been born a man I would most certainly have made my way as a shipmaster.

Lancaster Treat is the only other, besides Madras, who knows anything about navigation. It struck me, when I learned this, that Madras and the mate have upon them a very heavy burden. Were they to be felled by illness or accident, heaven forbid, the remainder of the crew would be helpless to steer toward land, and the ship would likely founder on some unforeseen rock rising out of the middle of nowhere. It is a very sobering thought, one I had never considered before.

Mother can navigate, for Father taught her on their first voyage together when I was still a baby. But she never had to use her skill, and I pray that I never will either.

Father used to say, "There are no newspapers at sea." He missed learning of current events as they happened, even though he, like most sailors, has no great interest in government and politics. I do not miss knowing what is going on in the larger world either, for we on the Boreas *are a world unto ourselves with our own small happenings.*

The weather has been uncommonly good and we are making great headway. In a few days we will make Rio de Janeiro, where we will stop a few days to take on a cargo of coffee and to see the sights.

July 10, 1872

*Rio is behind us now. We arrived early in the evening when
bells from little churches on the islands in the harbor were ringing
vespers. We anchored in the roads several miles from the city, but
even so, an offshore breeze brought us the scent of exotic flowers. The
mountains around the city are steep and rise like the backs of great
prehistoric creatures over the purple hills. For the first time, I felt as
if I had come a very long way from home and that I was now truly
a citizen of the world. And yet, as we make our voyage over the
great blue deep, I think little of geography, or of the vastness of the
world, for the* Boreas *is my realm, a tiny wooden town moving
from port to port where we visit, but do not intend to stay.*

*Even as I reveled in the new sights, sounds, and smells,
thoughts of home, of terra firma, of Grand Fan and Mrs. Maude
and Dr. Sam, came flooding into my mind, almost as if at that very
moment, they were thinking of me and Madras. As indeed they
were, for we found letters waiting for us in Rio. Letters are more
precious than any treasure the sea or foreign shores might harbor.*

*Grand Fan writes that the summer has been very hot and that
her boardinghouse has been filled to capacity. She mentions Ellis
Harding only in passing, saying that he has been much occupied
with duties at home—which, I believe, is her way of saying that she
has not seen much of him and misses his company. She writes,
"This summer I have had several visitors from Boston and one from
Philadelphia. The steamboat stops at the Point twice a day now, and
each time, any number of people from the towns along the Penobscot
stop to eat dinner and spend the afternoon sitting on the piazza or
wandering the road or the beach. I offer tea and popovers on the
piazza in the afternoon, and some come just for that. Perhaps, M, I
am the author of a stylish new trend!"*

Mrs. Maude and Dr. Sam write that they are well and sail about the bay in my little boat Zephyr, *and that Mrs. Maude has shown something of an aptitude for sailing. "Don't let anyone tell you an old dog can't learn new tricks," she writes. And beneath that Dr. Sam wrote, "And she leaves no doubt who is captain and who is crew!"*

We had letters from all the Mitchells, too, including old Mrs. Mitchell. Her note was very formal, containing no direct news. She did say, however, that she was happy to have letters from us and that Aunt Honoria is spending much time tending her roses. In a tiny, bird-like scratch at the end of the letter, Aunt Honoria wrote, "Yes, roses, roses, roses. Red, yellow, white, pink. H.C." I call that nothing short of effusive, coming from her! I told Madras that in some port or other, before we return home many months from now, we must find rose roots to take to Aunt Honoria. And perhaps an umbrella tree.

Pacifica's letter was full of news of parties and outings and dances—and of Hugh Chapman, who squires her to all these frolics.

Gordon writes that he is spending the summer learning to keep accounts in his father's office, that he has been allowed to go as cabin boy on several voyages to Boston, much against his Grandmother Mitchell's wishes, and that he finds himself much interested in steamboats, rather than sailing vessels, which have made the family fortunes since the War of the Revolution a hundred years ago. His father urges him to apply himself to mathematics so that when the time comes, he can attend the university upriver at Orono and study engineering. But Gordon says he is not interested in attending the university.

Zulema Mitchell writes news of Searsport and all the little family things she knows will interest us, although she says she can't think why we would be at all interested in news of church socials, the births of babies, and the deaths of citizens we don't know, except that she remembers her days at sea and how eager she was for any news from home.

I must write them of our brief stay at Rio. We visited Mr. and Mrs. Payson, who are from Portland, but live at Boston, although

*they have been living at Rio for several months and will remain
several more months until Mr. Payson's business interests in shipping coffee are concluded. Mrs. Payson, a pleasant woman in her
mid-thirties, took me in hand and showed me about. In the market
square, I bought lovely pieces of handmade bobbin lace for collars
and cuffs. She taught me a new embroidery technique, which is
much like hooking rugs, except it is done with a very fine hook and
fine silk thread. She called it Brazilian embroidery.*

*Madras was very much taken up with unloading and loading
cargo while we were in port and had only one afternoon to see the
sights, when we rode out with Mr. and Mrs. Payson in their carriage.*

*Now we are on our way again, headed toward Cape Horn and
the ordeal of getting around it.*

*We acquired one new man for the crew, a common seaman by
the name of Zulu Perez, who does not mix well with the others.
Already Madras has had to reprimand him for doing his work in a
haphazard way. He seems to have taken a great dislike to Marcel
DuPere. Both Mr. Treat and Mr. Nichols have spoken to Madras
about it. DuPere, for his part, goes out of his way to avoid Perez,
but the tension between them spills out to the rest of the crew, setting a mood that was not here before Perez came aboard. But there
is nothing to be done, for we will not make another landfall where
there is any civilization until we reach Hawaii several months from
now, perhaps as late as October or November.*

*Thus I am settled into the routine of life aboard ship. Madras
continues my lessons in navigation, and I find that I make the calculations with increasing accuracy.*

*One morning, when the weather was exceptionally fine, I
decided to air out a few blankets and other things, including the kapa
cloth. I was concerned that leaving it rolled up for so long and subject
to damp might cause it to mildew. I thought a bit of airing would do
it good. I had not looked at it since I'd shown it to my mother in*

New Orleans. I spread it on the deck and left it there for an hour or so. Just as I began to roll it up, I saw Hoku, the Hawaiian, come down from the rigging of the mizzen mast. He saw the kapa cloth and froze where he was, staring at it as if he had seen a ghost. He dropped to one knee in a kind of obeisance and said something in a musical language I had never heard before. His tone was both reverent and outraged. He did not look at me or speak to me, but he seemed incapable of moving away to go about his business.

Madras came to me and told Hoku to carry on. Hoku went without protest, but I saw him exchange a look with Madras that confirmed my sense that they are not strangers to one another.

"Madras," I said much later, after we had eaten supper, "what was it about the kapa cloth that caused Hoku to behave so strangely? Do you know him?"

Madras hesitated before answering. "I once shipped with Hoku many years ago, when I was part of my uncle's crew. The kapa cloth reminded him of home, that's all—just as that sampler hanging on Mrs. Payson's wall in Rio reminded you of Maude and the one she stitched when she was a girl. Remember how you were suddenly homesick in a way that you had not been before? Even sailors like Hoku have hearts that can be wrung by memories of what they left behind."

"Yes, perhaps, you are right, Madras. But I think it was much more than that. It was almost as if he were paying reverence to it. I did not feel at all threatened by his behavior. Quite the contrary."

"M, you are imagining things. Best to put the incident out of your mind. Sailors like Hoku and his ilk have no allegiances, not to their ships, the countries they were born in, nor the families that spawned them. True, they have feelings, but they are very superstitious, and in my experience such superstitions run to women, cats, and the weather. Not pieces of kapa cloth. Or knitting or hooked rugs. Best to leave well enough alone."

But I could not leave well enough alone. I began to brood about it, and the more I brooded, the more I wanted to know, and the more I resented Madras for his attitude toward my concern. I also brooded about my idea that he knew Hoku and had not mentioned it to me before.

For a few days I felt the old melancholy upon me. I dosed myself with St. John's Wort and began to feel better. But I could not stop wondering why Hoku had behaved so. I began to plot what I thought were harmless ways to speak to him.

July 17, 1872

We have just had our first serious fight, Madras and I. It happened like this: I told Lewis Andrews, the steward, that he was to tell Hoku to come to the galley one morning when I was there making a pot of tea. Lewis, to his credit, did not want to do as I asked, but I insisted.

Hoku began cursing Lewis when my message was delivered. Lewis cursed back, and then Zulu Perez put his oar into the altercation and shoved Lewis. Hoku grabbed Zulu and fists began to fly. Madras and Lex Nichols quelled the fight immediately. The three men were reprimanded and given extra duties. When Madras got to the bottom of the story, as I knew he would, he was merciless.

"You are aboard my ship, M, and you, like all the others, are in my command," he said. "Don't you ever take it upon yourself to go behind my back and give an order to one of my crew. Do you understand? For if you do not, I will lock you in your quarters as if you were a common mutineer. Is that clear?"

"Yes, Madras, that is quite clear," I replied. "But I see no reason for you to be so unfeeling . . ."

"My feelings have nothing to do with it, M. You have disregarded an unwritten code of the sea—you, the daughter of a sea *captain, who surely knows her place when she is aboard ship. I trust that you will not forget that in the future." I nodded dumbly to signify that I would comply with his order. He went above again, leaving me weeping and very ashamed of myself. I knew better than to do such a thing, of course, but my curiosity was so keen and Madras had seemed so uninterested, almost as if he did not want me to know any more about the kapa cloth and what it represents to Hoku, or the fact that he doesn't want to talk about Hawaii. The incident has not dulled my curiosity, I am ashamed to say.*

Madras did not come below that night. And he has barely spoken to me these last few days. I am miserable, and feel that he has carried his punishment of me too far.

Hoku, Lewis, and Zulu are under orders not to speak to me or approach me for any reason. For days now I have not dared show my face on deck. I have stayed below, knitting socks for Madras and reading Louisa May Alcott's Little Women.

We continue to make our way down the coast of South America toward Cape Horn. The seas are rougher now and the air is colder. Madras is much occupied with bending on sails that will withstand the gales we will soon encounter and seeing that all is shipshape.

July 20, 1872

This morning Madras brought me a pot of tea and we made amends. He says that I may walk on the deck when the weather is not severe, but I must keep to myself. I must resume my lessons in navigation. I must behave as if nothing happened.

"When we are home again, M," he said, "you may disobey me and question my judgment as often as you like, and I will thank you for it. But while we are aboard the Boreas *you must think of yourself as completely under my command, as indeed you are. I can't have it said among my men that I run a henpecked ship. It undermines*

my authority, an authority I must have when the going gets rough, as it always does at sea."

I stepped into his arms then, not exactly contrite, but knowing he was right.

"Madras," I said, "I do love you. I was so miserable alone in the bed without you." He grew passionate then, but there was no time for us to take delight in one another. That will come later tonight. "I long for your touch," I whispered as he left me. He turned and grinned and blew me a kiss. Now he is on the quarterdeck giving hell to one of the crew for stowing a piece of gear improperly.

When I walked the deck this morning, Lewis, Hoku, and Zulu did not look my way even once. I kept my head down, my eyes obscured by the brim of my sunbonnet. I glanced at them once or twice, for I am curious and seek a way to undo the harm that I have done. Madras does not think I can mend what happened, but I am determined to try. I shall be perfectly aloof and imbue my demeanor with contrition so blatant it will be like the beam of a lighthouse off a craggy cliff.

I did not stay on deck for long. I went below and began unpacking the warmer clothes Madras will need for rounding the Horn, where we will encounter icebergs and fierce winds from the South Pole.

Today the air is much colder and the seas grow increasingly heavy. Yet, we make good headway.

I have heard many stories of rounding the Horn, some of them from Madras, many from Dr. Sam. Most passages, they say, are tempestuous, some less so. But all encounter the hardships of icy rigging, seas that run high and heavy, and headwinds to beat against, for the winds blow east and we will be attempting to go west. They say it takes every iota of sailing skill to make any headway at all. Sometimes it takes months, but I try not to think about that. I hope it will be only a few weeks, not months.

Today, a few pangs of loneliness strike me, and I long for Grand Fan's front room, a soft breeze filtering through the open window, Mrs. Maude and Dr. Sam playing checkers at the table in the corner. I miss Mother and Father, too. I would like a long talk with Mother about my bad conduct, and to ask her advice. I think she would say, "Madras is your captain, M. Behave in a way that will do him credit. Obey him, for to do otherwise is to risk the safety of your ship and all who sail upon her." If only I had thought of that before!

Madras says that we may be among the last generation to go to sea in sailing ships—that I must remember that, and concentrate on keeping my log of this experience for posterity. It is better for me to be occupied in such a way, he said, than giving in to impulse and interfering with the workings of the ship. But at the same time, he said, I must learn the workings of the ship, must learn to plot a course and must learn the ship's business. I must tend to my women's business, too. Only in that way, he says, will I regain some of the respect that I have lost.

August 1, 1872

The wind screeches in the rigging and the Boreas *groans and complains. Madras is pushing canvas, using as much sail as he can as we make our way around the Horn. Soon, that will change, he says, and instead we'll be reefing in sails and running just enough canvas to beat against the wind. I sense danger everywhere, and instead of feeling secure in the knowledge that we are in this together, I feel as if I have severed an invisible hawser and we are all careening about in separate ships, none connected to the other. And it is my fault for being so headstrong. I do not know how to make amends except to keep to myself. Madras, I am glad to say, does not bear any grudge.*

It is very cold now, but we cannot have a stove going, for the seas are too high and the danger a fire presents is too great. I am bundled in long woolen underwear, thick wool socks, and a wool shawl wrapped and tied around my waist. I cannot go above. Madras will not allow it. I stay below. Even writing my log is difficult—see how my writing slants and drifts—as the Boreas *climbs one huge wave and slides down its backside, then rolls and heaves, even waddles from side to side in a most gormy way before being lifted and hurled into the next wave. But she takes it all like the stout, reliable ship she is.*

I have become a prisoner in the main cabin, with little to do but hang on and ride the bucking and rocking. There will be days, not so far from now, when I will have no choice but to stay in a bunk where there is a sturdy rail to hold on to, lashed to it, perhaps, to prevent my being thrown against the bulkheads.

The cold seas spew over us such huge amounts of water it is a wonder the crew can do their work. Madras has had the lifelines rigged and the men make their way fore and aft by holding on to the ropes. The men go aloft, too, in these mean conditions, which will only get worse as the weather grows colder and icy rigging and snow-covered decks become inevitable.

What I wouldn't give for a hot cup of tea.

August 7, 1872

Writing is all but impossible. I am in the bunk now where I must stay, for the pitching of the ship is unending and most violent at times. I try to knit, try to read, try to sew. I try to think home thoughts of Grand Fan, Dr. Sam, Mrs. Maude, Mother, Father . . .

No. Not Grace.

The piazza on a sweet June day. Sliding along calmly in the Zephyr *with Dr. Sam. Digging in the dirt with Mrs. Maude. Grand Fan's cat, Tennyson, in my lap. A party at Pacifica's house, a long walk up the road, breathing the scent of pine and a newly mown meadow. Those sweet weeks when we ran before the trade winds with hardly a ripple under us.*

Every day I pray that we will soon be past this freezing, furious, water-bound Hades.

I see Madras only for moments, day or night. I never know when he will appear. Sometimes he comes below long enough to sleep an hour or two. Chilled to the bone. Wet to the skin in spite of his oilskins. I leave the bunk long enough to bring him dry clothes and make him put them on. Everything is wet or damp or will be. I try not to despair . . . yet I can't help but want soft hands and murmuring voices cosseting me. I want to go home. I want Grand Fan.

Madras and I do not talk much. The wind shrieks and howls, drowning out our voices. We have little to say, anyway. We are tossed and blown. He touches my face, kisses my hand, then he's gone up the hatchway into that wind-and-water-pounded netherworld where at any moment he may be washed overboard, where he may be thrown against a bulkhead or a mast. Where he will order men to the very top of the masts which pitch and sway in arcs of forty-five degrees, or more. Where the crew, including Lewis and sometimes Oyster Duncan, must reef or release ice-covered sails. Madras won't tell me how bad it is. But I can guess. This is the first time he has made so difficult a passage around the Horn. I see it in his eyes.

I know nothing of how the men fare. Oyster Duncan brings me food at the usual hours. Salted meat, crackers. Something that might be coffee, only cold. He doesn't speak; he only nods and keeps his distance. He drips salt water. I look for fear in his eyes. I look for friendship, connection, sympathy. I see nothing. Nothing.

I am ashamed of myself for being such a coward.

Sometime in August, 1872

I have no idea what day of the week it is. The parameters of time no longer have edges or demarcation. Time simply passes, minute by wretched minute. Madras says we are making headway. He gives no details. But I know the details. A few miles forward, as many back. It is nearly a month since we began the passage around the Horn. I feel myself growing mad, crazy with fear and loneliness, crazy for the sound of another woman's voice, crazy for something to do besides tie myself to the bunk and pray.

August 30, 1872

All that keeps me sane is the geranium hanging from the transom. It has no light, has been given no water, but it has put forth a tiny green leaf. It gets no care, yet it thrives. I stare at that tiny green leaf as if it were the first hint of Eden. For surely this terrible passage will be accomplished soon.

September 5, 1872

Today, for the first time in more than a month, the Boreas *pitched less horribly. I felt it distinctly when I woke from a fitful sleep this morning. The wind is howling less loudly, too.*

Madras just came below to tell me that we have rounded the Horn, that from now on conditions will gradually improve, and we will find the seas growing calmer. Soon we will be in the warmer regions of the Pacific. Several of the men, he said, have suffered injuries, none seriously. Hoku, he said, saved the life of Zulu Perez when a great wave crashed upon the deck and Zulu was fair to being washed overboard. Hoku had made fast to the lifelines and managed

149

to grab Zulu and hold on until the ship rose above the water on the next swell. This does not mean, however, that the animosity between the two has been resolved. Zulu, in fact, seems to resent Hoku all the more. As for Marcel DuPere, he seems to be successful in his attempts to steer clear of Zulu. But it remains a troublesome situation. With conditions so bad these last thirty or so days, the men have had no time or energy to hone their grudges. But as conditions improve, that may change. Madras said he will keep vigilant and see to it that the troublemakers have more than enough to do.

September 20, 1872

Now I understand why it's called the Pacific Ocean. We cruise along on smooth seas under sunny skies at a good pace. I walk, sew, and read on deck. I do the washing. It is such a blessing to be able to do the washing. And though I cannot speak to any of the men except the mates and Oyster Duncan, I am well enough informed of all that goes on.

Lancaster Treat loaned me his copy of The Odyssey, *much annotated in his own hand, and I am doing my best to improve my mind by reading it. Each evening we discuss the chapter I have read. I suspect that Mr. Treat, at some point in his life, was a schoolmaster.*

Lex Nichols, the second mate, has begun to entertain us with stories of growing up on a farm in Nova Scotia. "We had a dog named Buddy," he said, "that understood what we said. If we asked him to go get a hammer, he would go to the tool shed and get it. If we asked him to fetch a chisel, he would get that." He told many other stories, too, of how in spite of living on a farm at the top of a great hill for many generations, the men in his family had a yen to travel, mostly up and down the island.

Mr. Nichols was afflicted with wanderlust at an early age. He felt the call not only of the rest of the island, but of the world. So he went to sea. "What I miss most," he said wistfully, "is that dog knowing every word I ever said to it." He does not talk about those he left behind on the farm. It's as if he has no ties to anything he once knew, and wants none. Mr. Nichols is a tall, spare man in his late thirties, I should think. His eyes are very dark, his hair black. He possesses a boundless kind of energy and a good nature that draw everyone to him. If he stayed alongshore and went into business of some sort, I have no doubt that he would do well, for he takes a genuine interest in people and all that goes on around him. Which makes it all the more puzzling that he has so little to say about his people. I keep such observations to myself, of course. I am learning to hold my tongue.

Madras says Mr. Nichols is a hard worker and is the best-natured man he ever shipped with. "There's not a mean bone in his body," Madras said. "And for that reason alone he's unlikely to ever be master of his own ship. One must have in him a backbone of iron to be master of a ship."

"Ah, but Mr. Nichols is surely the master of his fate," I replied.

"As we all are, M," Madras said, smiling at my pun.

Lancaster Treat is of a more quiet personality. He is in his early forties, I'd guess. He is courteous at all times, especially to me, but has about him a watchful air, as if he never trusts anyone fully, a trait that no doubt serves him well as a seaman. He is of middling height with pale brown hair and blue eyes, and a mustache across his mouth. He goes about his duties, Madras says, with great attention to detail. The men think he has eyes in the back of his head, but Madras says that is only because Mr. Treat is very perceptive and has had long experience at his duties.

It is a relief to get back to a normal routine after the terrible days of rounding the Horn.

October 5, 1872

Yesterday Oyster Duncan burned his hand so severely that he cannot perform his duties. Lewis is doing the best he can, but Madras said that I must supervise and do what Lewis cannot, like making biscuits and plum duff. We haven't much left in the way of food to work with. The flour has weevils. The pigs and chickens that came with us at the start of the voyage were eaten long ago. Even the water in the casks is brackish. But I do what I can with salt meat and root vegetables packed in sand that have kept well enough. I also have tinned fruits and vegetables, so we are not threatened with starvation. Daily rations of lime juice also packed in tins keep away scurvy. But I am sure everyone aboard is yearning for the fresh fruits of the islands. What I want most is a chicken dinner with mashed potatoes awash in cream and new peas drowned in butter. And cake. With frosting.

We are in such a dither of activity. Each day the decks are holystoned. Madras has set the men to shining brass and making the Boreas shipshape. The mood among the men is buoyant. We are nearing the islands. Yesterday we saw many flying fish, and tonight the sea glowed green with a strange, beautiful phosphorescence. Madras and I stood by the taffrail and watched a great orange moon rise and turn to silver. The hard, terrifying days of rounding the Horn seem as if they happened to someone else in some other world.

We made love that night in a way we had not before. Our connection was fuller, more satisfying and more deeply felt. Madras held me more tenderly and lovingly than ever. I feel ageless and wise, yet childish and giddy. Madras is becoming both more staunch and more spontaneous. He, too, seems ageless and wise, boyish and mischievous.

Madras and I grow closer in our ways of being with one another. I sense this not only in terms of intimacy, but in our daily, mundane interchanges. I am always reminding Madras to put on clean stockings. Sometimes I hang them on my ears and say nothing. He is always reminding me in silly ways to water the geranium, which I might add, has burst forth in great glory with an abundance of leaves and a profusion of magenta blossoms. Once, he put a little sign on the pot that said, "Water, water everywhere and not a drop to drink."

I have put away my woolen clothes and have unpacked once again the light cotton dresses the Misses Merrithew made for me, and the ones Mother bought for me in New Orleans. Grand Fan was right about the lace veil. It makes a perfect shawl to wear in the evening when Madras and I promenade the deck. "My beautiful, beautiful bride," he whispers when he is certain none of the men are in hearing distance.

The men have begun to make eye contact with me again. They nod their heads whenever their duties take them past me. I nod in return, and some measure of respect seems to have been reestablished. I have learned my lesson and retain my dignity.

I tend Oyster Duncan's burn each day. I apply to it one of the ointments Mrs. Maude gave me. It is compounded of aloe and other plants. I find jobs Oyster can do with one hand, like setting the table for supper, or clearing the dishes away, or stirring the oatmeal in the morning. He does not complain of pain, but I make him drink a willow-bark infusion several times each day. I see him talking to the other men, and I know he is telling them about what I do for his injury and how I make certain he still has work to do. It is for this reason, I believe, that the men have begun to respect me again.

October 10, 1872

I woke early this morning to the sound of one of the crew shouting, "Land ho!" I flung myself out of bed, threw on my dress, and ran headlong to the deck. And there I beheld the most beautiful sight— the green shores of Hawaii glowing like a blue-green and white jewel.

The men paused in their duties, and even those who were not standing watch left their bunks to come and gaze upon the sight. Hoku stood motionless, staring at the island, his face unreadable. But something about the way he stood spoke of his intense desire to set foot upon his native land. I saw him glance quickly in my direction, then away, before he fell to scrubbing the deck.

Madras joined me at the rail. He was oddly quiet, as if some great emotion were at work in him. And suddenly I thought of those little things I had been told, of the trouble he was mixed up in as a youth when he had first come to Hawaii. He seemed both deeply moved and deeply removed, as if he had drifted far, far away from me for a moment. I touched his hand and it startled him. Then he was himself again.

"The island looks as if it's barely five miles away, my dear," Madras said, *"but that's because the air is so clear. It is nearer twenty miles away. It will be afternoon before we reach our anchorage."*

Part 3
Hawaii

1.

The *Boreas* lay just outside the reef off Honolulu. The ship was alive with the duties of coming into harbor. Madras barked quick, efficient orders. The crew fell to with a will and determination that gave M a little thrill of pleasure and pride in her husband's aptitude for command.

Lex Nichols winked and saluted when he passed her on his way aft, a grave breach of shipboard decorum, but M knew his behavior was a manifestation of the joy they all felt. It pleased her that he had given way to momentary frivolity. She liked the Nova Scotian and his easygoing manner. He was a good seaman and did his work well and willingly; he had been an asset on the voyage. Madras had relied on him for many things.

Most of the crew, M knew, would take their pay and make for the nearest grog shop where they would drink and gamble away in a few hours what had taken them months to earn. They would find other berths on other ships in a matter of days, and sail away to the far harbors of the world, never to be seen or heard from again.

Lancaster Treat, Lex Nichols, Oyster Duncan, and Lewis Andrews had agreed to stay with the *Boreas* and make the homeward trip in a few weeks' time. Madras thought Marcel DuPere also would bide his time until he could ship with them again. Those men would help with the business of unloading cargo, which would allow Madras some leisure time. Oyster and Lewis would live aboard the *Boreas* while it was in harbor, acting as guardians of the vessel.

What appeared in the morning as a group of gray peaks floating on the horizon had become a detailed landscape of overwhelming beauty. M discerned dark shady ravines streaking the lush green hillsides. Touches of red volcanic earth dotted the flanks of the mountains shouldering the magnificent sky.

"Diamond Head," Madras said to M, indicating a promontory of land that claimed her attention. "And there's Honolulu." Wooden dwellings with grass roofs and deep verandahs hugged the green skirts of the mountains where they hemmed the sea. Shade from palm and banana trees deepened the greensward, and bright white sand added a sharp note of contrast. Two church spires and a few gray roofs, familiar in their New England shapes, but alien architecture in the tropical landscape, rose beyond, above the trees. Surf pounded and thundered—the heartbeat of the islands, steady and predictable.

M drank it all in—the indescribable beauty, the strange exotic land, the unfamiliar sounds. Her nose was assailed with scents that struck her as mysterious and beckoning, a blend of vegetation, salt water, wet sand, and something spicy and flowery. It was heady and exciting. Memories of her homesickness and the misery she had endured rounding the Horn evaporated like mist. She felt embraced by the landscape.

Soon, the pilot came aboard to take them over the reef.

M did not know where to look first, how to take in all that she saw. Coral fishermen dove and surfaced, droplets of water glinting off their strong, naked backs. Outrigger canoes, paddled with speed and dexterity by handsome men with dark hair and beautiful smiles, rode the transparent waves with grace and expertise, as if in some other life they had been finned creatures. She spotted Hoku standing in the ship's bow, staring steadily ahead, coming home.

M watched Hoku make his way aft, saw him salute Madras, and say something. Madras returned the salute and gave a curt nod, his face curiously devoid of expression. Hoku ran the length of the *Boreas* and dove into the Pacific. He swam easily toward shore. M watched him, wondering what would become of him, still curious about why the kapa cloth had so drawn his attention.

Would her questions ever be answered? At that moment she did not think so, and resolved to think of other things.

When the *Boreas* passed through a narrow channel in the reef and came to rest inside it, M spotted several American warships and a British naval corvette at anchor, all within two hundred yards of shore, where a crowd of people of all races and nationalities filled the air with a gabble of talk and laughter. Several hundred of those people made their way to the deck of the *Boreas*. They bore baskets of fresh fruit and fish, and carried garlands of flowers. M had no difficulty knowing which were Hawaiians. They were a handsome people, with lustrous dark eyes, the women with long black hair, open smiles, and brightly colored clothing. A tide of people dressed in white, crimson, yellow, scarlet, blue, and pale green garments that flowed and moved like draperies in a light wind engulfed M. Gentle hands touched her dress, her hair, her hand. She felt her spirit lift and soar, as if the salt in her veins acquired during the voyage had turned suddenly to honey.

The Hawaiians wore garlands of flowers on their heads, around their necks and wrists, flowers that scented the air with a sweet, spicy fragrance. M leaned toward the delicious smell, realizing suddenly that all she had smelled for months was bilge water, salt air, and the fish Oyster Duncan had cooked so often while they were at sea.

White faces appeared in the crowd, too. The men, clad in white linen suits, or in white shirts and dark-colored pants, seemed self-important and intent on serious errands. The women, dressed simply and tastefully in soft colored muslin and, like the men, wearing white straw hats to shade their fair skin, looked as if they were waiting for something. All the women wore amused smiles, as if they were constantly surrounded by clever, but slightly naughty, children.

A small woman emerged from the press of people.

"You must be Mrs. Mitchell," she said, holding out her hands in greeting. She slipped a pink and yellow garland of flowers over M's head. "I'm Ellis Harding's daughter, Mrs. Abel Davis. But you must call me Nancy."

Nancy Davis was in her middle thirties and had her father's wavy hair, pulled back into a loose knot with little curls escaping around her neck and face. She did not look like a missionary's wife at all—at least, not like M had always imagined a missionary's wife would look. She was a handsome woman, and her calm blue eyes regarded M with polite curiosity, her smile open and friendly. She seemed undaunted by the crowd milling about the deck. She looked like the sort of woman who knew how to put down roots anywhere, and thrive. A perennial, M thought, and liked Nancy immediately.

"Yes, I'm Mrs. Mitchell. But you must call me M, or I shall be looking around constantly for my husband's mother or grand-mother," M said, laughing. "Tell me, Nancy, why are all those horses there?" She pointed to a large herd standing in the heavy heat. They were saddled and bridled in the Mexican and American West manner.

"They belong to Hawaiian women, who love riding. They love to race at full gallop along the roads. No one knows how they do it—how they manage to look so at ease in the saddle, how they ride with such grace and such command. It's something in the nature of the Hawaiian spirit, I believe. They are all young women, the riders, none of them married. And each one a beauty. Many are members of, or distantly related to, the Hawaiian royal family. Sometimes they are arrested for riding too fast and they are jailed until friends or family pay six dollars to bail them out. They cannot be talked out of acting so recklessly, though many of us have tried. It has something to do with their childlike nature, I believe."

M introduced Nancy to Madras. They talked for a few minutes, exchanging news, and decided that M should go ashore at once. Nancy would take her to the Hawaiian Hotel. Madras would stay behind and see to the ship, pay the crew, and do other business.

As they walked along, M saw piles of fruit for sale—oranges, strawberries, bananas, and coconuts, and others unfamiliar to her. It made her mouth water. All she wanted to do was bite into something sweet and juicy. Nancy, sensing her wish, bought a banana and handed it to M.

"Welcome to the islands," she said, grinning.

Fish in a myriad of colors and weighing at least ten pounds each were for sale, too. M marveled at the abundance of food, the abundance of life, the abundance of beauty at every turn. "I am stunned by it all," she said. "It's like waking up to find that I am living in a jewelry box."

"It can be quite overwhelming at first," Nancy said as they climbed into a hired buggy. She spoke to the driver in Hawaiian, and the words fell on M's receptive ear like the purl of a brook on a fine May day back home in Maine. "One can become besotted just by the colors of the island," Nancy said. "Add to that the scent of the flowers, the taste of the fruit, and the sibilance of the Pacific, and there, my dear, you have the perfect recipe for Paradise—and, I am sad to say, many of the elements of perdition."

M sat back and basked in the sights and sounds so welcome to her after the long months at sea, where every day was the same, and the most pressing topics were what she thought of as the Ws—wind, water, and weather.

The thud of horses' hooves sounded heavy and rapid behind them as several dozen Hawaiian women, all riding astride, galloped past. One young woman slowed her black horse and rode beside the carriage. She looked directly at M, her eyes full of curiosity and something akin to disdain. Her long hair flowed out behind her, and the drapery of her loose white garment fanned out over the horse's rump. She was heavily bedecked with red and orange flowers, even wearing circlets of bloom around each ankle. M smiled at her, but there was no answering smile. With a proud toss of her head, the woman nudged her heels into the horse's sides and raced away to catch up with the others. Soon, she was galloping way ahead of them.

"How very odd," M murmured. She had the distinct feeling that the woman knew her, or something of her, and that the encounter was deliberate.

"Take no notice of it," Nancy advised. "The Hawaiians are a very curious and most independent people. And right now, Americans are not in great favor.

"Perhaps I should tell you a bit about the islands. The native Hawaiian population is nearly fifty thousand souls, decreasing by one to two thousand each year—mostly by death from diseases such as measles and other ills brought here by the ships. Infants and children die young, too. It is a great evil in this place that is so Edenlike in its beauty. The foreign population is more than five thousand people, increasing by about two hundred each year, most of whom are Chinese and Americans. Americans have the most money and the most influence here. The biggest part of the economy is sugar production, and it is almost completely in American hands. There are thirty-five plantations on the islands, and room for fifty more.

"Labor is hard to come by on the plantations," Nancy continued, "and usually comes from San Francisco, which means the plantation owners must pay a heavy import duty to the United States. If the islands were annexed to the States, then the duty would be taken off and the planters would reap great benefits, in terms of profits. But such talk has the native people crying, 'Hawaii for the Hawaiians.' I am ashamed to say that in all the rhetoric, the natives and their interests are being quietly ignored. King Lunalilo does not seem long for this world, and Kalakaua, who will succeed him, is the last chief with a strong claim to the throne. There is an uneasy mood here of late. You would do well to remember that and form no opinions, pro or con, on the matter.

"But there, I'm boring you with politics. My advice to you, M, is to see the sights, enjoy yourself, and think no more of what I have just told you."

M did not comment, but she thought Nancy wanted her to know there was much that went on in the island not readily apparent to a newcomer such as herself. She did not think it was knowledge she would need, but she understood such information was part of the life of a missionary, who had to factor in many things in order to bring souls to God. She saw, too, that such facts pained Nancy and was part of what moved her to want to bring comfort to the Hawaiians.

The carriage rolled up to the verandah of the Hawaiian Hotel, a three-story stone edifice situated under a large tamarind tree. The upper and lower verandahs were festooned with clematis and passionflowers. It boasted an English slate roof and twin exterior stairways that curved upward to the second-level veranda. Nancy said that open-air concerts given by a twenty-four-piece brass band often were given at the hotel.

Soon, M was installed in an airy, spacious room filled with sunshine.

"This is a new hotel," Nancy remarked. "Before, visitors were obliged to board with local residents. I think you will find it comfortable. Now I must leave you, but I will come for you later in the week and take you to see the local sights."

As Nancy drove away, it occurred to M that she had arrived in a world completely opposite from the sheltered existence she had known on the coast of Maine. At home, she knew the roads, the boundaries, friend from foe. Here, she did not have the ballast of common knowledge. She sensed ribbons of darkness waiting to entangle the unwary visitor. But what that might be, she could not imagine—unless, of course, it had something to do with "sowing wild oats," as the Misses Merrithew had said. The thought unsettled her for a moment, but she put it firmly out of her mind. After months at sea, all she wanted to think about was soaking in a tub of hot water and socializing with women she would meet at the hotel.

2.

"I can't linger any longer, as much as I would like to, M," Madras said the next morning, pushing himself away from the table in the hotel dining room. "I have a great deal of business to conduct. But I will see you this evening." He looked happy and rested, dapper in a white jacket and pants. They had spent a delightful night wrapped in one another's arms, and M almost blushed at the thought of it. He caught the expression on her face, read her thoughts, and a look of love softened his eyes.

"How you tempt me, M." He took her hand, kissed it, and hurried away.

M poured herself another cup of tea and turned to the pile of unopened letters Madras had brought the previous evening.

Darling M,
How quickly the summer has passed. I hardly know where the time has gone. Abbott's Reach was filled to overflowing in July and most of August. In terms of business, I am becoming quite well padded. Maude sometimes teases me about becoming a "capitalist." I assure her that I am not, but it is a very good feeling to know that if I wanted, I could buy shares in the Boreas or the Fairmount.

Abbott's Reach

I have kept so busy that the only time I think about how much I miss you is when I fall into bed at the end of the day. I have not yet stopped listening for your step on the stairs, but gradually, I am adjusting. I console myself with the fact that you must have arrived in Hawaii by now, and that in a few weeks' time you will be on the return lap of your voyage and most likely will be home again come June.

We hear that all is well with the Mitchell family, though Mrs. Mitchell has called Maude to attend her several times. It's the headaches, I believe, which trouble her severely from time to time. Maude says little about it, as is her way when it comes to her patients. No amount of inquiry will draw forth any more detail than what I already have told you. But perhaps Zulema Mitchell will tell you more, should the situation warrant it.

Sam spent much of his time this summer taking small parties out in the Zephyr—for a fee. He also taught several ladies and gentlemen to sail on their own, also for a fee. He is fast becoming a man of business, and of means! I point that out to Maude whenever she teases me about my penchant for making money. He and Maude spent much of the summer here and plan to spend the winter, too. That way we can take care of and be company for one another.

The Misses Merrithew are as chirpy as ever. They write me postcards inquiring after you. At the moment, they are cooing about making dresses for several local brides, including Lucia Griffin. She met a young man from Portland who stayed at Abbott's Reach in June. He went to a local entertainment, met Miss Griffin, and fell in love. They are to be married next April. Miss Griffin's young man is in the shipping business, I believe.

I have received several lengthy shipboard letters from you and look forward to hearing all about the sights of Hawaii. I have but one request—bring me a large seashell to add to my collection.

My love to you and Madras from your devoted,
Grand Fan

Ardeana Hamlin

M read through the rest of the letters in the stack, lingering over the one from her parents, saving the one from Patsy and the one from the Misses Merrithew to read later. But she tore open the one from Maude and Sam.

> Dearest M,
>
> *We keep a map tacked to the wall of the kitchen, and whenever we hear from you, directly or indirectly, we put a tack in the map so we can follow you on your voyage. It is, I suppose, a way to pray over you—by knowing your approximate whereabouts, we can direct loving thoughts toward you and thereby delude ourselves that we may keep you safe from blasting winds, combative whales, and the furious tempests stirred by the hand of Poseidon.*
>
> *We read your letters with great delight. We especially like reading between the lines, so we know that marriage agrees with you and that you and Madras are happy. Sam and I have been married for more than forty years, and are testimony that when two people are compatible and know the parameters of give and take, the marital state is one not only to be desired but also envied. Sadly, who will or will not be happy cannot be predicted; if only it could, there would be greater happiness in the world.*
>
> *Your grandmother wrote of her business dealings and Sam's, so let me say a bit about mine. I sold many a bottle of my herbal tonic this summer, and many dozens of little pills I concocted to alleviate pain and to restore sleep. I set up "shop" in the summer kitchen, and there I brewed and infused and dried herbs and shredded willow bark to my heart's content. Many of the boarders who come to Abbott's Reach complain of nervous disorders or other ills. For more complicated complaints or for injuries suffered while staying at Abbott's Reach, they consult Sam. He tied up more than one broken wrist this summer. It works out quite well to have medical attention available here, as the boarders feel they are getting a special*

service without having to travel all the way to Poland Springs—or to spas in Europe—to improve their health.

There, I have prattled on far too long, when all I truly want to say is that I miss you, that I think of you every day with great fondness. Sam sends his dearest love and promises to write at a later time. He has been much involved with learning to build a sloop and goes daily to Stockton Springs to work on it.

Write to us soon, M, and always remember that we are your loving,

Dr. Sam and Mrs. Maude

M's Log, October 1872—Honolulu, Hawaii

I have spent much of the last few days answering letters from home. It is sweet to read their loving lines, to hear news of friends and family. How far away they seem, yet how very near. When I am not writing, I am chatting with other hotel guests. They are an international community, to be sure. Nancy Davis told me that the hotel is something of a clubhouse, and I find this to be true. In the evenings, I meet English and American naval officers, sugar plantation owners and their families, Californians here to improve their health, whaling ship captains from Massachusetts, tourists from the Pacific regions of Canada, and a steady stream of local people roaming the corridors and lounging about the verandahs. Madras and I wade into the thick of it, talking and laughing. Not once have I been melancholy. He says the climate, so warm and lovely, does me good. Not to mention the food. At mealtime, great piles of fruit—bananas, guavas, limes, and oranges—decorate the tables. The food is very American, abundant and hearty. A wonderful change from the monotonous fare aboard ship—despite Oyster Duncan's best efforts.

I have met a lady by the name of Isabella Bird who has a very inquiring turn of mind and is writing about her travels here. She says this hotel may be as close to perfect as hotels ever get, and I take her word for it, this being one of the few hotels I have stayed in since I was a child. Miss Bird has taken me on several excursions about town, and I find her to be pleasant company, although she tends to be a bit bossy and very opinionated.

Lovely sights greet my eye no matter where I look—bright red flowers, lush green vegetation, the play of light on the mountains. Even rainbows in the distant reaches of the Nuuanu Valley dazzle my eye.

The hotel dining room, large and airy, has no curtains and is decorated in very pale blue with sea-foam green accents, cool and soothing to the mind. The windows look out on tropical trees in one direction and up to the mountains in the other.

The hotel host is German, the manager is an American, the steward is Hawaiian, and the servants are Chinese, each one dressed in spotless white linen. No women work here. The Hawaiian government, Nancy told me, built the hotel for a sum of $120,000. The charges to those who stay here are fifteen dollars a week or three dollars a day. Each night I fall asleep to the sound of the surf and wake feeling as if I were in Eden.

I am more impressed with Nancy Davis each time I see her. She is a practical woman and goes about her work of saving Hawaiian souls with great tact and gentleness. She has no children of her own and is especially fond of teaching the children here to read the Bible—both in English and Hawaiian. Her husband, the Reverend Abel Davis, is by contrast a somewhat taciturn man, but kind. Madras and I have been entertained at their house several times and will join them later this week for an outing into the mountains.

3.

The last brilliant pink and orange rays of the setting sun faded
to indigo over the frothy surface of the Pacific. A breeze sighed
through the palms, and the scent of earth and spicy blossoms drifted
in the air. M and Madras walked slowly, her hand tucked into his
elbow, toward Nancy and Abel Davis's house, where they would
enjoy pleasant conversation and eat Nancy's baked beans and gingerbread. The house was one of the few New England–style struc-
tures in Honolulu. It was sparsely furnished in the Maine way, with
braided rugs, graceful pieces of dark furniture, and blue willow
crockery. It felt so much like home it was as if, when one stepped
through the door, one had entered a magic machine that transformed that bit of Hawaii into a tiny fragment of Maine.

M wore a yellow muslin dress with sheer sleeves that stopped
just below the elbow. Her hair was swept back from her face in a
simple braid coiled at the nape of her neck. Short tendrils escaped
around her face, and she had tucked a red hibiscus flower in the
top of her braid. Madras said the flower made her look like a
senorita from Rio. He looked handsome in a white linen suit,
black tie, and captain's cap.

"Madras," M said, stopping suddenly. "There she is again. That
Hawaiian woman, the one I saw on horseback. I see her everywhere I go. It's as if she is following me. Sometimes she has a boy
with her." She stared at the lithe young woman standing under a
tree some distance from them. Her bright blue dress fluttered in
the breeze. Her expression was guarded and watchful, as if she had
something to say but was too proud to say it, but not too proud to
stand in the road and observe the movements of the very people
with whom she wanted to speak.

Madras glanced quickly at the woman. She gave a curt nod to acknowledge the glance and then melted away into the deepening shadows. For a moment M thought she had imagined it.

"She never nods at me, Madras, but she nodded at you. Do you know her? If you know her, you must tell me!"

She saw her husband's mouth set into a firm, straight line, so unlike him. As a rule, she had noticed, he often turned conversation away from the subject of the Hawaiian people, but M had attached no significance to that. Madras was very busy with the task of unloading the *Boreas* and arranging for another cargo and crew, which absorbed all his energy. He did not have time to listen to the idle gossip of the island.

M, on the other hand, was fascinated by Hawaii and its people—their physical beauty, their history, and their language, which fell on the ear like a brook falling over smooth stones.

Madras sidestepped her question.

"Surely you are mistaken, M. Honolulu is a very small place. It's only natural that you would see the same faces now and again."

"Not now and again, Madras. Every time I go out. The Hawaiian people are said to be curious, but there is nothing about me to incite curiosity. She doesn't stare at me. Mostly I see her as she passes me on the road, but always she looks into my eyes as if she knew something I ought to know. Sometimes when I am sitting on the verandah, I see her across the road from the hotel, watching."

Madras made an impatient sound and M withdrew her hand from the crook of his arm. It was an impatient gesture—and a hateful thought rose in her mind—Madras knew more about the woman than he was saying. The idea of the dark ribbon below the surface of things in Honolulu recurred to her. Clearly, Madras was evading something, hiding something. The thought lay heavily in her mind, a thought she knew would haunt her, cause her endless speculation and worry. Yet, she didn't want to be a nag or a shrew. She wanted Madras to speak without her asking directly.

"Madras, if you have something to tell me . . . "

"M, don't let yourself be troubled. In a month we will be gone from here, and you will have forgotten the whole thing. Surely this woman is not the only person who looks at you as you pass. Or stares at you when you are sitting on the verandah. No doubt Nancy Davis sings your praises to all and sundry, and now everyone—Hawaiian, English, American, and Chinese—wants to meet you." Madras tucked her hand back into his elbow. "Hawaii has many mysteries. Let it be."

"Like the kapa cloth your grandmother gave me? Should I let that be, too?" An edge had come into M's voice. She heard it and was instantly contrite. She did not want to pick a fight with Madras. He was her husband; they loved one another. Wasn't it her duty as a wife to trust that he would in time tell her what she was beginning to think she already knew? Perhaps. But she could see that this was not the moment to dig in her heels or pick a fight. She did not want to arrive at the Davises' in a snit.

Madras, sensing her pique, would not be drawn out by it. "Yes. Let it be. That cloth has nothing to do with you except that Grandmother gave it to you. You should have left it at home in the bottom of a trunk where it belongs. If you had, we would not be growling at one another on this lovely evening in the paradise of the Pacific."

For a moment, because he sounded so sanctimonious, M wanted to retort sharply, turn on her heel, and march back to the hotel. But she bit her tongue and made herself be calm.

"Forgive me, Madras. No doubt you are right." But she knew, even as the words left her mouth, that she would not give up trying to find out more about the kapa cloth, or the identity of the woman who watched her.

Soon they arrived at the Davises', where Nancy and her husband greeted them. Abel Davis was tall and slim. His hair was
white-blond and he had about him the calm air of a Maine
farmer who knows his cows and potatoes. He had, in fact, grown
up on a farm in Corinth, Maine. He had met Nancy when they
had both attended a revival meeting in Bucksport just before the
Civil War. He was a graduate of Bangor Theological Seminary, and
she was looking for a way to do God's work in a foreign land.
They had married within the year and sailed for Hawaii just
before Fort Sumter fell, launching the War Between the States.

While Madras and Abel sat in the parlor, M and Nancy went
out to the verandah. They talked of home, quilt patterns, cooking,
and life in Hawaii.

"What do you know about kapa cloth?" M asked.

"Kapa cloth is made of pounded mulberry bark and marked
with beautiful designs distinctive to a particular family. Sometimes
one can tell what family the cloth is from just by looking at the
designs."

"I have a piece given to me by my husband's grandmother. It
was given to her in the 1840s, I believe. She rescued a Hawaiian
woman from the clutches of a drunken sailor."

"I am no expert on kapa cloth, but I will take you to Queen
Emma soon. You can show it to her. She will be able to tell you
more about it."

"The queen?" M asked, suddenly awestruck.

"Yes, she often receives visitors. I have been acquainted with
her for many years. You will find her gracious, almost shy, with
lovely manners. There is nothing pretentious about her, nothing
about her that in the least resembles our notions of European royalty. She is the widow of Kamehameha IV and has English blood.
She was brought up by Dr. Rooke, an English physician here. Her
house is very English and she is the gentlest of women. She does

not rule, of course. There is a new king now. It is not unusual for a piece of kapa cloth to be given to someone who has done a deed of kindness. Mrs. Mitchell must have been very brave."

"And very ferocious," M said, without elaborating. Nancy smiled and did not pursue the subject.

They talked of other things, including the latest news from Nancy's father, Ellis Harding.

"I had a letter from my father only yesterday. My mother is in a state of steady decline, I was sorry to hear. He wrote that I must prepare for the worst. She may have died by now," Nancy said sadly. "I hoped for a long time, when I first came here, that she might rally enough to visit me. Father talked of it. The climate is so salubrious—I thought that perhaps it might restore her somewhat. But she was never well enough to withstand such a long journey."

"I miss all of them at home," M said, feeling the hand of melancholia squeeze her heart. "Grand Fan and Mrs. Maude. Dr. Sam. All my friends—the Griffin girls, the Misses Merrithew."

"Homesickness is to be expected," Nancy said. "One day we all go home, either to the arms of the Lord or to those we left behind on other shores. I find great comfort in knowing loved ones await me on the other side of the world, or in heaven."

They sat quietly a moment, each one thinking thoughts of home.

"Nancy, something troubles me. Wherever I go I see the same Hawaiian woman. She . . . watches me. It's as if she knows me."

Nancy gave M a questioning look and thought a minute before she spoke. "Was one of your crew Hawaiian?"

"Yes. Hoku." M told Nancy of Hoku's reaction when he saw the kapa cloth the day she had brought it on deck to air it.

"That is your answer then. The kapa cloth—and the woman—may be connected in some way to Hoku's family. In their eyes you may be something of a heroine simply because the story of old Mrs. Mitchell has been handed down in their family. They know the cloth is in your possession now. They may be in awe of you. Or, more likely, she may be watching over you, M, instead of merely watching you out of some strange curiosity."

"No, I don't think so—and Madras won't listen to me when I want to talk to him about it."

Nancy drew a quiet breath before she replied, as if she were thinking about what M had said and was fitting pieces together that she, too, did not want M to understand.

"Don't trouble yourself, M. Your husband is right. And he's very occupied with business right now."

"That's what he said."

"Then give him the benefit of the doubt until he sees fit to inform you in greater detail. Be patient. Now, shall we join our husbands and make them talk of other things besides business, the sugar plantations, and the big question of whether or not Hawaii will allow itself to be annexed to the United States?"

At the end of the evening, M and Madras walked out into the tropical darkness toward the hotel. M caught herself looking for the Hawaiian woman, but saw no one. How silly I am, she thought, and pressed closer to Madras's side. She could not shake the feeling that somehow Madras and the Davises had withheld from her something they did not want her to know. But she was resolved to bide her time as Nancy had suggested.

"Nancy is going to take me to meet Queen Emma," she said. "You will be impressed. She is a lovely, kind woman."

"You met her? You never told me."

"It was right after the War of the Rebellion. I was eighteen, I think. We were invited, as so many Americans and English are, to a garden party, where we played croquet, and no one mentioned the fact that thousands and thousands of men had just died at Gettysburg. It was as if such horror didn't exist in the world, although, not so many years before, various Hawaiian chiefs were slaughtering one another on a regular basis, and before that, too, when violence was a way of life because of the kapu system."

"What was the kapu system?"

"There were certain things those in power did not allow on pain of death. A common person, for example, could not let his shadow fall on a chief. Women were not allowed to eat with men, or to eat certain foods, like bananas. Certain places were off limits—*kapu*—and to set foot there meant instant death."

"When did that change?"

"It changed after the first Kamehameha died in 1819— because of his favorite wife, Ka'ahumanu. She convinced Kamehameha's successor, Liholiho, to break the kapu of women eating with men. They did so and nothing terrible happened. Breaking the kapu left the old gods of the Hawaiians powerless. The idols they worshipped were burned and the sacred altars were destroyed. The Hawaiian people were left without a life of the spirit. Enter the missionaries in 1820."

"And the old ways vanished forever."

"So the missionaries would have us believe. But there are those who say the old gods, despite the new gods—the American dollar and the New England Christian religion—still have power, and there are those who still honor them."

"Like Hoku."

Madras looked sharply at M.

"Whatever are you talking about?"

"When he saw the kapa cloth, he paid homage to it—or something akin to homage. I told you, Madras, but you keep pooh-poohing me about it."

"And I will tell you again, M—you misinterpreted Hoku's gesture."

A hot streak of anger stirred in M's mind, and she wanted to stamp her foot in disagreement. But she made herself be calm. She could not prove the intent of Hoku's gesture. It was pointless to argue and spoil the evening. Soon, Nancy Davis would take her to meet Queen Emma, and she would learn more. And she would keep what she learned to herself. Madras was not the only one who could keep things to himself, she thought spitefully.

4.

For the next few days, although she looked, M did not see the mysterious Hawaiian woman. She began to feel relieved, as if that part of her mind, prone to dark thoughts and feelings, had played a trick on her. Her mood grew lighter.

When Nancy Davis called for her one afternoon for the promised visit to Queen Emma, M was full of energy and looking forward to the expedition. She was, however, a bit nervous about meeting the queen. She felt overawed, like a schoolgirl, a feeling she would have scorned in anyone else. Then she remembered her grandmother's dignity and Maude's treat-everyone-alike attitude, and that bolstered her courage.

M wore her pretty yellow dress, a color that went well with her fair skin and the red-gold lights that played in her red-brown hair. She wore her lace wedding veil as a shawl, which she really didn't need because the day was warm and fair. But the lace was fine and elegant, lovely enough, she felt certain, to wear to visit a queen. She also wore a broad-brimmed straw hat tied with ribbons to match her dress.

M took with her the kapa cloth wrapped in white cotton fabric and tied with a length of braid work she had fashioned from the same material. She held it in her arms the way one cradles a newborn infant. She told Madras of the impending visit, but she did not tell him that she would take the kapa cloth with her.

"We are going to what is known as the Summer Palace," Nancy said as M stepped up into the carriage that would take them to the queen's residence. "But it's really just a house, not so different from what you'd see in Searsport." She wore a long-sleeved gray silk dress with lace at the throat and cuffs. A small hat covered in matching gray silk and bedecked with a few wisps of blue feathers completed her outfit. Although the dress and hat were plain, they suited Nancy well.

"And what do I do when I meet her?" M asked, her nerves starting to overtake her. Americans didn't curtsey to royalty, but it did not seem fitting to shake hands with so grand a personage.

"Just be yourself."

"How do I address her?"

"You may call her 'Ma'am.' "

The queen's house was square with a low, slightly pitched roof. A row of columns supported the roof of the verandah, giving the house a Greek Revival look. Lush vegetation blooming in red, white, yellow, and purple made a lovely green setting for the white building.

Queen Emma opened the door and greeted them before they could ring the bell. Nancy gave M an "I told you so" look. The queen was known for her simplicity of style.

"Welcome. Come in," Queen Emma said. She was dressed in a fashionable black silk gown with little embellishment. It reminded M of a dress she had seen Madras's mother wear. The queen's wavy hair, caught back by beautifully carved and bejeweled combs, fell loose and long down her back. She was tall, like most Hawaiian nobility. Her figure was Junoesque, neither too thin nor too heavy, merely well-fleshed. Her face was oval, her nose straight and beautiful. She had a finely modeled brow and chiseled lips.

Her large eyes were dark and lustrous, alight with an expression of kindness and a hint of what M felt certain was sadness.

Surely, M thought, the queen suffered from bouts of melancholia. After all, she had lost her child, the prince, when he was only four. Nancy had told M that after the child's death, the queen had sat beside his grave without moving for four days. A year later, the queen's husband, King Kamehameha IV, had died—so much tragedy for a woman only thirty-six years old.

M noted the queen's innate dignity and grace of movement—the way she held her head, the lift of her hand, the set of her back and shoulders. She was regal, but in an unconscious way, like a lioness.

The queen led them into a drawing room furnished with heavy furniture, covered with plump cushions worked in needlepoint. The walls were hung with portraits of her late husband and of her son. M glanced around quickly and felt as if she had left the exotic, brightly colored culture of the island and entered the sepia- and gold-toned civility of a London house, just as Nancy had described. Nancy handed the queen a jar of strawberry preserves and a tin of gingersnaps. The queen smiled graciously with evident pleasure.

"Thank you so much. You know how I love jam with lemon scones at teatime," she said, kissing Nancy on the cheek.

The queen indicated that they were to sit on overstuffed chairs upholstered in dark leather. M laid the bundle containing the kapa cloth on the floor beside the chair.

"I understand you are a bride and come to Hawaii on your wedding journey, Mrs. Mitchell," Queen Emma said as she poured tea into delicate Sevres china cups, a gift from the nation of France. She spoke in a lilting, supple way.

"Yes, ma'am. I was married on May Day aboard our ship, *Boreas*. My husband, Madras Mitchell, took on bales of cotton in

New Orleans, which he sold in Rio. There we got a cargo of coffee, which he sold here. Now he is loading sugar for California."

"You have traveled much?"

"When I was a child I sailed with my parents on the
Fairmount, and I went to England and Italy and North Africa. We
also sailed to cities up and down the East Coast of the United
States. This is my first trip to the Pacific."

"One day you must steer your course for London and Venice.
Especially Venice. When I was in Venice I was constantly drawing
my breath with pleasure and excitement each time I rounded a corner and beheld the beauty of a cathedral across a cobbled square, or
gazed upon the frescoes depicting the saints and our Savior. Words
cannot describe the rapture of the idle hours the king and I spent
with our small son in a gondola upon the canals." Queen Emma
glanced at the portraits on the wall and a little catch came into her
voice. "London, too, holds great charm for me, for my aunt and
uncle Rooke, who raised me, are English. I have not, I am sorry to
say, ever been to Maine in America. You must tell me about it, Mrs.
Mitchell, though Mrs. Davis has already told me very much."

"I am sure she has told you, ma'am, that Bangor, on the
Penobscot River, smells of pine and evergreen from the sawmills
that run day and night, making boards and shingles that are sent all
over the world, even here to Hawaii. Ships from all over the world
come to Bangor, too. My grandmother lives on Penobscot Bay,
twenty or so miles downriver from Bangor. She keeps a boardinghouse where people from cities like Boston and New York come
to spend the summer. Her house is on high ground and many
windows look up and down the river. We often see eagles, seals,
and harbor porpoises. In winter the snow is very deep, and the
beautiful blue-green hills turn white for many months, but we get
about in sleighs drawn by horses and on snowshoes. We burn
wood in stoves and fireplaces to keep warm. I have a small boat,

the *Zephyr*, and I sail it on the bay with my dear friends, Dr. Sam Webber and his wife, Mrs. Maude Webber."

And so the conversation went for nearly twenty minutes. The three women chatted about places in the world they knew and loved. They talked also of music and horses, two of the queen's favorite subjects.

"But you must tell me what is your impression of my home-land of O'ahu," Queen Emma said. "Mrs. Davis has fallen in love with this land and its people. She has aided me greatly at Queen's Hospital." The queen had established the hospital as a charitable institution for the benefit of her people. Each ship that came into port was assessed a fee of two dollars to benefit the hospital.

"I love the way O'ahu smells—spicy, earthy, and of the ocean. The colors of the flowers, the mountainsides, the plants and trees—it all enchants me, ma'am. The kindness of your people impresses me very much. It is truly paradise."

"Well said, Mrs. Mitchell." The queen smiled at M and delight played across her face.

"Ma'am, we have taken up far too much of your time," Nancy said, "but I wonder if we might ask you to indulge us a moment longer. Mrs. Mitchell has brought with her a piece of kapa cloth that belonged to her husband's grandmother, Mrs. Augusta Mitchell, who gave it to this Mrs. Mitchell. Old Mrs. Mitchell was given the cloth many years ago for interceding when a young Hawaiian girl was set upon by seamen, intent on mischief. Perhaps you would look at the cloth and tell us something of its history."

"How very curious," Queen Emma commented, nodding to indicate that she would look at the cloth. M reached for the bundle, undid it, and rolled the kapa cloth out on the floor.

Queen Emma sat very still, a look of shock and amazement on her face. She placed her hands on her cheeks, drew a sharp breath, and opened her mouth to speak, but no words came. After a moment, she regained her composure, lifted her head, and took a deep breath. She was visibly moved, but with dismay, delight, or something much more devastating, neither M nor Nancy could say.

M was horrified by the queen's reaction, and she could see that Nancy was distressed, too. What terrible thing had she unleashed by showing the kapa cloth to the queen? Was this some hateful trick old Mrs. Mitchell had played—something that would make trouble for her and Madras? Her thoughts veered crazily. Madras was right, after all. She should have left well enough alone. She wanted to speak, to apologize, but her lips would form no words.

"Ma'am, what is it? We had no idea . . . we only want to understand . . ." Nancy stammered. "We mean no disrespect."

The queen stared at the kapa cloth and lifted her hand in a gesture to indicate that she had taken no offense. Tears welled in her eyes and she slid from the chair to her knees.

"Ka'ahumanu," she whispered.

M's Log—October 20, 1872

In those moments when Queen Emma fell to her knees and reached for the kapa cloth that lay on the floor at her feet, I wished for a tidal wave to engulf me, to wash me off the face of the earth. I was appalled at what my simple desire to know more about the kapa cloth had unleashed.

Nancy Davis has a far more level head than I, and is not at all beset by the sharp welling up of intense emotion that so frequently overtakes me. She went to Queen Emma, spoke quietly to her, took her hand, helped her back to her chair, and stayed by her side until the queen had quite recovered her composure.

Tears streamed down my cheeks, but I could not speak, so great was my distress. I braced myself for a harsh dismissal, for banishment from the islands, for some terrible wrath to descend on me. For surely, I had committed a dreadful, though unintended, offense.

"Tell Queen Emma everything you know about the kapa cloth," Nancy said quietly and kindly. "Leave nothing out." I told the story again, adding a few details I had not remembered to tell before. I told about Hoku and how he had reacted when he first saw the kapa cloth.

Queen Emma, composed now, spoke only in Hawaiian directly to Nancy, but when she looked at me, I saw tenderness in her expression, like I have seen in the eyes of my mother, Grand Fan, and Mrs. Maude.

"She says you are beloved of the old gods of Hawaii and a true daughter of the islands," Nancy said, translating. "I will explain later. But now we must take our departure and let the queen rest. You must leave the kapa cloth here with her, for it is a rare object and, therefore, sacred to the queen and her family."

I rose from the floor where I had been kneeling, my legs unsteady. Queen Emma came to me and kissed me on both cheeks. She took my hands in hers and held them for a long minute. "Daughter," she said.

I don't know how to tell Madras about all this. But tell him I must, just as I must write his grandmother when I have learned what more Nancy has to tell me. I feel certain there is more to this story, pieces that link the cloth to Hoku and to the mysterious Hawaiian woman who watches me. Somehow, I feel certain, they are links to the woman Old Mrs. Mitchell aided all those years ago. Madras, too, is a link in this chain. He will not want to talk about it. He has never wanted to talk about his first time in Hawaii.

Nancy has not given me the details of what Queen Emma told her about the kapa cloth. She said she must speak with her husband first and get his counsel. She took me directly back to the hotel and said she needed to spend time in prayer, and that I was to call on her tomorrow; then she would have more to say about the kapa cloth and its origins.

I write this as I sit on the verandah, shaded from the sun, a breeze sighing in the leaves, the sound of birds scribbling melodic notes into the air, guests promenading up the drive. Madras will be here soon and I long for his arms around me, long to tell him of all that this day has brought me. But I cannot speak. I must keep from him the contents of my heart, close another small door against him, as I did when I did not tell him that I was taking the kapa cloth to show Queen Emma. I do not like closing doors against the man I love, lest they become locked for good, creating barriers, no matter how small, between us. A husband and wife must always be free to walk into one another's heart and soul. But I forgot that in my hasty pursuit of satisfying my curiosity.

It is late in the afternoon. I have re-pinned my hair, put on a fresh dress, and composed myself. Madras and I have no social engagements this evening. We will talk of the events of his day, read the letters that have come for us, and go for a walk, as is our habit since arriving here.

Tomorrow, after I have talked with Nancy, I will tell Madras everything. But for now, I must keep my thoughts to myself.

I am thinking of what the wise women in my family—Mother, Grand Fan, Mrs. Maude—would say to me if they knew of my dilemma. I believe they would say that it's all right to withhold what has transpired until I have learned more, but I must not let another day go by without confiding all to Madras.

5.

M slept poorly that night, but Madras fell asleep quickly and deeply, never noticing that anything was amiss. He was preoccupied with the final details of selling the cargo of coffee brought from

Rio, and with the additional business of provisioning the *Boreas* for
the next leg of the trip, going over the contracts for the cargo of
sugar that was in the final stages of arranging before being loaded.
There was also the matter of finding crew members, too.

Oyster Duncan and Lewis Andrews had proved useful in any
number of ways, Madras said. During the weeks in harbor, they
lived aboard the *Boreas*, served as guards, made lists of foodstuffs to
be purchased, holystoned the deck, and attended to matters of rigging and other tasks that needed to be done to get the ship ready
for departure.

The mates, Lancaster Treat and Lex Nichols, reported to
Madras each day. He had given them the tasks of inspecting sails,
ropes, and pulleys, assessing the bilge, arranging to have cracks in
the hull sealed, and repairing or replacing worn gear. In their
many off-hours, they toured the islands, visited Americans of their
acquaintance, and occasionally stopped at the Hawaiian Hotel to
eat supper with Madras and M.

M only half-heard what Madras said of the ship's business. Her
head ached, her heart was sore, and all she wanted was to talk to
Nancy. She was glad when Madras drifted into a deep sleep.

M woke to find Madras gone and a note on his pillow:

*Don't look for me before nightfall, M. I have decided to take a
trip to a sugar plantation some miles inland to make final arrange-
ments. I trust you will find an agreeable way to spend the day.*
My love and ten thousand kisses,
Madras

M rubbed the sleep from her eyes and dressed quickly. It was
already past ten o'clock. She ate a sparse breakfast of fruit and tea,
went back to her room to fetch a parasol, and set off for Nancy's
house. They had set no time to meet, but M could not wait for

social niceties to set the day in motion. Not far up the road, standing in the shadows beneath a tamarind tree, she spotted the Hawaiian woman who watched her.

M judged the woman to be around twenty-five or thirty years old. She was small in stature, with abundant black hair falling loose to her hips. She was clothed in a piece of brightly colored fabric that left her shoulders bare but covered her body to just below the knee. She wore a wreath of red flowers on her head and several garlands of red and yellow flowers around her neck, wrists, and ankles. Her feet were bare. Her face was exquisitely beautiful, and there was about her an air of serenity and solidity that made her seem statuesque despite her size, as if she had grown from the roots in the earth beneath the tree.

M stopped. Instead of pretending she did not see the woman as she had done in the past, M looked directly at her. The woman met M's eyes and a long moment passed between them. M took a step toward the woman. The woman turned suddenly and followed a path into the vegetation behind her. M had the distinct impression that the woman wanted her to follow, but M was unwilling to be led away from the road. She watched the woman disappear up the path. Though she felt unsure of what the encounter meant, she did not feel threatened. A part of her wanted to follow the woman, to speak to her, to ask, "Who are you? Do you know my husband? What do you want of me?"

M composed herself and continued on her way to Nancy's.

Nancy made a pot of tea and they sat down at the kitchen table. Nancy was the very picture of the sensible, practical Mainer. Yet M sensed that beneath Nancy's composure there lurked a certain level of trepidation, as if M had lifted the lid of Pandora's box, allowing something chaotic and potentially threatening to escape. Inwardly, she chided herself for such thoughts, blaming her fear on her guilt at not speaking to Madras about the situation, and her anger at Augusta Mitchell for starting the whole sorry business about the kapa cloth.

"Madras told me about Ka'ahumanu before we went to visit Queen Emma," M said, "how Ka'ahumanu broke the kapu, so I understand why the kapa cloth is sacred. But I fear that I offended the queen—that somehow I breached a boundary that I did not know existed . . ."

Nancy looked sharply at M. "Offended her? Quite the contrary. You've restored to her a piece of her heritage. Apparently, the woman your husband's grandmother rescued was blood kin to Ka'ahumanu. Ka'ahumanu is a cousin of some sort to Queen Emma. Ka'ahumanu is revered as the Mother of Hawaii. She is the bridge between the old ways and the new. Because of her, the days of idol worship, constant warfare, and indiscriminate killing were transformed into these peaceful, modern days of Christianity and commerce, of civilization and serenity. Indeed, it is believed that Ka'ahumanu was the first Hawaiian to convert to Christianity."

"Is that the end of it then, Nancy?" M asked, relieved. "Is it as simple as that?"

"Nothing in Hawaii is simple, M. Once it is learned that the kapa cloth is in the queen's possession—and you may be sure word will get out, perhaps it already has—the faction that wants to return to the old gods, to preserve Hawaii as a sovereign nation, and to eject Americans and Europeans, will use it as a rallying point. And the faction that wants Hawaii annexed to the United States—the planters and those of us who have brought the word of God to the islands—will say that it is proof positive that Hawaiians are still too primitive in their beliefs to be allowed to govern themselves. Every man of religion in the islands, including my husband, will preach against the kapa cloth. It will be called an instrument of the devil, a tool of the pagan past. It will feed into the political turmoil that seethes beneath what appears on the surface to be Paradise."

"But is the danger of political upset so great, of the Hawaiians returning to the old ways?" Even as she asked the question, M realized how silly she sounded. It was barely fifty years since the kapu system had been broken. It still existed somewhere, if not in actual practice, then in the spiritual fiber of a people, especially among those who could remember those times, who had lived by it, for good or ill, for thousands of years. And as for the politics of the islands, Americans saw fortunes to be made by raising sugar and cutting the sandalwood forests, and in the sale of goods and stores needed by every one of the hundreds of ships that came into harbor. Those Americans were, indeed, already making fortunes.

The islands, which had once belonged exclusively to the Hawaiian people, had been broken up into plots of land and sold to the highest bidder. Land speculation already had made fortunes for many. It was part of the inevitable process of dispossession that had been taking place since Captain Cook's arrival in the islands in the 1700s, the same process that was going on against Indian tribes in the United States. And while M understood all that only vaguely, she found it troubling, and did not like to think that she had done something to stir that seething pot.

"M, I must abide by what I believe—and what my husband believes," Nancy said. "We, and so many others like us, are here to do the work of God, not to reinstate the idols of the godless past. What you must understand is that no matter where we are, the old, godless ways are always with us, especially here. Nothing lasting can be accomplished in one or two generations. That is why God sent Abel and me here—to cultivate the vineyard of faith, to root it deeply, so deeply that things such as idolatry can never again find life in this place."

M's thoughts whirled with new questions. "But how would Hoku, who sailed with us, know that the kapa cloth was sacred?"

"Perhaps he, too, is from Ka'ahumanu's line, or allied in some way to the woman who gave the kapa cloth to your husband's grandmother. It seems to me that the fact he recognized the symbols on the cloth is proof that the old, idolatrous ways are still taught to the young here. This is what we must prevent."

"What will Queen Emma do with the kapa cloth? She is, I understand, a devout Christian."

"I don't know what she will do with it, M. She will be advised."

"By whom?"

But Nancy did not answer that question. She poured more tea and firmly changed the subject. "These things are best left to the men, M," she said. "It's not a woman's place."

She added with a small smile, "There is much you do not understand about Hawaii. Let us talk of other things and not be troubled by it."

A sharp retort rose to M's lips, but she squelched it. Still, the question lingered in her mind: The kapa cloth had been made by women, was given to one woman by another as a token of gratitude, was later given as a gift from an old woman to a young woman, and was now in the hands of yet another woman. Why, then, was it not a woman's place to have a say in the politics of the situation?

"But I am troubled by it, Nancy. I feel as if I am being treated like a child, even conspired against to make certain that I am not told anything that might put to rest the questions I have—not only about the kapa cloth, but about the woman who watches me . . . My grandmother and Mrs. Maude taught me to ask questions and to confront what it is I fear. I am not accustomed to being left in the dark about the things I want to know about."

"Then you must spend time in prayer, M, until you can discern your path in this matter. I have told you as much as I can, and I feel certain that Madras, as your husband, knows what is best for you."

At that, M clamped her mouth shut, knowing full well she had run into a wall of silence that Nancy imposed . . . as well as one of her own, since she had yet to tell Madras what had transpired. Very well, she thought, there is more than one way to get to Bangor. She would leave the subject for now, as Nancy insisted.

That evening, Madras returned to the hotel earlier than M had expected. To her dismay, Lancaster Treat and Lex Nichols accompanied him. The opportunity to discuss frankly with Madras all that troubled her would have to be set aside yet again.

"A bit of diversion for the supper hour," Madras said cheerily as they came onto the verandah.

In the dining room, the tables were filled with all manner of Americans, English, and Europeans. Conversation in several languages, including French and German, welled up in the room. M thought she sensed a certain expectant edge in the air and on the faces of some of the men. The ladies seemed to be as airy, cool, and feather-light as always, their manners perfect, their demeanor gentle and compliant. M felt defiance course through her, but at what, she could not say. She calmed herself and spoke in a civil manner.

"Have you made progress today toward provisioning?" she asked, knowing that it was in her best interest to steer the conversation toward a subject the three men preferred to talk about.

"That we have," Madras said, "and two or three weeks from now we will weigh anchor. I had an excellent trip to the sugar plantation, and the rest of the cargo is arranged. I've found a couple of men who should prove reliable hands."

"And just in time, too, I should think," Lancaster Treat said as he reached for the sauceboat. He looked dapper in his mariner's jacket, the silver buttons shining in the lamplight.

Lex Nichols glanced up from his plate, his dark eyes and handsome face alert and curious. He was known as a talker, and possessed the ability to spur his listeners to divulge a great deal of information they otherwise would not tell someone they hardly knew.

"Yes," Lex said, "there's bound to be some nasty politicking and unrest among the natives, considering."

"What do you mean?" Madras said.

"It's about Queen Emma and Ka'ahumanu," Lex said, glancing at M. She felt alarm grow in her middle.

"Not more ancient history," Madras said dryly.

"In a way, I suppose it is," Lancaster said.

"A piece of kapa cloth that belongs to Ka'ahumanu's family has been given to the queen," Lex said. "They say the Hawaiians are already starting to get ugly toward the Americans and the British. They say the old pagan priests, the kahunas, are coming out of hiding—that the appearance of the cloth is a sign, as if the shroud of Christ himself had been found and delivered to the Pope."

"I see," Madras said tersely, with a tight smile. "Just a squall, no doubt."

M kept her eyes on her plate, but could not refrain from asking, "And did you learn where this kapa cloth came from?"

"Well, yes and no. From an American, but no one knows who. Couldn't have been from any of the missionaries or their people, and it sure wouldn't have come from the planters, no matter what their nationality," Lancaster said. "They have fortunes at stake."

"Any guesses?" Madras asked, glancing at M, the expression in his eyes making it clear that he knew precisely who had delivered the kapa cloth to Queen Emma.

Both men shook their heads no, and resumed eating.

"Well, thank God for that," Madras said, looking directly at M, his face unreadable now.

M wanted the very floor to swallow her up and spit her back out at Abbott's Reach. She felt a dark blot of emotion filling the edges of her vision. She wondered wildly if she had remembered to dose herself with St. John's Wort that day, and thought surely she had not.

After supper, they went outside to sit on the upper verandah where many other hotel guests also had gathered. The sound of a guitar drifted into the night. All along the shadowy verandah the fiery ends of the cigars the men smoked winked and blinked like fireflies on a hot July night at Abbott's Reach.

M was grateful for the dark, grateful that the men spoke in low tones of the business of the coming day, and left her to say little or nothing. She felt an awful dread building within her, and she longed for home. Why am I such a coward about this, she thought, chiding herself, always wanting to run home the minute I find myself in difficult circumstances?

6.

"What have you done, M?" Madras asked quietly when at last the evening was over and they were in their room. He leaned against the door, as if to prevent her from fleeing. A wave of claustrophobia engulfed her, but she gained control and faced him. She told him the story of taking the kapa cloth to Queen Emma.

"Damn and blast!" Madras said. "Didn't I tell you to leave well enough alone? Can't you do as I say when I tell you not to meddle in things you know nothing about?"

Fury rose in M's body, refusing to be contained. "You are my husband, Madras! Not my captain!"

She saw a hard look come into his eyes, a look she had seen before when he was toe-to-toe with an insubordinate sailor. The steel in his eyes passed quickly, but she had seen it, and it had stunned her to think he could so far forget himself and the love they shared to train so mean a gaze upon her, if only for that instant.

Madras opened his mouth to speak, thought better of it, and sat down, leaving M to pace up and down, giving action to the anxiety she felt.

"M," Madras said more calmly, "do you have any idea that what you have done can undermine the stability of the government here?" His words shocked her.

"Madras, what do you mean? I did not act rashly. I consulted Nancy Davis."

"One of the very people who could use a good reason to point out to the powers that be that the Hawaiian people aren't chosen by God to manage their own political affairs."

M could not argue with that, for Nancy had referred more than once to the "childlike" nature of the Hawaiians.

"But I meant no harm, Madras. I was merely curious . . . about the kapa cloth and . . . other things."

"Even the smallest storms can become hurricanes . . . and if you don't know how to take in sail, you might go down. This is especially true when you don't have all the . . . answers . . ."

"Is there nothing to be done, Madras?" M interjected impatiently.

"Probably not. Things like this tend to take on a life of their own." He drew a breath and gazed at her, as if judging what else he ought, or ought not, to say. "Well, we'll be away from here in three weeks, two if I push hard enough. That should give me time to get you out of here before some zealous reporter finds out you're the one who handed over that accursed kapa cloth and smears the Mitchell name all over the newspapers between here and Maine. Yes, Maine, M. News travels, you know. And if your name comes to the surface, so will other names, including your grandmother and her colorful past."

M felt herself grow white with anger.

"How dare you speak of Grand Fan like that?"

"You should have thought of that before you went behind my back and brought the cloth to the queen," Madras said coldly, that hard look flitting around his eyes again. He fought to get control of himself, succeeding to a small degree.

M faced him, made herself speak calmly.

"You are quite right, Madras. I should not have kept a secret from you. But isn't that like the pot calling the kettle black? What about your secret?" M, of course, alluded to the Hawaiian woman who watched her. She stopped speaking abruptly, unwilling to say more, not knowing what else to say.

A wary, defensive look crept into Madras's face, and M saw that she had touched a nerve.

"You go too far, M," he warned.

"And you don't?"

"Then let me apologize for being crass."

"Have you nothing more to say, then?"

"For the moment, no."

M felt the fight drain out of her. She was weary, confused, hurt, and still angry. But more than that was the feeling that love, if she were not vigilant, could flee, could be conquered, routed, in that tidal wave of emotion that had grabbed her so fiercely.

She did not know how to bridge the terrible space that separated her from Madras, her husband, her love. But she knew what her grandmother and Maude and Sam would do. They would hold out their arms and she would run to them for comfort, forgiveness, and safety.

She did not want what she and Madras felt for one another to become soured by what she had done, what she suspected he had done. She heeded her heart.

She opened her arms to Madras, and he opened his to her. "There is only you, M. Now and forevermore, there is only you, and always will be," he whispered hoarsely, pulling her to him with tenderness and passion. She molded her body to his, and understood more deeply what it meant for husband and wife to cleave together. That they were of one flesh, she had no doubt. Learning to be of one mind was something else again. That would take a lifetime to learn.

For the next several days, M stayed close to the hotel, reading newspapers, fearing she'd find her name in a headline. To calm herself, she engaged in social conversation with the ladies who sat on the verandah in the late afternoon. Sometimes, she sat in her room doing embroidery, stitching a new shirt for Madras or darning his socks. But nothing about the kapa cloth appeared in the press, much to her relief.

She and Madras had made up, but she sensed a slight change in the way they related to one another, a tenseness that hadn't been there before, a hesitant quality that served to remind them of their differences instead of their common ground.

M did a lot of thinking during those few days, and she knew she would never feel at ease until she knew what there was to know about the Hawaiian woman who watched her.

"Madras," she said one evening, several days later, "who is the woman who watches me? Please, let us have no more secrets between us."

Madras regarded her with a level look, gauging her capacity to understand what he knew he no longer could avoid saying. He weighed the risk in his mind as he might weigh the color of the horizon when assessing the weather. She had been moody and unhappy the last few days. Not exactly melancholy, but on the verge of it. He did not want her to become ill. He did not want to be the author of that. And yet, what he had to tell her might very well propel her toward a fit of the gloomy blues. He took a deep breath before he spoke.

"I fathered her child."

M stared at him. She tried to speak, but could not. She felt suddenly betrayed, oddly disconnected. And yet, it confirmed what she had known instinctively.

Madras let what he had said sink in. He had told her what she wanted to know. If she wanted to know more, then let her ask. He felt certain she would; M was nothing if not curious. He waited, wondering how she would react, knowing that his words had hurt her deeply, had fractured her view of him, perhaps even putting into question his love for her. It was misery of the acutest kind.

M's thoughts raced as she remembered what the Misses Merrithew had said about men sowing wild oats. She remembered overhearing someone at a party in Searsport allude to "Madras Mitchell and that business in Hawaii years ago." Now it all made sense.

She could not be angry. Nor could she wrap herself in a cocoon of hurt feelings and outraged sensibility, though every fiber of her body wanted to give in to hurt, to betrayal. But she had asked a direct question and he had given her a direct answer. That was what she wanted. No more secrets.

"I don't know what to say," she whispered.

He saw the questions in her eyes, questions she had yet to find words for.

"It's the usual story," he said. "I was young, inexperienced, and foolhardy. She was young and beautiful. And marriage was out of the question."

"You wanted to marry her?"

"I wanted to do the right thing."

"Did you know about the child?"

"Yes."

"And Hoku?"

"He is a cousin of some sort to Kapiolani. One of her people."

"Kapiolani?"

"That is her name."

"And the kapa cloth is connected somehow to them."

"Kapiolani and Hoku are of the royal clan, of Ka'ahumanu's people. But they have no claim to the throne."

"And do you . . ." M paused, trying to frame the question. "Do you see Kapiolani and her child?"

"No, M, I do not."

"How are they provided for?"

"Until I came of age, my father saw to it. Now I do. Through an agent."

"So if the whole thing about the kapa cloth comes out . . ."

"Then my connection to Kapiolani might be revealed publicly ... to my shame and embarrassment, and to that of my family and her family—even though they all know about what happened."

Suddenly, it all struck M as hideously hilarious. Her grand-mother's shameful past, the shameful past Madras and Kapiolani shared—even the shameful incident all those years ago when Augusta Mitchell protected a Hawaiian woman from the shameful advances of a drunken sailor. Shame had stalked them for years, and now, they were back where it had all begun. Shame—it went all the way back to the Garden of Eden, literally and figuratively. And here they were, a part of that eternal, great whole.

M began to laugh hysterically. She could not control it. She tried to speak, to explain why the thought of all that shame—the foolishness of it—was so amusing, but she could not stop laughing. She sank to her knees on the floor, tears of laughter streaming down her face.

Alarmed, Madras took her by the shoulders and gave her a little shake.

"M," he said firmly. "Stop. You'll make yourself ill."

She laughed harder, laughing until she was crying more tears than there was laughter. Then she could not stop crying.

Madras tried to comfort her, tried to get her to listen to him, but she held up her hands in front of her face, palms out, as if to ward him off, as if he had become suddenly a stranger to her. He did not know what to do. He was not in command, could not control the situation, and that caused him to doubt himself, to question himself, and finally, to step away from her to let her cry.

M's Log—October 21 , 1872

At last I know the truth. The woman who watches me— Madras and that woman had a child. His son. I can scarcely write the words. Madras is asleep and I am alone, the moonlight spilling in the window, the ink so black, the page so white, and I, so invisible. My husband sleeps while I write. This agony in my heart. I want to still myself, but I cannot. I cannot.

I want Grand Fan, I want Mother, I want Father, I want Mrs. Maude and Dr. Sam. I want my dear sweet sister, Grace, who sleeps in the deep. I want them all gathered around me like a fortress to beat away this clawing beast that has come to maim and scar me.

I try to name the volcano of emotions that erupt from me, this scalding flow of tears—betrayal, shame, shock, abandonment, hurt, fury, helplessness, distrust, disrespect. St. John's Wort be damned, I am, indeed, sliding down the vertical chute of melancholy.

Yet, I must stay sane, for I am alone in this. It will do me no good to write home at length, for no letter will get to Abbott's Reach for weeks, and no reply can come for several months. I cannot speak of this to Nancy Davis, though I believe I would find her a sympathetic listener. She might confide in her husband, or write to her sister, who might write to Ellis Harding, their father, and thus word would filter to Grand Fan and set off an alarm of worry. No, I must firm my backbone and captain my frail craft through this tempest.

What would Father do? He would reef sail and keep the bow headed into the waves to guard against capsizing. He would order all hands on deck. He would put on wet-weather gear and stare the tempest squarely in the eye. He would weather it. As for Mother, she would go below, surround herself with books and needlework, and lash herself to the bunk to ride out the storm. She would not lose faith in Father's ability to bring the Fairmount *safely through the boiling seas. I have seen her do this. I have been lashed to that bunk with her more than once. She would be afraid, but she would not let Father know it. She would say prayers and think of home. She would sing to me and make me laugh. She would not let me sink.*

I must not founder and go down. I must stay afloat.

But a ship is only as good as what the captain knows, what the captain has learned and can apply to the situation. A captain never stops learning. Nor does a woman, for that matter.

The moon has drifted beyond the window and I can barely see to write. Madras tosses restlessly in his sleep and speaks my name. In his sleep he reaches for me.

The first step toward forgiveness, Grand Fan says, is to take the hand that seeks your own.

7.

Madras woke to find M curled up in a ball and asleep in the far side of the bed. He reached out to stroke her arm and rearrange the sweep of her auburn hair spread out on the pillow in a tangled skein. She did not stir.

He had wanted to say so much more to her before she had become incoherent and unable to listen or talk, unable to do anything except feel the intensity of her own emotions. He saw evidence of her despair scattered about the room—crumpled handkerchiefs thrown on the floor, a blot of black ink staining her index finger, and her log tucked under her pillow.

In truth, he was glad of the reprieve, was glad another day would pass before there would be time and leisure to talk with her. It would give him time to think and understand, time to frame a way to make her see that she was dearer to him than anything, or anyone else, on Earth. It had pained him to admit that ever since they had arrived in Honolulu, he had been haunted by memories of Kapiolani and all that had happened between them so long ago. Those memories would take him unaware when he least expected it, and he knew his mood had darkened and that he had closed a part of himself to M.

He had been barely eighteen the year he had sailed as a newly minted mate with his uncle, Lebbeus Mitchell, master of the *American Eagle*. It was 1862 and Isaiah had wanted Madras out of the way of the Civil War—not that Madras felt any great sense of patriotism or heroics that might have impelled him to join up. He had grown up at sea. The world, in many respects, was his home. His sense of allegiance to any country, even the United States, threatened as it was by the secession of the South, was less important to him than his sense of allegiance to his father, his family, and the business of going to sea. There was another difficulty: Because so many men were signing up to join the army and navy, it was hard to find a decent crew to ship with them. At that time, seafaring families looked even more closely to their own ranks to man the helms of their vessels. Loyalty to family was far more important and necessary than loyalty to country. He believed he served his country best by fueling its commerce. He did not need to serve in the army to be of use to his country.

And so he set off on a voyage that would take him around the world, from Searsport to Boston, South America, Hawaii, China, India, Africa, Spain, England, Ireland, and back home to Searsport. He would be gone for more than three years.

It was, for the most part, a routine journey. The crews didn't need much driving, there were no real fights to break up. Madras had plenty of time to carry out his duties and to study for the day when he would apply for his master's ticket. Even the trip around the Horn was accomplished in a reasonable amount of time and hardship. But when they were only a few days from Hawaii they encountered a savage storm that tore away the foremast. The required repairs made their stay in Hawaii last more than four months.

Madras spotted Kapiolani almost from the moment they anchored. She and a group of other women, both old and young, came aboard the *American Eagle* to sell fruit. Uncle Lebbeus had warned Madras that Hawaiian girls were "forward" in their dealings with sailors, but Madras saw no evidence of that in Kapiolani. What he saw was a beautiful, dark-eyed girl whose smile warmed his heart and whose grace captivated his imagination. Clearly, she was not one of the so-called "harbor women" his uncle had warned him about.

Madras's path crossed Kapiolani's almost daily, often three or four times a day, and it was not long before their hands met, then their lips. And before the first month of his time in Honolulu had elapsed, Madras had disappeared into the lush countryside with Kapiolani. After they had lain together for the first time, it was as if some demon had possessed Madras, and all he thought about was the joy his body knew when he was with Kapiolani.

Lebbeus warned Madras to cool his passions, told him that there was a difference between love and lust. It was only later, when Kapiolani told him that she was with child, that Madras understood his uncle's words. He knew Kapiolani would never feel at home in the kitchens of Searsport, that she would never be accepted there, but Madras wanted to marry her nonetheless. He wanted to do the right thing for her and for their child. He could stay in Hawaii, go into business, and start a new life with Kapiolani, he reasoned, even though he understood that white men with Hawaiian wives were never truly welcomed as members of white society.

Now, it was ten years later, and he had left M sleeping to go about the business of the day. He dressed quietly and went down to the dining room where he found coffee and fruit. He ate quickly and hastened toward the docks. He already knew that he must add another errand to his round of duties. He must call on Joseph McTeague, his agent, and ask him to tell Kapiolani that she must not watch M, to remind her that her needs and that of the boy were amply taken care of. McTeague must make it plain to her that if she did not do as she was asked, compensation could be greatly reduced or withdrawn altogether.

It upset Madras to think in terms of punishing Kapiolani by withdrawing financial support. She had, in fact, behaved admirably under the circumstances. She had told him of her pregnancy. She had not expected him to marry her, nor had her family expected it. They knew how to live on the bounty of the land and how to provide for themselves. And children were always welcomed in Hawaiian families, no matter what. He knew her family would take care of her, that they did not want their daughter to leave the island to live in a land they could never visit. It was better for all that she had stayed with them . . . they had welcomed her child and helped her care for the boy.

Madras tried to shake his thoughts of the past, but they persisted. He had done the right thing and had confessed to his uncle, saying he intended to marry Kapiolani. Lebbeus, aghast, forbade marriage and ordered Madras confined to quarters, though not under lock and key. There had been a terrible row. As Madras remembered that night, a vein of anger swelled within him, making him feel off balance and out of step.

Kapiolani was the first woman he had ever loved. He told Lebbeus that he had no intention of giving up Kapiolani just to satisfy some outmoded convention about the mixing of the races, words that rang hollow even as he had spoken them. Differences in color mattered, he knew that. It was the way of the world—and his family. They would sympathize, they would do the right thing, but they would not understand, and they would not allow him to deviate from the path his family had trod for centuries.

One night, Madras jumped overboard and swam ashore. He and Kapiolani sought a justice of the peace to perform a marriage ceremony. When that failed, Madras looked for the next best thing: a sea captain in his cups who would take them aboard his ship and say the proper words to make them husband and wife.

But as they emerged from a grog shop, a gang of men grabbed Madras, bound him, and carried him back to the *American Eagle.* Lebbeus locked Madras in the hold, charged him with mutinous conduct, and there Madras stayed until the ship sailed the following week. Madras was surly and ill-tempered for weeks afterwards, but when he promised to discharge his duties as he was bound to by the articles he had signed at the beginning of the journey, Lebbeus released him.

Madras plotted to jump ship in China and make his way back to Kapiolani, but Lebbeus anticipated that. He engaged Madras in long conversations, sympathizing with him and the predicament he was in, until gradually Madras came around in his thinking and saw his actions in a new light—he had committed a youthful folly that had borne a regrettable outcome. He was not the first, nor would he be the last young man to behave in so rash a way. Madras let himself be guided by his uncle's wisdom, and in time he came to accept his fate. But he always remembered Kapiolani with affection.

A few years later, Madras learned that his father had provided
for Kapiolani and the child through McTeague, the agent, a
responsibility Madras insisted on assuming when he was of age
and had the means to do so. He knew that such an action was
unusual and he was grateful for it.

Madras had not seen Kapiolani again until the recent night
when she had appeared like a ghost under the tamarind tree. It
had unsettled him to see her. He had felt both a deep sense of
shame and a deep sense of affection for her, feelings that left him
confused and charged with guilt, the same feeling that had beset
him all those years ago when he had been forced to part with her.

As Madras walked to the docks, it came to him how stupid he
had been to think that he could return to Honolulu and simply
ignore his past there. How could he have thought that M would
not be affected by what he had done all those years ago? He realized with chagrin that secretly he had wanted to see Kapiolani, if
only from a distance, to satisfy himself that his heart had truly
mended, that she was well—that what had happened between
them had not ruined her life. Yet, at the same time, he had wanted
to wipe the slate of memory clean, forget Kapiolani, forget that he
had a son. What he had not foreseen was how difficult it would be
to speak to M of that time with Kapiolani, or that his involvement
with the Hawaiian girl would come to light in such an awkward
and unforgiving way.

Madras knew he had hurt M, and here he was, running away
from the sight of her searching, troubled eyes. Damn and blast, he
thought. He hurried on down the road, forcing himself to think of
the business of the day and not the follies of the past.

M woke to the empty side of the bed. Her eyes were heavy
from lack of sleep and her head felt evil, as if demons had taken
up residence in her skull and were beating against the bone.

Misery swept over her, became entangled with homesickness, with grief for the honeymoon that had ended so abruptly and in such an unbelievable way. She did not think she could get out of bed. Her stomach hurt and her arms and legs felt numb. But she must attend to her needs.

Carefully, she crawled out from under the covers and stood at the window for a long time, staring out at nothing, her thoughts sluggish and dull. She kept thinking of water, water deep enough to enclose her, water blue enough to match her mood, the watery deep where Grace now dwelled, the water over which her parents sailed, the water of the Penobscot which flowed past Abbott's Reach in its never-ending stream. *Water, water, water,* she thought. She drank some, dressed, pinned up her hair, and stumbled out of the room and into the late-morning light. She blinked and wished she had remembered her hat. She did not know where she would go or what she would do except walk toward the deep, enfolding water.

The day was growing warm and M felt herself flush with heat. She felt dizzy. But she kept walking, unmindful of where she went, moving along the dusty road, then away from the road until she found herself on a deserted white beach where the blue-green water slid up to the toes of her brown shoes. She sat down on the sand, unbuttoned her shoes, and took them off. She flung them away in a sudden fit of temper. Somehow, the action made her feel better. Then she walked deliberately into the surf, ankle-deep, knee-deep, thigh-deep. Warm water, not icy like the water at Abbott's Reach. Her long skirts surged and snaked around her legs. She struggled against the pull of the surf until she was waist-deep, chest-deep, neck-deep.

Grace, she thought.

A sudden heavy wave knocked her off her feet, and in an instant she was underwater, flailing, yet alert, the cobwebs in her head washed away. And now she knew she was drowning and it came to her with crystalline clarity that there were far worse things than being wed to a man who had withheld from his wife a secret from his youthful past.

She clawed her way to the surface, took a deep breath of the precious, precious air. "Madras," she whispered, then screamed his name, and screamed it until the light began to narrow and water filled her mouth and the weight of her clothing dragged her down, down to those terrible depths where her sister lay. Her last coherent thought as her strength drained away was, *I am dead.*

M's Log—October 25, 1872

It startled me to learn that I had not died. I woke to the sight of a thatched ceiling and the sound of Hawaiian voices speaking softly, musically. I lay on a woven mat upon the floor of the dwelling. I was covered with a cloth, which I knew to be kapa cloth just from its texture beneath my fingers. I was dressed in a loose cotton garment with a high neck and long sleeves, the kind the Hawaiian women sometimes wear. My hair had been unpinned and spread out around my head to dry like laundry on the grass. Gentle hands massaged my arms, legs, hands, feet. I was too weak and too disoriented to feel anything but relief that I was safe and on dry ground. I could not determine if I had been there a long time or only a few minutes. A shaft of sun slanted through the window opening, creating a misty yellow light. I think it was afternoon, but I could not tell.

The faces of the women floated into my field of vision—women with long white hair, women with strands of gray in black hair, women with glossy black hair—old, young, and in between. One of the white-haired women knelt beside me and gently laid her hand first on my cheek, then on my belly. She spoke softly in Hawaiian, and though I could not understand her words, I felt comforted, as if

Grand Fan or Mrs. Maude had touched me. She held a cup to my lips and nodded her head, indicating that I should drink. It tasted like coconut milk. I tried to speak, to ask for Madras, for Nancy Davis. I tried to thank everyone in the room for their kindness, but words would not form in my mouth.

Another woman knelt beside me, a young woman, the woman who had watched me. Kapiolani. *I managed to whisper her name and her eyes grew soft with kindness.*

"We have sent for your husband," she said in English. "My son Naihe saw you in the water. He ran to us, and we pulled you out. We brought you here to this house where my family lives."

I glanced at the white-haired woman kneeling on the other side of me.

"Kamamalu, my grandmother. She is a healer," Kapiolani said. "She says you carry a child."

Her words registered in my mind, but I was so overcome by fatigue, I barely comprehended, except in a distant, almost detached way.

I don't know how long I slept, but when I woke again I felt more like myself, though still weak, as if I had been ill a very long time. The women were gone and Madras sat beside me. His face registered intense concern, and he held my hand in his strong fingers. It was evening and a lantern glowed outside my range of vision. I glanced around, looking for the women.

"They have gone, M," Madras said gently. "They saved your life."

"I know," I whispered, tightening my hold on his fingers. "Kapiolani. Naihe." The names lay in the air between us, and I saw with sudden clarity that it was as it should be. The past that had belonged only to Madras now belonged to me as well. The circumstances of Madras's past had commingled with my present circumstances, and in the wake of this event, a new kind of awareness and trust had been created. He no longer had to pretend for my sake that his son did not exist. And I no longer had to resent the fact that the

child and his mother existed. I told him that, and a surge of emotion raced across his face. He kissed my hand. "Did Kapiolani tell you?"

"Her grandmother told me." Madras laid his hand on my belly in a gesture of awe and protection. "Madras, I believe Kamamalu is the woman your grandmother saved all those years ago." I could not say for certain how I knew this, but I knew it to be true.

A look of shock came over Madras's face. "It can't be," he said.

Soon after, I heard the wheels of a carriage and the voices of Lex Nichols and Lancaster Treat. They helped Madras bundle me into the vehicle and they drove us to Nancy Davis's house. She had prepared a room for me at the back of the house, on the first floor. It reminds me somewhat of Grand Fan's back bedroom off the kitchen at Abbott's Reach, simply furnished, comfortable and welcoming. The walls are whitewashed and the bed is spread with a pieced quilt in the log cabin pattern. Rag rugs cover the floor by the bed and in front of the dresser. Curtains of sheer fabric hang at the windows.

During the day, when Nancy is busy with her housekeeping, I hear her moving in the other rooms, hear her voice speaking softly to her husband, or talking to someone who has called. Sometimes I hear her speaking Hawaiian. The sound of birds and the sigh of the wind come into the room all day. It is like a blessing to be wrapped in this room, in those sounds.

When I asked Nancy about Kamamalu, she said it was quite likely that she was the woman Augusta Mitchell had saved all those years ago.

"God works in mysterious ways," Nancy said as she brushed my hair.

M's Log—November 1, 1872

I have been here for several days. They sent for a doctor the day after they brought me here, and he pronounced me no worse for the *experience, but advised a week of bed rest. I am up and about a bit more each day.*

Nancy is a good nurse and the soul of patience. She brings my meals on a tray and sits with me. She brings her sewing and allows me to do a bit of hemming. She does not speak of what happened to me. She speaks only of general things—the subject of her husband's latest sermon, the news that a British ship is in port, and that Isabella Bird, the woman who is writing about Hawaii, has gone to one of the other islands to visit the place where Captain Cook was killed.

8.

Melancholy claimed M and the dark parameters of despair tied her in knots. She cried for no reason, she could not sleep, and food was like sawdust in her mouth. Her arms and legs felt heavy and incapable of movement. She could not bear to look at Madras or talk to him, and a terrible sense of anger gripped her so strongly she thought she might lose her mind entirely.

It would have been better if I had died, she thought miserably, her face turned to the wall of the room in Nancy's house, the tray of food on the table by the bed left untouched. Her mind wandered and roamed, and her thoughts were often jumbled and incoherent.

I am becoming someone else, she thought wildly, the idea so terrifying she wanted to scream. She did not want her being to change, she did not want her body to change as she knew it would in pregnancy, and she did not want her perception of Madras to change. But everything had changed, except her ability to grasp what those changes were, and what that would mean in her life. She could not fit the new garment of perception to herself.

She swallowed St. John's Wort faithfully several times each day, but it did not seem to help. It was as if her spirit had embarked on a subterranean journey of its own, one her physical and mental being had not gone along with. She found her state of mind confusing and infuriating, and the inner conflict left her weak and disoriented.

Word of M's illness filtered out into the community of women in Honolulu. Each day Queen Emma sent a small basket of fruits and bouquets of flowers in hues of bright red, orange, and yellow. She wrote encouraging notes and sent uplifting books for M to read.

Some of the American ladies sent tins of molasses cookies, and the British ladies sent packets of tea and layer cakes. The ladies also paid brief calls and talked of the recent croquet tournament at the hotel, a party one of the British naval officers had given, and what they planned to wear to an upcoming ball. Other people called, too, but Nancy kept visits to the sickroom brief.

One morning in mid-November after M's sojourn in bed had passed the two-week mark, Nancy said kindly, "We have all been solicitous of your health, M. Two weeks is long enough for you to mope and feel sorry for yourself. Today I will comb your hair and help you dress. Then you will come into the parlor and sit with me, and help me sew for the poor. You will find the hems simple and easy to do. And tomorrow, you will do the same, and each day after that until you have turned your thoughts outward instead of inward."

M obeyed reluctantly, but returned exhausted to her room after an hour. Nonetheless, she repeated the effort the next day, and sat with Nancy for nearly two hours.

That evening, M heard Hawaiian voices singing and the sound of softly strummed stringed instruments floated through her window. Nancy sat nearby reading a chapter from the Bible. "Some of Kapiolani's family are singing you well," Nancy said, closing the book. "They are dancing you well, too, my husband says. It is their custom, an ancient one. My husband does not approve of it and does his best to lead them away from such pagan ways. But I can't help but think it is simply another way to celebrate God's goodness. At church each Sunday we sing God's praises at worship service. Surely, the music that comes from these kindhearted people, who also come to church to sing, can be construed not only as a gift from God, but a gift to God. And it is most assuredly a gift to you, M."

M listened to the music in spite of her effort not to. It seemed to seep like perfume into her skin, her mind, her heart. Gradually, she felt lulled and soothed, as if she had been wrapped in something healing. She fell asleep with the sound of the voices and the music echoing in her heart.

That night she slept so deeply that she did not have frightening dreams and did not wake in the middle of the night, panic-stricken. And when she woke the next morning, refreshed, she found Madras sitting by her bed. She could not look at him without crying, and found that her heart was overflowing with more love for him than she had ever thought it was possible to feel again.

"Madras," she whispered, "my love."

"M, darling M," he said as he folded her into his arms. "I have missed you. Oh, how I have missed you."

She nestled against his chest and felt that she had come home from the miseries of the water at last.

She thought, then, of the child she carried, marveled that it would be born in six months. She lifted Madras's hand and laid it on her belly on the spot where the child had fluttered for the first time in its watery nest. Tears brimmed in his eyes, and in hers. But the next moment they were laughing with so much joy it took her breath away.

M's Log—November 20, 1872

Madras comes several times each day. I see him in a new light now—not simply as my husband, the man who belongs to me, but as one in whose depths I am slowly learning to immerse myself.

Immersion such as this, I find, does not make us interchangeable or intertwined in some evil, entangled way. Rather, it deepens us equally, and brings us to an understanding that makes us more fully husband and wife.

We have not yet spoken of Kapiolani and Naihe, for there has been neither time nor opportunity. But the time for speaking grows near. I will ask Madras to take me to see Kapiolani and her son as soon as I am well enough to do so.

M's Log—November 21, 1872

We have weathered this terrible storm, Madras and I. We have found safe harbor in one another once again, even though I was in great danger of being bashed insensible against life's reefs. But I know now that the reefs are always out there, no matter how vigilant is the sailor in the crow's nest or how bright the beam from the lighthouse. We are frail craft, we humans. We are easily blown off course into the path of danger.

I told Madras that I was ready now to visit Kapiolani and Naihe. He said he would have his agent McTeague arrange it. McTeague does not think much of the idea, but when he learned that I would not be deterred, he went about the business with great care, tact, and circumspection. He brought us word that Kapiolani and her family will receive us.

For the visit, I had two objectives in mind: First, I would thank Naihe for saving my life, and second, I would thank Kapiolani and her family for ministering to me with such kindness.

All I have with me of any worth besides my wedding ring is the gold lapel watch Mother gave me on my sixteenth birthday. This I decided to give to Kapiolani. I also have several quilts made for me as parting gifts by friends in Searsport. These I will give to Kapiolani's people. To Naihe I will give the miniature painting of

Madras, a wedding gift to me from his parents. It seemed only right to me that he should possess an image of his father.

As for Madras, I required that he acknowledge Naihe as his son by giving him a sketch of the Boreas and an offer to enroll the boy, when the time came, at Oahu College, a school in Honolulu founded by the Congregational missionaries for the education of their children, should he wish to go.

We set off with McTeague early in the afternoon, walking along the road that skirted the ocean. McTeague had combed his gray muttonchop whiskers into perfect symmetry and his shirt was nicely starched. He walked a step behind us and said little.

When we came to the place where I had nearly lost my life, we found Kapiolani, Naihe, and their family waiting for us. They were dressed for the occasion in brightly colored wraps of cloth. Both men and women wore leis around their necks. The women also wore garlands of flowers in their hair and around their ankles and wrists. As a group they possessed a regal and noble air. They seemed at one with sand, sky, and sea.

After a few greetings and much hesitation on everyone's part, I stepped forward to Kapiolani. "Take this watch as a sign of my gratitude," I said to her. "I owe you my life and the life of the child who will be born to me."

Then I offered the miniature of Madras to Naihe. He looked at it with a shy kind of pleasure, glanced quickly at Madras, and nodded his head to indicate that he accepted. "You are my husband's son," I said. "For that, and for saving my life, I honor you." He took the miniature and held it against his heart.

Madras held out his hand to Naihe and they embraced for the first time as father and son. They fell into a somewhat awkward conversation, and Madras learned that Naihe already attended school and aspired to be a teacher.

"Naihe is a curious boy with a great desire to learn—not only about his own world, but that of his American father," Kapiolani said.

And just when I thought that we had accomplished all that we had set out to do, Kapiolani, Kamamalu, and several of the women led me to the water. They took off my shoes, held up my skirts, and urged me toward the edge of the ocean where the water lapped gently at my toes. Taking turns, they spoke in Hawaiian, addressing the ocean, the sky, the warm air. I have no idea what they said, but it seemed to me they were praying. So I bowed my head. Kapiolani removed a lei from her neck and set it around mine. She gave me another lei and indicated that I should toss it as far as I could out into the sea.

"We have made peace with the gods of the water," she said. "They will trouble you no more."

9.

"What can this be?" M said as she and Madras went toward the door of their hotel room, where a wrapped parcel waited for them. They had just returned from a going-away party at which they had been the guests of honor. Nancy Davis and the ladies of the church had planned and carried out the gathering.

"I have no idea, M," Madras said as he picked up the parcel to measure its heft. "It's not very heavy." The parcel was wrapped in brown paper and tied with twine. Madras tucked it under his arm and unlocked the door to their room. He handed the package to M. "I guess you'd better see what this is all about."

M tore away the wrapping and shook out a quilt made in the Hawaiian way, appliquéd with a large central motif cut from folded cloth, much the way one cuts snowflakes from folded paper. "It's the breadfruit design," M said, having seen several such quilts at Nancy's house. She had, in fact, been covered by such a quilt as she lay abed, regaining her strength after her close call with drowning. This quilt, however, was not in bright red on white; instead, it was indigo blue on white. M shook it out fully, the better to observe it. The stitching, she noticed, was fine and even.

"Very nice," Madras said approvingly. "And whom do you think we have to thank for this?"

M gave him a long, level look, as if to suggest he had taken leave of his intelligence. "Kapiolani, Kamamalu, and the women of her family is my guess," M said. "Look—here in this corner. It's a little piece of kapa cloth. And there's a leaf pattern stamped on it and a single word: Aloha. Madras, that leaf is the same as the one on the kapa cloth your grandmother gave me."

Tears started in M's eyes as she gathered the folds of the quilt in her arms. "We must do more for these island people, Madras. We have taken their land, we govern them, yet we treat them like social outcasts. They could not even attend our going-away party! We have disrupted something that was ancient and—"

"And in many ways destructive, M," Madras interrupted.

M had had several conversations with Nancy and her friends on the subject, although the missionaries took a rather more conservative view, and were, in fact, the ones who wielded a great deal of power in the government and commerce of the islands.

"The old ways were not Eden, you know," Madras continued. "And neither is what has replaced it, but at least heads no longer roll when a commoner dares to look at the king. And warfare here is a thing of the past. Yes, there are still many evils—I know that firsthand, for in my youthful folly, I contributed to it. But you have made me see where my duty lies, and what I must do to right the wrong I so carelessly set into motion."

"I don't think you were careless, Madras. Quite the opposite. I think you cared very deeply for Kapiolani. Otherwise, you would not have tried so hard to marry her. But I think, in the long run, you cared more deeply for your family and their wishes for you to live as they do, to believe in the things they believe. I wanted you to be perfect, Madras, even though I know that none of us are perfect—certainly not me, not Grand Fan, certainly not your grandmother." They grinned at one another. "I was wrong to judge you, Madras—for that was what I was doing—judging you because I did not know your story or Kapiolani's. But now that I do, I see that—oh, this will sound so foolish—that all stories, mine, yours, everyone's, are connected in some small way. And for that reason, it behooves us to think before we judge."

"I'm grateful for your wisdom, M." But more than that, he was grateful for her practicality, for her loving-kindness and hard-headed insistence that a wrong be righted, even if it meant that the ladies in Nancy Davis's circle disapproved, as he felt certain some of them did. But that mattered little to him. What mattered was that the breach between he and his wife had been closed and that they had weathered the storm without foundering—that they had, indeed, been strengthened by the turbulence.

M folded the quilt and set it with several valises that would be taken to the *Boreas* in the morning. The rest of their luggage was packed and stowed aboard the ship. Their sojourn in Hawaii was at an end. They would sail the next day for San Francisco.

Early the next morning, Nancy and Abel Davis and a few others gathered on the hotel verandah to see M and Madras off.

"I have greatly enjoyed spending time with you," Nancy said as she embraced M. "Queen Emma sends her love. And as you go down the road, be sure to look seaward."

In a flurry of good-byes and alohas, M and Madras stepped into a carriage to be driven toward the docks. When M looked seaward, as Nancy had told her she must, she saw a cluster of Hawaiians in their canoes, and they were waving.

"Look, Madras," M said, pointing, and waving in return. "It's our Hawaiian family." Tears trickled down her cheeks, even though she was smiling.

Madras smiled and waved, too, his heart lighter for having made peace with the past embodied in his son, Naihe. The beauty of the island had seduced him as a youth, but now it had saved him as a husband, a father, and a man. He felt a strange pang of regret, a moment of "what if," and the quick thought of what it might have been like if he and Kapiolani had married and made a life together in Honolulu. He turned and looked at M, and he knew in an instant that the course he was on was the right one.

M sensed his feelings of the moment, took his hand, and kissed it.

"I'm glad to be going to sea again, Madras. It won't be the same as when we were so newly married and on our honeymoon, of course, because we have learned so many new things. And we are not quite the same as we were on the day of our wedding. But I think that is as it should be. We must deepen—as husband and wife, and as individuals. Life will do that to us if we let it."

"Good heavens, M, that sounds almost like a sermon. I fear you have spent far too much time in the company of missionaries," Madras said teasingly. He grinned at her and she gave him a playful nudge on his arm.

"I suspect, my dear, that you will change your tune quite considerably when I get you alone in our cabin this evening," she said archly. "When we are rocking in the cradle of the deep." She gave him a coy look to make certain he took her meaning.

He pulled her to him, disregarding anyone who might see them, and kissed her in a way he had not done since their quarrel, before M's incident in the water.

"That, my dear, you may have on account until the moon is over the yardarm."

Part 4
At Sea Again

1.

Entries from M's Log, 1872–1873
Aboard the Boreas

Compared to the immense distance we covered from Searsport
to Honolulu, this leg of our journey, to California, will be short,
indeed. It seems strange to be upon the sea again, bereft of the bril-
liant hues of Hawaii, and the kind society of friends we found there.
But I love the great expanse of blue sky over us, and the sound of
water swishing beneath the hull. I love the way we are rocked and
swayed by the motion of the ship day and night.

I am regaining my sea legs more quickly than I thought I
would. I notice, too, that my middle is expanding to accommodate
the child growing within me. I have let out the waists of my skirts
and dresses. Nancy Davis saw to it that I had several new dresses
made with a high waistline, tailored with much gathering of fabric to
hide my changing shape.

When Madras came aboard, Oyster Duncan, Lewis Andrews,
Lex Nichols, and Lancaster Treat were lined up, dressed in their best
navy blue jackets, the buttons polished and shiny, to welcome us.
Oyster has not changed. He is as gruff as ever, but I saw a twinkle
in his eye, and know he is glad enough to see me. Lewis has grown
taller and has filled out some. There is something in his bearing now
that makes one know he considers himself a man. Mr. Nichols and
Mr. Treat welcomed me with great respect and kindness. I found that
reassuring. They, like Madras, represent home and safety to me.

We had not been at sea more than a few hours when we spot-
ted a ship off the starboard bow. We seemed to be gaining on her. As

219

*I stood at the railing, watching, Madras came to stand beside me.
"Shall we speak her?" he asked.*

*Speaking a ship is generally done to allow the exchange of
news and reading material, or to dispatch letters—in this case, letters
to those left behind in Hawaii. It also works the other way. When
we get to California we can report that we spoke the ship and the
news will be telegraphed to its owners, then published in the newspapers, and in that way all will know that as of a certain day, everyone aboard was safe. In return, the other ship will report speaking us
when it arrives at its destination.*

*But it really wasn't necessary to speak the ship since we had
barely begun our journey. It surprised me that Madras wanted to do so.*

Madras raised the spyglass to his eye, then passed it to me.

"The Empress*!" I exclaimed, barely able to contain my excitement. "India, China, and Persia Havener!"*

*"The very same," Madras said. "I knew they were in
Honolulu, but I had no idea they were to sail today."*

"Why didn't you tell me?" I demanded.

*"I only heard of it a day or so ago. The Havener sisters don't
usually broadcast their comings and goings—as you well know."*

*That was true. One almost never read of them in the shipping
news. It was only by word of mouth that one knew whether or not
the* Empress *was in port or asea.*

"I wonder where she's bound," I said.

"Judging by her current course, I'd say California."

*Madras loosed a bit more canvas, and after another hour had
passed, we found ourselves abreast of the* Empress. *That, too, surprised me, because I knew the* Empress, *with her leaner, clipper-ship
lines, was faster than the* Boreas. *Clearly, whoever was in command
of the ship wanted to speak us, too.*

*I stood by the rail, craning my neck in the most shameless way,
hoping for a glimpse of the sisters. But all I saw was what I see*

every day on the Boreas, *the crew going about its business, the mate giving orders, and a man at the wheel beneath the billowing, wind-filled squares of canvas.*

Madras shouted, "Ahoy the ship," through the megaphone, and the mate replied, "The Empress, *Captain Havener, bound for San Francisco."*

"All is well?" Madras asked.

"All is well," the mate replied.

A cabin boy ran up to the mate carrying a package wrapped in oilcloth. The mate tied it to a line and threw it across the space sep-arating the two vessels. It could not be letters, since both ships were bound toward the same destination. Perhaps it was books and a request for an exchange.

"For the captain's lady, compliments of the Misses Havener," the mate said.

Madras caught the package and handed it to me.

The mate pulled back the line, nodded to Madras, and slowly the Boreas *fell back and away as the* Empress *pressed on a bit more sail and sped away.*

"Apparently," Madras said, "you have made an impression on the Havener ladies without your even being aware of it."

I tore the wrappings away and found a lovely wool baby blan-ket crocheted in a pattern of lacy shells, and bonnet and booties to match.

"But how could they know?" I asked Madras. "We've told no one but the Davises."

"In Hawaii, M, the very air has ears."

A small rill of anxiety stirred in my mind. What was being said about me, about Madras? Even though we had made our peace with Kapiolani and her family, we had tried to keep it private. Yet, how silly it was to think that such a thing was possible. Hawaii was in many ways like any small town, like Stockton Springs or Searsport.

Nothing was ever kept secret for long. Not even the wide expanse of an ocean could guarantee that word of our doings would not filter back to Madras's grandmother. I shuddered at the thought. And yet, hadn't I been born of scandal—my grandmother's irregular life, my mother's illegitimate birth, and indeed, my own? I had much to hide, yet the bones of it had not been hidden from me, and I lived an upright life among upright people who were not afraid of the truth.

Our first night at sea, Oyster and Lewis prepared a special supper—roast chicken and gravy, potatoes, carrots, and a vanilla cake topped with strawberries. Lewis carried the food in to us with great ceremony. I told him to convey my thanks to Oyster. We were a merry party that night. Mr. Nichols and Mr. Treat told stories of their days at sea, and Mr. Treat played a few tunes on the harmonium.

When it grew dark I retired below, waiting for Madras to join me. I felt slightly queasy from the motion of the Boreas *and, no doubt, from my condition.*

"The Empress *seems to be holding to the same course as we are, so the man at the wheel reports. But she disappeared below the horizon about the time the moon rose," Madras said when he came below, at last.*

"Do you think we will see her again when we get to San Francisco?"

"Hard to say. But one thing is for certain—they will reach California before we do and report that they spoke us."

"And everyone at home will breathe another sigh of relief."

We are churning and rolling in a tempest that blew in upon us in the night. Mr. Treat called Madras at midnight and I knew we were in for a wild time. Before he left me, Madras made certain that I was properly lashed to a bunk so I would not be thrown around like a rag doll every time the Boreas *pitched and rolled. Now all I can do is wait for the hours to tick away. Writing this log is a challenge—I can scratch only a word or two before the vessel lurches, then I must raise the nib from the page. The ink bottle is secure in its well, but I must take care in choosing the moment I begin to make marks on the page lest I make blots and scribbles.*

The wind is howling to such a degree that it deafens me. The bulwarks creak and groan so that I fear the timbers might break at any moment. My heart pounds with fear greater than I have known in all these months at sea, even when we were rounding the Horn. I feel disoriented and slightly crazed, as if the calm hours I knew so short a time ago were merely a dream from which I have now awoken. Twice I have had to undo the lashing and stumble to the commode. I have redone the lashings, but still I am tossed and bucked no matter how hard I brace myself.

I think of the child I carry and long for the comfort of Grand Fan's house and the eventual hour when the seas will calm, the Boreas will resume her easy motion, and Madras will come in out of the weather to sit with me in the evening.

Several days later—I have lost track of the days . . .

My hands tremble and I don't know if I can calm myself enough to write. But write, I must. Madras lies upon the bed, his body broken, in an unconscious state. But wait—I must begin from the beginning, must write this logically and carefully in order that I might make sense of it.

The storm was fierce, more fierce than anything we had endured rounding the Horn. It seemed to come from nowhere, engulfing us and flinging us into a vortex of ceaseless, unending motion. Once, Madras came below just long enough to see that I was properly lashed to the bunk and to reassure me. But I saw in his face something I had never seen before—fear. All he said was, "Pray, M." He kissed me and went back to his post. I don't know how much time passed, but suddenly I heard a terrible rending, then a violent impact. I felt the Boreas lurch and roll in a sickening way, then right herself. I heard cries, which might have been the wind, but in my heart I knew that it was not. I wanted to untie the knots that held me and run to the deck, to find Madras. It was at that moment, though, that the child I carry stirred. It was no more than a flutter, like a tiny finger brushing again and again on the other side of my belly. I wept then, for I was certain that this tiny new life would never see the light of day—that it, and I, and all aboard the Boreas would sink beneath the mighty power of the waves and be lost forever. "Grace." I said that aloud. And almost immediately, I heard her voice answering me. "Not time yet, M," she said. And I saw her face, the blonde curls falling across her forehead, her blue eyes twinkling with mischief as they often did when she was bent on having me play a game with her. I closed my eyes and prayed, not for deliverance from the storm, but in thanks for having had such a sister as Grace.

Soon, I perceived from the motion of the Boreas that the wind had abated slightly and the ship was wallowing in a way it had not done before I heard the terrible crash. All I could do was wait.

After what seemed like hours, Lex Nichols appeared, water running in rivulets off his sou'wester, his face a mask I could not read.

"Mrs. Mitchell," he said, very correctly, very formally. "We've lost the foremast."

"Where is Captain Mitchell?" I demanded.

Mr. Nichols hesitated and dropped his head so that he would not have to look at me. I felt fear gnaw at my middle and my unborn child fluttered again. I laid my hand upon that place as if to protect it from whatever awful truth I knew was bound to come.

"He was struck by a falling yardarm, ma'am. He is senseless."

I could not speak.

"Not dead. Badly injured."

"Unlash me," I said. "Do it now. Then bring the captain down here. At once."

"There's more. Mr. Treat was injured, too. He is insensible, also."

"Then bring him here, too. Is anyone else injured?" I kicked away the lashings and stood unsteadily, obliged to hang onto the bulwark to keep from being pitched about.

"No, nothing serious." Mr. Nichols hesitated as he turned to go. I waited for him to speak. "There's no one to navigate."

"But you are second mate . . ." Still, I knew that did not necessarily mean that he possessed the depth of skill to get us to San Francisco.

"The captain was teaching you . . . we've been driven by the wind for more than two days now. If we are still on course it would be a miracle."

"No," I said. "I am not skilled enough . . . I can't possibly—"

"Someone must take command."

"That is you, Mr. Nichols, by virtue of the fact that you are now the senior officer aboard this ship."

"The men I can handle, ma'am. But I can't navigate."

Suddenly, I could not think. My mind refused to take in any more. But I knew I must think, must gather the dangling ends and knot them together. "Have the captain and Mr. Treat brought here, Mr. Nichols. I will see to their injuries. You must determine a few things. Are we shipping dangerous amounts of water? Does the rudder respond to the wheel? If we allow ourselves to drift and be blown for another few hours, will that deepen our danger? Bring those answers to me as soon as you can."

"Aye, ma'am," he said, saluting quickly. It was then that I knew that I had, for all intents and purposes, become the captain of the Boreas.

Mr. Nichols, Marcel DuPere, the Aroostook County man, and John Bear Neptune, the Penobscot Indian from Old Town, carried Madras and Lancaster Treat below. They placed Madras on the bed and Mr. Treat on the sofa in the saloon. I saw at once that I would need help and sent for Lewis Andrews; I felt he would take direction from me, and that his physical strength would be of use in lifting the injured men. This proved to be true.

First, I had to assess the seriousness of the injuries. I began with Mr. Treat, for it was clear that his were more extensive. His left shoulder was dislocated, he had a great gash on his head, with tiny splinters of bone showing through, and his right leg was broken. I was not able to determine if he had internal injuries.

Madras had broken ribs, a broken thighbone, and a wound on the left side of his head that clearly included concussion.

More than once I gave silent thanks that Dr. Sam and Mrs. Maude had sometimes taken me with them when they visited the sick and injured, and that I had paid attention to one degree or another when they had discussed such things. I had learned from them how to clean and care for wounds, how to stitch and bandage them, how to put dislocated joints back in place, and even how to set a broken bone. Even so, I had small practice at doing such things. Knowing how and doing so without their aid were two very different things. But I could not let that deter me, given the graveness of the situation.

I barely knew where to begin, but decided to start with Mr. Treat's shoulder. With Lewis's help it was a simple matter to pop it back into place and bind the arm to his side. His leg is set, too, splinted, bound, and propped on pillows. With tweezers I sterilized in alcohol and boiling water, I picked from Mr. Treat's head the worst of the bone splinters, cleaned the wound, and bandaged it. If there is bleeding within his cranium, or swelling . . . but I dare not even imagine such a thing.

I do not know if I set Madras's thighbone properly. I did the best I could. It was impossible to assess the broken ribs—I do not know if his lung has been pierced. I wrapped his chest in wide strips

*I cut from sheets in hopes that would be enough to hold the breaks
in place, but not so tightly that the pressure would cause more harm
than good. As for his head, that was the worst. I shaved the hair
away from the wound. I saw no bone fragments, and hope this is a
good sign. I stitched the edges of the wound together with silk
embroidery thread, placed a compress against it, and bandaged it.
When there was nothing more I could do to make the two men
comfortable, I instructed Lewis to watch them and report to me any
change he might notice.*

"Aye, ma'am."

*Just as I felt I might collapse from fear and fatigue, Mr. Nichols
appeared.*

*"We're shipping some water, ma'am, but the pumps are taking
care of it. The rudder is responding to the wheel. Repairs to the
mast, sails, and rigging are under way. We can drift a few more
hours, but that is risky because I do not know for sure if we have
been blown north, east, or south, or somewhere in between," he said.*

"Very well, Mr. Nichols," I replied.

*"The men are working with a will now, ma'am, but it's been
an ugly twenty-four hours. They will want to know who is in
charge. Otherwise, there's apt to be unrest."*

*"You are in charge . . . Captain Nichols. As for the matter of
navigation, I will do what I can, and perhaps together, with you as
captain and I as a silent mate, we can make headway toward San
Francisco."*

*The relief that came over his face was the most splendid thing I
had seen in days.*

"Aye, aye, ma'am."

"You must choose a first and second mate," I continued.

*"DuPere and Neptune," Mr. Nichols said without hesitation.
"They are good Maine men, loyal and true for all their rough edges.
The crew respects them."*

"I leave it to you, then, to convey that news to them." He turned to leave, but as he did he hesitated.

"You must speak to the crew, ma'am. Soon."

"In the morning," I said. "In the morning." He left and I felt myself sag with the immensity of it all. A black wall of melancholy hovered at the back of my eyes, and I found my breath coming in little gasps of despair. My dress was stained with blood. My hair hung in a wild tangle tied back with a piece of yarn. My mouth felt furry and my head ached.

Oyster, who, no doubt, had been keeping an eye on me, appeared with a pot of tea and crackers. He folded a blanket around my shoulders. He said nothing and disappeared in the direction of the galley. Lewis appeared in my line of vision.

"Rest, ma'am," Lewis said, his face so young and earnest. "There's nothing more to do but watch, and I'll do that." He regarded me with a look that was both compassionate and respectful, and I saw reflected in his eyes a vision of myself that I never thought to see. He saw me as a leader by whom he was willing to be led.

I barely had time to register that thought before I laid my head against the back of the chair. The next thing I knew, light was coming through the transom. It was the dawn of another day, a clear day, a day without a tempest roiling the waters and pitching us about. But there was much to do, and only I could do it.

I assured myself that neither Madras nor Mr. Treat were in worse condition than before. I changed the dressings on their wounds and saw that infection had not set in. I bathed their faces, searched anxiously for signs of consciousness. Madras muttered something and moved his head slightly. It occurred to me then that I should devise something to keep him and Mr. Treat from moving their heads, for fear of compounding the hurt they had already suffered. I sent Lewis into the hold to retrieve ballast stones. These I wrapped in layers of towels, which I then positioned at the side of each man's head, making head motion next to impossible.

That done, I sent for Mr. Nichols and told him to assemble the men on deck, and that I would speak to them.

I glanced at the clock. It was not yet seven o'clock. No one had eaten. I sent word by Lewis to Oyster Duncan that the men were to have a liberal ration of maple syrup on their oatmeal, and that breakfast was to be served as soon as possible.

An hour later, Mr. Nichols conducted me above.

I stood at the rail looking down on the circle of faces. They were a rough-looking lot, some wearing navy blue watch caps, others bareheaded, old and young, most with the deeply tanned, battered-looking complexions of men who spend their lives at sea and days on land in the drinking dens. Weariness was etched into the lines of their bodies. None of them smiled. Nothing about them betrayed anything they might be feeling.

Behind them, forward, lay bits and pieces of the wreckage of the foremast, a tangle of ropes and other gear that had not yet been made shipshape.

I had no idea what to say or how to begin, but I thought it best to simply tell the truth as I understood it. I also had to make it sound as if nothing was amiss in terms of the chain of command. They did not need to know that the duties of navigator now fell to me, but they did need to know that they would see me each noontime with a sextant in my hand, taking the angle of the sun. Therefore, I mixed at least one small falsehood into my remarks.

"Captain Mitchell and Mr. Treat are both badly injured," I began. "They have not, as yet, recovered their senses. I have seen to their wounds and have every hope of their eventual recovery. Mr. Nichols, as senior officer, is now in charge of the Boreas. *The storm blew us off course, but Mr. Nichols is charting corrections that will aid us on own way. The captain taught me the rudiments of navigation.*

It is my intention to practice those skills for the rest of the voyage against the unlikely event that Mr. Nichols should fall ill and be unable to discharge his duties as navigator. On behalf of Captain Mitchell, I thank you for the hard work you did these last few days, and for that which is before you these next few days. Let us all heave to with a will in order that we may safely arrive, in a few weeks' time, at San Francisco."

At that point, Mr. Nichols stepped forward and sang out orders that sent the men back to their watches or other duties of the day.

As soon as it was practicable, when the sun was at the proper point in the sky, I took readings with the sextant and charted the calculations, comparing them to the last Madras had made. As near as I can determine we have been blown five hundred miles north-east. That, in itself, is not dire. We do not have to worry about icebergs from Alaska or crashing into any islands in our immediate vicinity. We are simply adrift in the Pacific, less than halfway between Hawaii and North America.

In the worst case, all Mr. Nichols has to do is steer east by the compass, and eventually we will run into the western coast of North America. But that is a rocky and treacherous coast, often filled with fog. It will not do to sail blindly to it. We can reverse our direction and sail back to Hawaii, but that will gain us nothing, and presents a rather small target to hit, whereas the entire western coast of North America ensures that, even if my calculations are seriously off, we will arrive somewhere.

I conferred with Mr. Nichols, and he agreed that we should resume our course and not turn back. I checked my calculations several times, and we pored over charts and maps. When we were satisfied that the numbers were correct, Mr. Nichols gave the orders, the sails were set, and the man at the wheel steered in the new direction.

We limp along, hampered by the fact that in place of the foremast has been rigged a timber far shorter than needed. The men *hung from it a gaff-rigged sail that takes the wind, but adds little to the speed the Boreas could attain. It will be, I determined, at least a week before we regain the longitude and latitude of our proper course. After that, it should be reasonably easy to stay that course.*

But given the plodding rate at which we can make headway, it will be at least four weeks before we come into San Francisco harbor, a month before Madras and Mr. Treat can be seen by doctors—provided, of course, they survive that long. But, no, I will not allow myself that terrible thought, for it drags with it a darkness that fills me with dread and a panic the luxury of which I cannot afford.

On the fourth day, as we tried to regain our former course, Madras opened his eyes for a moment. He looked at me without recognition, but I took the opportunity to spoon into him a liberal dose of laudanum, which I knew he needed to assuage the pain of his wounds. He swallowed it, and I managed to get a few spoons of broth into him, too.

Mr. Treat continued very bad, not sensible enough to take more than a few drops of water. I knew that dehydration had already set in, and he grew thinner. Miraculously, neither his wounds nor Madras's show signs of infection. Lewis and I work diligently to keep it that way, sterilizing in a steam kettle Oyster rigged for the purpose the scissors and sugar tongs with which we cut away and handle the dressings we change each day. We scrub our hands with hot water and dip them in spirits to further purify them.

On the fifth day, Mr. Treat spoke, though he did not open his eyes. He said, "Water." I held an invalid feeder to his lips from which he sipped water that contained drops of laudanum that would ease his pain, which must have been considerable.

In the ensuing days, I used laudanum as liberally as I dared, knowing full well its addictive properties. But I wanted to lessen the men's suffering, to keep them as quiet as possible, yet leave small windows of time in the day when they could be given food and water.

Meanwhile, during those five days, we fought to regain our course. Contrary winds buffeted us and impeded our progress. Clouds made it impossible for me to take the sun at noon. The crew watched me with a strange attitude that was both respectfully cool and hotly suspicious. When it was necessary for me to appear on deck, I kept my time there as brief as possible. Mr. Nichols always accompanied me, writing down the coordinates I gave him, making a pretense of doing calculations. In truth, he was quick to learn and had a head for mathematics that was greater than my own. I knew that with the proper instruction and study, he would learn the navigator's craft and rise to first mate and, eventually, captain. But those were fleeting thoughts, for the bulk of my energy was taken with nursing Madras and Mr. Treat.

In my few spare moments, I attempt to ease my mind by re-reading the letters I have received from home. Patsy and the Mitchells have written faithfully, giving me news and tying me to the pleasant days of Searsport. Patsy hints that she expects to be engaged by the time Madras and I return home. Lily Griffin and Mindoro Matthews were married in September. Patsy and Hugh stood up with them.

Letters from the Misses Merrithew detail the slow turn of the seasons at Stockton Springs. Strawberries, they wrote, were excellent this year, and they have put up ever so many jars of jam.

Mother and Father write that they plan to arrive home for good in the spring. Father says that it is time he tried dry land, but has not yet decided exactly what he might turn his hand to once he comes alongshore.

The letter I received from Grand Fan the day before we sailed said that Ellis Harding's wife had died, and that she had not seen him for weeks. He has gone to visit his daughter in New Hampshire and plans to stay there indefinitely.

Mrs. Maude and Doctor Sam write of outings they took in the
Zephyr during the summer, of the pumpkins they planted, and
how Mrs. Maude roasted the seeds and offered them for sale, with
great success, at a store in Stockton Springs. Twice they were called to
deliver babies in town, and once to mend the broken leg of a child
who fell from a haymow.

By the seventh day after the terrible storm, Madras stirred in a
way that he had not done previously, and I was obliged to ask
Lewis to secure him to the bunk with bands of cloth I cut from a
sheet to prevent movement of his head and leg.

Knowing that both men were in danger of becoming addicted to
laudanum, I eased back gradually on the doses until they received
only several drops per day. I had no idea whether or not this was
enough to ease their pain, but they slept on, stirring only when
Lewis and I changed dressings, put clean sheets under them, washed
them, and tended their personal needs.

Each day, I gave a report on their progress to Mr. Nichols,
which he conveyed to the crew.

On the eighth day I woke, as usual, from a fitful sleep when
the morning light sifted through the transom. I had a terrible crick
in my neck. My unborn child seemed to be dancing a jig against my
backbone. I felt the keenest sense of despair, fearing as I had not
before, that neither Madras, nor, indeed, Mr. Treat, were likely to
come to their senses. I did not want to be limping through the Pacific
Ocean on a course that might, or might not, be accurate enough to
carry us to San Francisco. I started to cry, and I felt my melancholy
take hold. It was then that I heard what I had been longing for
even more than home.

"M." It was hardly a whisper. But it was Madras, and his eyes
were open. His lips struggled to shape another word, but could not. I
took his hand and held it against my heart.

*"Squeeze my hand if you hear and understand me, Madras," I
said. His fingers moved; the motion was not strong, but clearly he
understood. "You have been hurt, my love, more than a week ago in a
terrible storm. Do you remember?" His fingers did not squeeze mine.
"You have been unconscious. Mr. Treat is hurt, too, but he is gaining, I
think." The expression on Madras's face grew agitated and he drew in
a sharp breath. "You mustn't worry, Madras. Mr. Nichols is in charge. I
have been taking the sun and I believe we are on course. And heaven
willing, within the month we will be in San Francisco." He relaxed his
fingers then, and his hand slid to the mound of my belly. "All is well,
Madras." And he lapsed into what seemed to me a natural sleep.*

*Mr. Treat was more coherent that morning, too, though terribly
weak. I asked for a dish of oatmeal, which I thinned with water,
sweetened with molasses, and fed to him. I asked if his pain was at
ebb tide or high tide. "Rising," he answered, and I saw the suffering
in his eyes, but it was more than two hours later before I dared give
him a tiny dose of laudanum. After that, he slept the rest of the day,
as did Madras.*

*That day the clouds lifted, and when I took the sun and made
the calculations, I saw that we were on course.*

*There was little time to do much else than care for the injured
men, take the sun, reread the old letters, and write my log, which I did
in odd moments during the day when Lewis needed to be in the galley helping Oyster Duncan, or in the evening when it was my
"watch" with Madras and Mr. Treat. Lewis relieves me at midnight
and I sleep until dawn. He helps with caring for the invalids, sleeps a
few hours, carries out his duties in the galley, and returns at mid-after-
noon. The routine we have established propels us through the day.*

Broken as the Boreas *is, her repairs hold up, and Mr. Nichols
sees no reason why the jury-rigged sail and mast should not get us to
our destination. "I've seen worse," he said, but did not elaborate.*

This noon, as I was taking the sun, I estimated that we were at least halfway to San Francisco. Mr. Nichols agreed. As I readied to go below, John Bear Neptune, who is now the mate, approached Mr. Nichols. "We're shipping water, sir," he reported.

An hour later, Mr. Nichols came below to share the details of the situation with me.

"Those weak seams have opened more. We're shipping quite a bit of water," he said, a concerned look passing across his face. "The pumps can handle it for now, but there's no knowing if those seams will hold. Repairs are being done. I've assigned men to oversee the job. If the pumps can't keep up, or the seams give way again, they'll sing out. Then it would be weeks before we arrive in port. Can the captain and Mr. Treat stand that?"

I glanced at Madras and the mate. Both were sleeping. "They can stand slow progress better than they could stand being removed to lifeboats and cast away in the middle of the Pacific Ocean," I said, making it clear to him that I understood the extent of this new danger.

"And if it comes to that?"

"Then we'll do what we must, Mr. Nichols, and do it as well and as bravely as we can."

He nodded and went back to his duties.

I do not feel brave. I feel frightened and set upon by forces over which I have no control. So much has happened in these last few months that I cannot yet incorporate it into my sense of self, my sense of the world as I understand it. I am no longer the carefree girl who sailed away with the handsome captain. I am wife, nurse, soon-to-be mother, and in charge of, to a very great degree, the fate of the lives aboard this ship, especially for the father of my child and Mr. Treat. It weighs upon me.

We have not yet spoken any ships. This troubles me, for it suggests that I have miscalculated our course. If we were on course, surely by now we would have crossed paths with other ships. But we have not. I spoke to Mr. Nichols about this yesterday, but he was not unduly worried. Ships may have passed in the night, he said. But I do not think so. The night watch would have reported lights if another ship had passed our way. I must check the coordinates and go over the mathematics again.

Another week has passed. We are still shipping water, but the repairs are holding. Our progress has slowed even more, however, and Captain—I must remember to call him that—Nichols worries that our supply of water will run low. I have used a great deal more from the rain barrels than I ought in order to keep Madras and Mr. Treat clean and comfortable. But we are not in such dire straits that we must ration water.

Madras is increasingly coherent and awake, though still weak. Mr. Treat gains each day, too, but is still too weak to sit up. He too sleeps less. Both men are stoic, but I know they suffer.

A few days ago, Asa Savage, one of the crew, spoke to Oyster about talk that was going on in the forecastle. Apparently much of the talk is about the ineptitude of Captain Nichols, and the fact that he is nothing more than a "petticoat sailor," meaning, of course, that he takes his orders from me. Oyster conveyed this intelligence to Captain Nichols and he told me.

"Do you think this is a prelude to mutiny?" I asked.

"Could be," Captain Nichols replied. "But it may only be that they are jittery, and want the voyage to be over and done. I think we must be on our guard, and if any man behaves in any way that suggests his unwillingness to go along with things as they are, then he must be made to understand it will not be tolerated."

We did not think it wise for me to address them again, or indeed, to show myself on deck any more than was absolutely necessary.

I kept my fears to myself as best I could, but Madras, as he
gained strength, sensed my unease.

"I'm still the captain of this ship," he said one morning in a tone
that surprised me. Until that moment he had been patient, and willing
to rest and recover. But now he seemed restless and unable to lie still.

"No, you are not," I said firmly, "not until your bones are
healed." And, heaven help me, I increased his dose of laudanum.
Not by much, but enough to keep him quiet.

The mutterings in the forecastle continued until one day Brian
Magee gained the support of six other men. They confronted other
members of the crew, demanding that they fall in with a plan to
take control of the Boreas. But Asa Savage went immediately to
Captain Nichols. When Mr. Magee came to take his watch at the
wheel, Mr. Neptune and Mr. DuPere seized him. There was a scuf-
fle, Mr. Magee calling for his cohorts, who seemed unwilling to come
to his aid. Mr. Magee was taken below and locked up. The other
men, lacking a leader, saw no more need to challenge the powers
that be, and went about their duties.

"They were ashamed of themselves, I think," Captain Nichols
told me later. As for Mr. Magee, he has a reputation for surliness
that even Madras has remarked upon, though no one thought that
the man had it in him to foment a mutiny—for that is what it was,
at least in intent, if not in actual practice.

I don't know how much more drama and worry I can take. I
am tired of being brave, if indeed, that is even the right word. I am
tired of the endless work and tired of the anxiety and tired of the
cursed snail's pace of the Boreas. But I must not give in to despair.
Madras and Mr. Treat are mending. The mutiny did not occur.
Captain Nichols is proving his worth. And if our calculations are
correct, we are within two weeks of San Francisco. The mere thought
of setting foot on terra firma floods me with a sense of relief, and it's
as if I had within my grasp the Holy Grail.

Part 5
Alongshore Again

1.

Even before the *Boreas* was within sight of land, M and the ship's crew knew it was near. The birds told them so; gulls and terns wheeled in the sky. M and Lex Nichols pored over their calculations and felt certain that when they sighted land, they would be right where they wanted to be—or close enough. The mood on the ship became lighter and the hands worked more diligently. Even Oyster Duncan saw fit to smile.

It was Christmas morning when they saw the first green face of land, and spilling across it, the houses and buildings of San Francisco. M stood at the rail gazing shoreward, her thoughts darting and tumbling. Relief washed over her in waves. Doctors would come to attend Madras and Mr. Treat. She would send a telegram to Grand Fan and Isaiah Mitchell. She would be able to sink into a tub of hot bathwater in a hotel room that did not heel over or move under her feet. She would sleep and sleep and sleep. She felt her backbone sag, as if suddenly the weight of all that had been hers to carry had become too great a burden. But she drew a deep breath, squared her shoulders, and lifted her head. It was Christmas Day. They had been given the gift of safe passage and arrival, and she was grateful for it.

The *Boreas* was still miles from the harbor when a steam launch approached and a pilot came aboard. He conferred with Nichols, then went below to meet with Madras and M. He sized up the situation, brought the *Boreas* to her mooring, and made his report. That report was soon the talk of San Francisco, and it wasn't long before reporters got wind of the story. Tall headlines marched across the evening edition of *The Chronicle:* MUTINY ON THE HIGH SEAS; COURAGEOUS CAPTAIN'S WIFE CHARTS COURSE ACROSS PACIFIC; SEA-FARING WIFE BECOMES ANGEL OF MERCY. The details of the story were sparse and based solely on what the pilot had reported.

M stared at the words, not knowing whether to laugh or cry, aghast at the publicity. It had not occurred to her that their story would become public. She and Nichols had merely told the truth, which both felt they were obligated to do. What she had done, while not routine, was not unusual. She knew the story of *Neptune's Car*, the ship navigated safely from the rounding of the Horn to San Francisco, by the captain's wife, Mary Patten, in 1856. But it had never entered M's mind to compare herself to Mary Patten, who also had been expecting a child. Or to any of the other navigating women she had heard stories about—not even the Havener sisters.

As the furor of a sensational news story brewed, the harbormaster sent Dr. Charles Barrett to attend Madras and Lancaster. Barrett was a small, compact man with dark hair cut close to his head. His hands were finely made, his nails very clean. He was known for his expertise with broken bones. He was a calm, thorough man, and M trusted him immediately.

"I did the best I could," she said as Barrett lifted a dressing, examined splints, and assessed the situation.

"It's almost miraculous that there's no infection," Dr. Barrett said. "But both men must be hospitalized until I can be certain no surgery is needed. The broken bones need to be in plaster casts. I want them moved within the hour. I'll arrange it."

Barrett also sent Dr. Matilda Drew to attend M. When M expressed her surprise at being attended by a woman doctor, Dr. Drew explained that her father was a doctor, and that after learning what she could from him, she had studied at the Women's Medical College of the New York Infirmary founded by Dr. Elizabeth Blackwell in 1868. Dr. Blackwell had been the first women to receive a medical degree in the United States in 1849.

Mrs. Maude would be so proud, M, thought.

"Clearly," Dr. Drew told M, "you are healthy as a horse in spite of all you've been through. But you are exhausted, and I prescribe a week in bed and plenty of fruit to eat."

Before the day was over M found herself tucked up in a boardinghouse a few streets beyond the harbor area. Mrs. Rebecca Goodwin, the owner, who knew a good story when she heard one, asked M all kinds of questions, enjoyed the tale immensely, offered motherly sympathy, and kept her mouth shut. She assisted M in sending telegrams to Fort Point and Searsport. She mailed the letters M wrote. She discussed train schedules and helped M form a plan for coast-to-coast travel by rail; the transcontinental railroad had been completed within the last several years. She even called in a dressmaker to alter M's clothing to fit her expanding figure.

Within hours after the *Boreas* had docked, reporters knocked at Mrs. Goodwin's door, asking to speak with M. Mrs. Goodwin sent them packing. When they failed to gain access to M, they frequented the hospital, waylaying Dr. Barrett as he made his rounds. They swarmed around the *Boreas*, too, but Lex Nichols gave no details except to confirm that yes, there had been a terrible storm at sea that had crippled the ship, injured the captain, and slowed their progress. He refused to discuss the mutinous acts of Brian Magee, who was now in jail awaiting the pleasure of the courts. He said nothing about the fact that it was M who had navigated the *Boreas* safely to harbor.

To their credit, Oyster Duncan, Lewis Andrews, John Bear Neptune, and Marcel DuPere also kept their own counsel and gave no details. But other members of the crew were more than happy, for the price of several pitchers of beer, to dish out all the details it was the reporters' job to get. And get it they did.

Each day some new headline blazed across the front page of the newspapers. Brian Magee told his story in dramatic detail, making himself out to be not a villain but a hero whose sole intent had been the safety of the ship and those aboard her.

To a man, even the ones who had been drawn into Brian Magee's point of view and supported his actions, all on board praised the "old man's wife" for her bravery in binding up the wounds of the injured. Several surmised that it was she who had done the navigating and not Mr. Nichols, but they didn't know for sure. That tidbit took the reporters a while to confirm, but when they did, the story became even more sensational.

"Looks like you're a heroine," Mrs. Goodwin commented as she laid a copy of *The Chronicle* on M's lap.

"More like a wife who had no idea what she was getting herself into when she went to sea," M said a bit sourly. She did not want publicity and attention. She wanted Madras well again, and she wanted to go home.

Meanwhile, as M's exploits were delineated in the newspapers, M received replies to her telegrams. Her grandmother, Dr. Sam, and Mrs. Maude wanted to know if they should take the next train headed in the general direction of the Far West. Isaiah and Zulema Mitchell telegraphed the same question. M responded with reassurances and asked them to await further details of her plans to travel home. To spare them additional worry, she did not mention the fact that she was expecting a child.

Going home depended, of course, on how quickly Madras would be well enough to travel. Dr. Barrett thought another two months of recovery was in order. Although Madras's leg was healing well, the head wound had left him with diminished vision in one eye and a weakness in one arm. The doctor said Madras would have a limp once he had regained his ability to walk. He did not recommend that Madras return to sea. M received that news with great dismay, knowing that it would break Madras's heart.

M also disliked the thought of staying in San Francisco for another eight weeks. She was in her fifth month of pregnancy, if she had calculated correctly, based on the fact that she believed she had become pregnant sometime in September. It would take a month of slow travel to get home to Maine. By then—counting the two months Madras would spend recuperating, and a month of travel—she'd be close to her eighth month, perhaps a bit beyond. By then the rigors of travel might well be beyond her.

"You mustn't fret so, Mrs. Mitchell," Rebecca Goodwin said as she sat knitting socks. "You're a strong, hardy girl. Why, when my mother came to the West back in 1848, she walked across the prairies of Nebraska while expecting my brother, Seth, and thought nothing of it. She walked ten miles just hours before he was born. She gave birth in a covered wagon with only me and my father to help."

Dr. Matilda Drew said much the same thing. "You are healthy, Mrs. Mitchell, and it follows that your unborn child is, too. Traveling by train is not as uncomfortable as it used to be, and it's also much faster than it was. I see no reason why you should not attempt it when the time comes."

"But the snow in the mountains," M said. "Won't the tracks be impassable?"

"Perhaps," Matilda said. "But I am told that plows of immense size and large crews of men with shovels manage to keep the passes open. We live in an age of transportation marvels, Mrs. Mitchell. I'll make inquiries." Relieved to know that she had friends to aid her in formulating plans to start for home, M gave herself up to the kind care of Mrs. Goodwin and Dr. Drew.

Once this problem was solved, she set her mind to another. Someone had to sail the *Boreas* back to Searsport. She went to the hospital to visit Madras to discuss it with him. She found him getting about in his wheelchair, as he was not yet able to bear weight on his injured leg, which was encased from thigh to foot in plaster. The head wound had left a thin, red scar above his left eye. But he was in good spirits and more than able to discuss the problem of what to do with his ship.

"We'll engage a captain," Madras said. "I'll recommend Mr.
Nichols, Mr. Neptune, and Mr. DuPere as officers, and Lewis
Andrews and Oyster Duncan for the galley." He saw no point in
making a fuss about the fact that he was not well enough to make
the ocean voyage himself. He understood how close he had come
to death, how lucky he was to still have his mental faculties and
the surety that he would walk again. "It will be hard to bear, M,
being a landlubber, but many a man before me has crossed this
same great divide, so it isn't as if I haven't had the lesson from better men than I."

"I am greatly relieved to hear it, Madras," M said, taking his
hand and pressing it to her cheek.

Madras advertised in *The Chronicle*, and the day the advertise-
ment appeared, a captain, a Maine man no less, from Boothbay
Harbor, applied for and was accepted for the position. The *Boreas*
was even to have another cargo—hides from the many steers
raised in the vicinity of San Francisco. Also aboard would be several paying passengers who wanted to go to points in Chile and
Brazil. By the end of the month, the *Boreas* had stepped a new
mast, other repairs had been made, and she had gone to sea.

Lancaster Treat also made headway in those weeks, but it
would be a long time before he fully recovered from his injuries.
He would not be an invalid, but he would need someone to look
after him for many weeks to come. M notified his sister in Old
Town, and she telegraphed that she was more than willing to take
her brother in. She had a big house and several strong sons to help.

With her immediate problems solved, and Madras and
Lancaster improving in health each day, M refined her plans to
begin the long journey home.

M's Log—March 1873

*How odd it is to be here in San Francisco. It's as if I embarked
on this journey as one person and have arrived on the other side of
the United States as someone else entirely. I cannot say precisely
how it is that I have changed or become other than I was. But this I
know: I am less inclined to fight what I cannot change, less likely to
fall down the dark slide of melancholy when the tides of life dash
me against the rocks.*

*Given the fact that Madras may never go to sea again, it stands
to reason that I will not either, unless we take a voyage for the fun of
it when our children are grown and we want a change of scene. I
have thought much of that these past mornings while I have lain in
bed. I have concluded that I will not mind. I have had my adventure, and except for a few very unpleasant parts of it—like rounding
the Horn, my near drowning in Hawaii, and the storm that blew
away the mast—I have enjoyed every second of it. The experience
has seasoned me in ways that will surprise Grand Fan, Mrs. Maude,
Dr. Sam, and my parents. From now on, I will be content to sail the
Zephyr around the bay on fine summer afternoons.*

*Still, I am not all that brave, and I want to be at home with
my people when my child is born. I am not at all plucky about giving birth. Mrs. Maude will be there to help me, of course, but it will
hurt a great deal. And even though much more is known about giving birth than when Grand Fan gave birth to my mother, it is still
a dangerous time for mother and child.*

*Mrs. Goodwin, who is the dearest soul, says I must not think
of such things. I must think of planning the journey by train, first to
Omaha, then to New York, and finally, to Boston, where we will
take a steamer to Searsport. Madras agrees that this is the best
course of action.*

Matilda tells me that snowfall in the mountains this year has not been nearly as heavy as in other years, and that the mountain passes are expected to be open. That, of course, can change before we are ready to depart, but I feel certain that all will be well, for somewhere in Hawaii, kind people are singing us safely home.

The child rolls and taps a hand or foot against my belly. It swims in its own small sea, sailing toward the light and air of life. And I . . . I curl into the cocoon of this room, grateful for the kindness of strangers and the good fortune that has brought us safely home from the sea.

2.

After several weeks of slow travel through Nevada, through the snow-shrouded mountains and passes that were barely wide enough to let the train pass, and across Wyoming and the high plains of Nebraska, the train rolled into the station at Omaha. The entire way, whenever they passed through or stopped at even the smallest town, people turned out for a glimpse of "the sea captain's wife," as the press had dubbed M. The attention embarrassed her, and she stayed hidden from view as much as possible.

Matilda Drew had anticipated such attention, however, and, wearing a veil and waving from the window of the train coach, often stood in for M. She had insisted that she accompany M, Madras, and Lancaster on their journey. She had family in Omaha whom she had not visited in several years and gave that as her excuse. But M suspected there was more to it than that; she was convinced that a certain level of affection had begun to bloom between Matilda and Lancaster.

Matilda proved invaluable on the trip. She saw to it that Madras and Lancaster were comfortable, and made certain that M ate properly and rested. She also served as go-between when local reporters came snooping around, asking questions. She handled every situation with polite but firm resolve, refusing to let the reporters speak to anyone.

But nothing had prepared M, Matilda, and the others for the reception awaiting them as the train hissed to a stop in Omaha. A band played "Anchors Aweigh," and children waved small American flags. Women tossed single flowers at the train car as M stared out the window in astonishment. A cadre of reporters, pencils and pads in hand, milled around, looking for a way to gain access to the celebrity—albeit, one they had created out of whole cloth.

"Dear me," Matilda said, settling her chip hat more firmly on the back of her head and buttoning her leather gloves. "This won't do." Swiftly, her skirt hem snapping, she stepped to the doors at the front and back of the car, slid home lock bolts, and took charge. The other passengers in the car sat frozen in their seats, uncertain what to do. "Ladies and gentlemen, as you can see, we are the cause of all this commotion," she said. "I suggest that you wait patiently until someone from the railroad or the police arrive to take this situation in hand."

Madras reached for M's hand. "That's the last time I teach you to navigate," he said in her ear, laughing.

"Really, Madras, I had no idea," M replied, so amazed by the to-do she could hardly take it in.

"Looks to me like you've become a notorious woman, my dear," he whispered, grinning at her. "Must run in the family." M stared at him in mock outrage, and whacked him gently on the arm.

"I have not! All I did was get us ashore in one piece. Masters of ships do that every day. Why, Father is doing that at this very moment."

"But masters of ships, M, my darling, are never women."

"Well, maybe they should be." She laughed, too. "Look, rein-
forcements have arrived."

A contingent of policemen on foot, and what appeared to be
several cavalry officers in blue uniforms and mounted on shiny
black horses, caused the crowd to part. The policemen ranged
along the platform holding the crowd at a proper distance. The
military men rode back and forth along the track. M had no idea
what it was they were doing or why their presence was needed.

"Rescue, at last," Matilda said. She turned from the window
and said to the others in the car, "I do apologize for the delay."
She unbolted one of the doors and several policemen entered.
They escorted the other passengers out of the car, and, shortly
afterward, assisted M and her entourage down the steps to the
platform. As M emerged, the crowd applauded and cheered.
"Speech, speech," someone yelled.

"I think you should say something," Matilda whispered. "It
might keep the reporters happy for a while."

M gripped Madras's hand and looked at the crowd. Almost
instantly a hush descended.

"Thank you for this kind welcome, ladies and gentlemen, but
I am no heroine. It is my husband, Madras Mitchell, who is the
hero of this situation. For it is he and his first mates, Mr. Lancaster
Treat and Mr. Lex Nichols, who risked their lives, not only in the
storm, but in the many storms that seamen everywhere endure on
a regular basis in order to do their work. Cheer them, and the
crew of our ship, not me, for they and all seamen are the true
heroes of the deep."

"How about a word from the captain?" a reporter called out.

M stepped back from Madras to let him be the center of attention. Madras, sitting erect in his wheelchair, straightened his spine
and looked directly at the reporters. "None of us are heroes, sir.
Where we come from, the grand State of Maine, men and women

go to sea in ships every day. We raise our families at sea. Our wives have traveled to ports all over the world, and in doing so, they learn the workings of a ship. What is remarkable about my wife and other women who sail the world with their husbands is their intelligence, their sense of adventure, and their common sense. Enough said."

The crowd cheered loudly, and the band struck up another maritime tune. M and Madras were put into one closed carriage, and Matilda and Lancaster went in another. The carriages, escorted by the officers on horseback, pulled away from the station and headed for the hotel.

3.

It was the same at each stop as they made their way east, through Chicago, Detroit, Buffalo, and Syracuse. Crowds assembled at every station. Newspaper reporters elbowed their way through the crowds, trying to get as close as possible to M and Madras. One newspaper published a map of the train's journey, describing many of the stops in detail. Sketch artists made hasty drawings of M, Madras, and Lancaster, and their likenesses appeared in newspapers across America. Fortunately, M was able to hide her impending motherhood from the public eye by wearing a loose black cloak.

At last, after a month of traveling, their party—including Matilda, who had decided to continue along to Maine with them—arrived in Boston. The commotion of publicity was so overwhelming that M and her party kept to their rooms in the hotel as they rested and made preparations to take the Boston boat Down East to Searsport.

"But not one of us is going to stir until we have rested for a week at least," Matilda declared. She kept the press at bay, but by this time, reporters and editors had found another angle—the history of the *Boreas* and her voyages, and keeping track of the current progress the *Boreas* made as she plied her way through the Pacific, headed for a passage around the Horn.

Each day Matilda brought them the shipping news, and they scanned the pages eagerly, elated when they found an item reporting that another ship had spoke the *Boreas* or reported sighting her off the coast of Chile. It disappointed them when no news of the *Boreas* appeared.

"It's only a matter of time," M said one morning as she and Madras ate breakfast in their room. She rattled the newspaper roughly, folding it into a more manageable size.

"What do you mean, M?" Madras asked.

M sighed heavily. "Grand Fan. It's only a matter of time before our story leads to her story, and, worse, your story—in Hawaii."

Madras grew silent a moment. "Yes, I've thought of that. I suppose it's inevitable."

"It's not something either of us could have foreseen, Madras. I only did my duty toward you and the *Boreas*, as any wife would do."

"Well, there's no point in worrying about it now, M. Your grandmother is tough as nails. She'll continue to paddle her own canoe. As for my parents, they stick together no matter what."

"But your grandmother, Madras."

"Ah, yes . . . now that's entirely a horse of a different color."

"There's nothing she can do to us anymore, when you think of it. You are done going to sea, we're married, and there's no way she can deprive you of employment in your family's shipping firm."

"But she can raise holy hell and make things miserable for the rest of us until the day she dies."

"Do you think she will?"

"Hard to say. Only Grandmother knows for sure what she will or will not do."

"It seems to me, Madras, that we should not anticipate anything untoward on your grandmother's part. I believe that she is good at heart, and that when she blows and blusters as she did before we were married, it's because she has the best interests of those she loves in mind."

"As long as it suits her purpose, and as long as she gets her own way."

M's Log—April 1873

We keep holding our breath, convinced each morning that The Globe *or one of the other newspapers will unearth Grand Fan's story and my connection to her, and that it will be splashed all over the front page. This fear is the only thing that has marred my joy at being in New England again. Sometimes, I think it would be easier if I just consented to an interview, to tell my story, such as it is, or that Madras should speak to the press and tell his story. Then they would leave us alone, and the reporters would hurry away to some new sensational story of mayhem, murder, or disaster.*

We have telegraphed everyone at home that we will arrive in Searsport next week. They will all be there—Grand Fan, Mrs. Maude, Dr. Sam, the Misses Merrithew, the Mitchells, the Griffin girls, everyone. They will rally around us, and we will be folded into their care. How amazed they will be when they see that I am with child and that I am so near my time.

I have had a letter from Mother that she and Father will arrive in Portland next month and will come immediately to Searsport. They will go to sea no more. Father still has property in Bangor, which many years ago was his foster mother Hannah Bailey's boardinghouse. They have decided to live there instead of at Belfast. Mother says Father has made prudent investments so they will not starve, and he expects to find work at a shipping firm, although Mother says he has a secret desire to teach the mathematics of navigation to boys like Gordon Mitchell, who have a yen to go to sea.

I don't know what we would have done without Matilda. She has seen to everything—tickets for the boat home, a new dress for me to accommodate my growing girth, barring reporters from our door, and tending Lancaster Treat. Mr. Treat, I am glad to say, continues to improve. I think it has as much to do with his regard for Matilda as it does to the care she gives him. I see the look in his eyes whenever she is around, and she looks back at him in the same warm way. I have said nothing to her, but I will not be surprised if she decides to set up shop in Old Town to be near him, and that a wedding will be announced before the year is out.

I have done nothing this entire week but lay about in bed. I grow heavier with child each passing minute, I swear. Matilda says resting this week will prepare me for the trip Down East and for the excitement of arriving at home. Madras says I am more beautiful now than ever I was. I tell him I am no longer his mermaid, more like his own special whale, and he laughs. It is good to make Madras laugh.

4.

The steamship *Bangor* approached the dock at Searsport, its paddlewheel coming to a sudden halt as it slid to its mooring. A crowd had gathered at the pier. A band was playing and the ladies waved white handkerchiefs.

"I think we must be home at last," Madras said to M, Matilda, and Lancaster.

"I was so hoping to avoid all this," M whispered, glad she was enveloped in her black cloak to hide her expanded waistline. She noted that several closed carriages waited nearby. Without doubt, someone in the family had anticipated the excitement and made a plan to whisk them away.

"I think the least we can do is stand at the rail and wave to them, Madras. But don't you dare think that I will step out into their midst."

"No need to, Mrs. Mitchell," the steamboat captain said. "You can rest in the saloon and greet your relatives there. No one will be allowed aboard but your family, until you are safely away. By that time the crowd will grow bored and leave." He escorted them to the boat's "parlor," where the furnishings were upholstered in red plush.

They did not have to wait long.

Fanny burst through the door with Maude, Sam, the Mitchell family, and the Misses Merrithew close at her heels. The Mitchells grabbed Madras, enveloping him in handshakes and fond embraces. Fanny reached for M and pressed her closely into her arms. Her eyes widened as she felt the unaccustomed girth of M's body. She took an abrupt step back, drew aside the cloak enough to confirm what she already knew. She tried to shape words, but her mouth merely hung open for a second before she closed it.

"My dear girl," Maude said. "Why ever didn't you tell us? Never mind, I already know. You didn't want us to worry."

"Well, what do you know," Sam said. "Another young one to show the ropes of sailing the *Zephyr*."

M looked around at the smiling, joyous faces. They hadn't changed—but something had, and it took her a moment to realize what it was. She was the one who had changed. She had grown up. She saw that realization register in their faces, and saw, too, that they regarded her with deeper affection and a respect that granted her, in their eyes, this new mantel of adulthood.

Augusta Mitchell stepped out of the swirl of relatives. She was dressed in black and leaned on the ebony cane with the silver knob.

"Home at last, and in one piece. Not the first time a Searsport woman has had to navigate a ship to port. Won't be the last."

"Did you navigate your husband's ship, Mrs. Mitchell?" M asked.

"Once or twice, in a pinch. But in my day such things were not spoken of, let alone get into the newspapers." Augusta pressed her lips together, not saying more, but making her disapproval clear.

"I did not seek . . . " M began hotly, forgetting suddenly that she was grown up now, no longer the naive girl she had been nearly a year ago, when she and Madras had married and set off on their great adventure. Madras laid a hand on her arm and she closed her mouth, knowing full well that the last thing anyone wanted on this wonderful day was to rile Old Lady Mitchell.

"Oh, dear me," one of the Misses Merrithew chimed in, "no lady ever wants to take the wheel of the captain's ship, but when it must be done, we must rise to the occasion. Don't you agree, Sister?" The other Miss Merrithew nodded her head in agreement, the little curls at the front of her head bobbing jauntily. They flanked M and Madras, as if shielding them from anything more Augusta might have the bad manners to say.

Honoria materialized out of the crush of family, pressed her tiny gloved hand to M's cheek, and murmured, "Home, my, yes, home."

When the crowd showed no signs of dispersing, Isaiah and Gordon Mitchell devised a plan to take M, Madras, Matilda, and Lancaster away by smaller boat, hardly bigger than the *Zephyr*, upriver to Abbott's Reach, where, everyone agreed, they would be safe from the commotion of the crowd and less likely to be hunted down by the press.

"We have found you a house near town," Zulema murmured in M's ear. "Not quite as near your grandmother as you might like, perhaps, but not so far that you can't visit one another, and the rest of us, easily. It will be waiting when you and Madras are ready. I have asked your grandmother to help furnish and decorate

it. She has, I find, exquisite taste. Now we must decide which
room will best accommodate our grandchild."

In the flurry of leaving, Patsy kissed M's cheek and whispered,
"Hugh Chapman and I will be married in June."

M's Log—May 1, 1873

*Home, home, home! I revel in it; I want to dance and sing and
toss my hat into the air! But I am in no condition to trip the light
fantastic, with the weight of this unborn child leaving me without a
shred of graceful movement.*

*Matilda and Lancaster have left us, going on to Old Town,
where he will reside with his sister and where she may open a medical practice. They are not officially engaged, but Matilda confided
that when Lancaster is well enough to find some sort of employment, they will marry. I had not been home more than a day before
Mrs. Maude and Dr. Sam sat me down with them to inquire after
my health and to ascertain just what is what in terms of my
approaching confinement. Mrs. Maude examined me thoroughly, and
Dr. Sam peered into my mouth, drew down the lower lid of my eye,
felt my pulse, and listened to my heart and my breathing. Neither
found anything amiss and they pronounced me healthy.*

*While Maude was mapping my belly with her small hands, the
child rolled and kicked. "Already dancing a jig," she remarked. "Is it
always this lively?"*

*"No, not always," I replied. "Sometimes it's much more active,
especially when I try to get comfortable when I settle down to sleep
at night. And sometimes it's quiet, usually when I am walking
slowly and humming to myself."*

*Maude looked at me and smiled with satisfaction. She handed
me a brown bottle. "This is a tonic," she said. "A shipboard diet is
never the best, although I am sure you ate well while you were in*

San Francisco. And I know Matilda took very good care of you. Still, it won't hurt to take a teaspoon of this once a day. It's one of my simples—rose hips and extract of kelp. Oh, my dear, it is so good to have you at home again." Dr. Sam nodded his agreement. He took one of my hands and Mrs. Maude took the other. They led me out to the piazza and sat me down in a rocking chair.

"Rest for a quarter of an hour," Dr. Sam said. "Maude and I are going to look over that patch of ground on the east side of the house where I believe your grandmother wants to put in more dahlias."

And so I sat, rocking, gazing out at the bay, taking in every nuance of the delicate color that was just beginning to creep over the countryside, for it was, indeed, May Day, precisely one year since Madras and I had married. I knew that Grand Fan was in the kitchen concocting a cake to mark the day. Madras, assisted by his brother, Gordon, had hailed the steamboat as it came past the point and gone to Searsport for the day.

Poor Tennyson, the cat, wanted so much to get into my lap, but, alas, I have no lap left.

I must have dozed, for I when I came to, I found Grand Fan sitting in a rocking chair beside me, my hand held gently in hers. She smiled at me and laid her head back against the chair. "Oh, M," she said, "what a year it has been."

I noticed that there were more lines around her eyes and mouth than had ever been there before, but she seemed as youthful as ever. She wore her hair more simply than a year ago, and I saw that she had left off the henna rinse. A streak of gray made light-colored ribbons at her temples. It was rather becoming, I thought.

"Yes," I replied. I understood then that there were many things we would never tell one another—how I had nearly drowned, or how terrified I had been rounding the Horn, or how panicked I was after the storm in the Pacific when I learned that I must navigate all hands to safety. But I knew that I would tell her of Kapiolani and

Naihe one day, after Madras had taken a stand on that subject with his grandmother and the rest of his family.

I thought it likely that there was much she would not tell me about what had transpired between her and Ellis Harding during the past year, and since his wife's death. He had gone away, first to New Hampshire to visit his younger daughter, then to Hawaii, no less, to visit his daughter, Nancy. That much I knew. But it was not the time to talk of these things. It was the time to wait for events to evolve, for the seasons to ripen and unfold, for my child to be born, and for the daily parameters of life to take shape.

5.

"Are you hoping for a boy or a girl?" Maude asked as she and M walked along the road not far from the house.

"It doesn't matter one way or the other to me, Mrs. Maude, as long as it's healthy. I think Madras has his heart set on a boy. He says if it is a boy, he wants to name it Lex Lancaster Mitchell. I have no objection to that."

"And if the baby is a girl? Have you chosen a name?"

"Yes, but I want to keep it to myself until I have seen her face—if it turns out to be a girl."

It was mid-May and the leaves only that day had unfurled to cast shade over the road. The bay was deep blue under a powder-blue sky. The tide was running full, and everything in M's world seemed poised on the brink of expanding, opening up, growing green with promise.

"I don't think it will be much longer now, M. The child has dropped the last day or so. I'm thinking by the end of the week, or sooner."

M said nothing and reached for Maude's hand, holding on tight. "A girl can't have too many mothers, or grandmothers. Or fathers and grandfathers, for that matter."

"Do you include old Mrs. Mitchell in that equation, M?" Maude asked, with a mischievous grin on her face.

"I haven't decided yet."

M passed the next few days in a haze of comfort, waited on by all her family, and her husband's family. A stream of visitors arrived at the door, each bearing something for the expected baby. The Misses Merrithew paid a call and brought with them a little white baby dress beautifully embroidered in white. Patsy and Zulema brought a large basket decked out like a May basket, filled with diapers, tiny shirts, and flannel blankets.

The next afternoon, Augusta Mitchell arrived in a carriage driven by a hired man. She was dressed in mauve and wore a plumed hat with a wide brim, which made her look all the more like Queen Victoria. She offered no smile of greeting.

M watched the old lady approach with a sense of dread. She was sitting in a rocker on the piazza. Getting into the chair had been something of a task, and getting out of it to stand was impossible without a strong arm to assist her. Her grandmother and the Webbers were somewhere in the house, busy with the tasks of the day.

"Mrs. Mitchell," M called out in greeting. "Forgive me if I do not rise."

"Quite," Augusta said, as the driver assisted her from the carriage and then drove the vehicle to a tree, where he and the horse could wait in the shade. Augusta came up the piazza steps carrying her ebony cane, not leaning upon it. Yet, she seemed frail in a way M had not anticipated. Perhaps it was a trick of the light, or that the color of Augusta's dress did not suit her complexion. M found it impossible to gauge Augusta's mood. What did it matter anyway?

"I think Grand Fan and the Webbers are not far away. I can call them . . ."

"That won't be necessary, Mrs. Mitchell. It's you I have come to see." Augusta handed M a small black velvet box. In it was a carved ivory circle with a silver bell hanging from it, a rattle for the expected baby. "It belonged to my daughter, Isabelle, who did not live beyond her third birthday."

M fingered the rattle. The little bell tinkled sweetly. "Thank you," she said, touched by the gift, knowing that it was a great honor.

"Your time is near."

"Yes, Mrs. Maude thinks it will be any moment now."

"I understand you caused quite a stir in Honolulu."

"No, Mrs. Mitchell, it was you who caused the stir."

Augusta's eyes grew icy as she regarded M.

"For which I thank you, Mrs. Mitchell," M continued. "For if the incident with the kapa cloth had not taken place, then Madras and I might never have gotten things out into the open. You see, Mrs. Mitchell, you are already a great-grandmother. His name is Naihe, and he is about ten years old. And one day he will come here to visit us. I will see to that. I really don't know why, of all the rewards you might have given me for my duty to you, that you gave me the kapa cloth. I would like to know."

Augusta looked down at her hands, clad in black-lace mitts. "I gave it to you because it once belonged to a family of spirited, strong women who were being exploited in the worst possible way. Their very way of life was being stolen from them. And I was as much to blame for that as anyone, simply because I had set foot on their shores. I gave you the kapa cloth because I knew you were a worthy recipient. That is all."

"Then you knew nothing of Madras and Kapiolani?"

"Oh, I knew there had been mischief. And I suspected that there had been a child. But Isaiah was very close-mouthed about it, and I never could get anything out of him. Not that I didn't try. But sometimes Isaiah can be as stubborn and determined as I am."

"Then forgive me, Mrs. Mitchell, for thinking that your motives were unkind. 'So long as we can say this is the worst.' "

"Shakespeare. I might have known you'd try to rout me with a quote I couldn't place." And in that moment, Augusta Mitchell grinned. Laughter erupted from somewhere in the most subterranean levels of M's belly, and Augusta joined in. They laughed until tears rolled down their eyes. Augusta reached for M's hand and they sat there, laughing like two fools, hands clasped, the moment so full of joyous hilarity that M thought they might never stop laughing. It was so good to laugh and laugh.

"Oh!" M exclaimed, her laughter stopping abruptly. "Oh."

Augusta rose and bent over M. "Your face has gone white as a sheet," she said. "Is it a headache?"

"No, Grandmother Mitchell. It's the baby. I think the water . . ."

Augusta turned on her heel and sailed through the screen door and into the house, calling, "Mrs. Webber, Miss Abbott, come out to the piazza at once! It's M!"

Maude took one look at M and knew the time had come. "Fanny, help me get her out of this rocking chair and into the back bedroom. Mrs. Mitchell, if you'd be so kind, Madras is in Searsport. He needs to be sent for."

"I'm on my way," Augusta said, already halfway down the piazza steps, headed for the man who had driven her to Abbott's Reach. She dispatched him to Searsport at once. She went back into the house to the kitchen where she took off her delicate mitts, reached for a big white apron, and began stoking the fire in the stove, intent on making a pot of tea and knowing that Maude would want water hot enough to infuse herbs.

"Fanny," Maude said, "Sam is somewhere outside, probably in the dahlia beds. Find him and bring him. Not that there's any hurry; you know as well as I do that a first baby doesn't come hastily into the world." With her arms around M, she steered her toward the bedroom off the kitchen.

"I don't think I can do this," M whispered after her grandmother had gone outside.

"Little late to think of that now, my dear," Maude said. "Come, I want to get you out of that wet dress and into a comfortable bed gown. You don't need to go to bed or lie down yet. I want you spry around the room until you enter the third stage of travail. It's better for you and better for the child that way. No sense in working against gravity when you can make it work for you."

By late afternoon Madras had returned, with Isaiah, Zulema, and Aunt Honoria Cobb not far behind. In the evening, the Misses Merrithew arrived bearing doughnuts and a basket of eggs. Augusta and Honoria presided in the kitchen, fixing a meal that could be eaten on the run or sitting at the table.

"It feels like old times," Maude said to M, "all the women arriving to take over the duties of the household. That's how it was in the old days. That's how women learned to bring babies safely into the world, and how they took care of one another."

Madras stepped into the bedroom on tiptoe, as if he feared something might break or flee at his approach. M was "walking through her pains," as Maude put it. M reached for Madras's hand and the strength of her grasp shocked him. "Does it hurt that much?" he asked.

"Yes," M panted, "yes, damn it, it does." But it relieved her to have him there, to have his arms around her, to have him to lean against. "Maude says this could go on all night."

Please, God, no, Madras thought. "I'm right here, M. I'll be right here every minute until the baby comes."

"That you will not, Madras Mitchell," Maude said. "You are going to leave right now. This is women's work. M has some things to learn before we can work effectively together to get this child into the world. But I will call you when her time is closer." Maude pushed Madras gently out the door.

Sam and Isaiah took Madras in hand. "We won't be wanted much around here, Madras," Sam said, "but we must stay close by in case Maude needs us for anything, or if M sends for you. I think the best thing for the three of us to do is go outdoors and pitch a few horseshoes. The women will call us when they want us."

The night wore on, and gradually M's soft moans became louder and more vocal. "I can't walk another step, Mrs. Maude," she gasped. "Let me go to the bed now."

"Indeed, I think it's time."

At midnight Maude sent for Madras. "It won't be long now— by dawn, I should think." She showed him how to rub M's back and how to keep M's gaze focused on his face when another pain struck her. "She knows you are here, Madras, but all her energy and concentration is on travail, the work of giving birth. Speak quietly and encourage her."

The Misses Merrithew had fallen asleep on sofas in the parlor. Augusta and Honoria went upstairs to sleep. Sam and Isaiah retreated to comfortable chairs in the summer kitchen. Fanny and Zulema kept a vigil in the kitchen, taking orders from Maude as the need arose. They steeped an infusion of willow bark for pain. They carried baskets of clean towels and sheets from the linen cupboard. They brewed pots of tea for Maude to sip and cups of coffee for Madras. They brought cold-water compresses for M's face and pitchers of hot water for Maude to wash her hands in.

At five o'clock in the morning, just as dawn was breaking and birds had begun to throw silvery notes of song into the sweet golden air, Maude stepped into the kitchen and summoned Fanny and Zulema.

"Support M into a sitting position," Maude instructed. Fanny and Zulema lifted M's shoulders and cradled her in their strong arms, murmuring to her, stroking her face with loving hands. "Madras, I want you here by me, just there by her knees, where M can see you and where you can gently, very gently, apply a bit of pressure to help her keep her knees apart."

Madras gazed at Maude, his face full of questions that he dared not ask. Maude nodded and smiled in reply, and he relaxed into his task.

"Big breath, M," Maude said. "Big push, big push. Breathe . . . breathe. Good. Now, rest a moment, and get ready for the next one." She slipped her hand under M's lower back and laid the other on M's belly, the better to anticipate the next contraction. "Here it comes, another one. Big breath, big push. Yes, yes. I see the baby's head. Here we go—one more push."

"You have a daughter," Maude said, laying the child on M's abdomen while she cut and tied the cord. Fanny and Zulema eased away and placed a mound of pillows under M's shoulders. Maude dipped the baby in a pan of warm water and the infant let out a wail. Maude wrapped the tiny girl in towels and handed her to Madras. Tears of relief and wonder ran down Madras's face as he leaned down to show M their child.

"All right, everyone out while I get the new mother cleaned up," Maude said, taking the infant from Madras and putting her to M's breast. "Madras, you can stay."

"What shall we name her?" Madras murmured in M's ear.

"Blythe. We'll name her Blythe Nuuanu Mitchell."

M had never forgotten the dazzling rainbows she had seen in the Nuuanu Valley when she had first arrived in Hawaii.

6.

"I might have known I'd arrive too late to be with you, M," Elizabeth Giddings said to her daughter when Blythe was a month old. "I have missed many of the important events of your life, and I deeply regret that."

"It doesn't matter, Mother. You are here now."

"And will be from now on, to such a point that you will come to wish your father and I were not around so much."

"No, Mother, not at all; I am so happy that none of us will ever have to go far away from one another for years at a time. After I came alongshore when I was a child, I learned what it meant to be raised by more than one set of loving hands. I want Blythe to know that feeling of safety and belonging, to feel at ease being passed from one set of warm arms to another. A child cannot be loved too much."

"Don't you worry that she will become spoiled with so much attention?"

"No, because in all of that attention, she will be learning who she is and what life is about. She will know the history of her family as well as the history of this place. Think of it—Maude will tell her stories of the British invading Hampden in 1814. You and Father will tell her about your adventures at sea. Blythe will even learn about roses from Aunt Honoria."

"And Augusta Mitchell? What will Blythe learn from her?"

"How to respect her elders." And they burst into laughter at the thought. But the fact was, Augusta was besotted with the child and visited as often as possible; she enjoyed spending an afternoon sitting on the piazza, rocking the baby. Fanny had accepted only a few guests that summer, and sometimes Augusta engaged in conversation with ladies from Boston and gentlemen from Portland, entertaining them with stories of her days at sea. On those evenings, M sat on the steps of the piazza with Blythe on her lap

and listened, filled with a sense of belonging to the great contin-
uum of life.

One afternoon a trio of tall, middle-aged women were spotted coming up the road that led from the dock where the Boston
boat put in each day, to take on and leave off passengers. "Can't
think who they could be," Fanny said to Maude, drawing aside the
curtain to look out the window. "I'm not expecting any guests."
She waited for a knock at the screen door before pulling off her
apron to go to the door. She greeted the visitors with a pleasant
hello and ushered them into the parlor.

"I'm sorry to say that I am not taking any more guests this
summer, ah, Miss, Mrs. . . . ."

One of the women stepped forward. She, like the other two
women, wore a white cotton dress, tucked and frilled, but in a
restrained sort of way. And, like the other two women, she wore a
braided straw hat with a wide brim, tied under her chin with pale
blue silk ribbon.

"We are the Misses Havener—China, India, and Persia."

M's Log—June 1873

*When Grand Fan, with a great air of mystery, called me down
to the parlor and ushered me into the room, I had no idea what she
wanted, but the moment I saw those three ladies, some instinct told
me who they were.*

*"We have come to pay our respects," said Miss China Havener,
who seemed to do most of the talking. I barely paid attention to
what she was saying, I was so caught up in looking at them. All
three look remarkably alike. They have oval faces, blue eyes, hair that
once must have been very blonde, but is now more of a sandy shade.
They dress alike, and wear their hair in simple coils at the nape of
the neck, and they are the same height—tall and slender. I think*

they may be a bit older than Grand Fan, but it is difficult to know. They seem ageless.

I noticed that each Miss Havener wore a bangle bracelet. Miss China's is gold, and engraved with initials. Miss India's is ivory, carved with rosettes, and Miss Persia's is silver, set with a small amethyst flanked by two tiny moonstones.

At first the conversation was general—Blythe and her health, the weather, the fact that they had taken the steamer at Brooksville earlier that day in order to visit us. They were very correct in their remarks and manners, and drank the tea Grand Fan brought in, remarking that Darjeeling is their favorite. They drink it sweetened.

When Mother and Mrs. Maude drifted into the room and were introduced, the sisters seemed quite at ease. They had, in fact, spoken the Fairmount, *once or twice, and they knew Mrs. Maude and Dr. Sam by reputation. They seem to know everyone by reputation, but have had no direct contact with anyone but their father and the crews and mates the* Empress *shipped. I wanted to ask a great many questions, but Grand Fan fixed me with a look every time I opened my mouth, and I knew that my curiosity was not to be satisfied, at least not that day.*

Finally, I could contain myself no longer. "Why are you alongshore?" I blurted out with no preamble and no manners before Grand Fan could shush me. I handed Blythe to Mother the better to concentrate on what the Havener sisters might have to say.

"Captain Havener died at sea a few weeks ago," Miss China said. "He was well past eighty."

No one knew what to say for a moment.

"Was it a sudden illness?" Maude asked.

"No," Miss Persia said. "He fell overboard in the night, and we were unable to rescue him."

"Now he sleeps in the deep," Miss China said. "And so my sisters and I must stay alongshore."

The sisters glanced at one another, a look that I could not read precisely, but I felt they were communicating without words, as if they had suddenly reached out and grasped one another's hands, something they must have done many a time as they sailed the world with their father, aboard a ship where they were the only women and had only themselves to rely upon, to speak to, to be comforted by. I think I stared because Grand Fan cleared her throat and nodded at me every so slightly.

"But where will you live?" I asked. "And why must you stay alongshore? It has been said that it is you who are masters of your ship."

"M," Grand Fan interrupted, "Miss Persia's cup needs refilling." I had stepped out of bounds.

"We have a house near Cape Rosier. Father had it built before Mother died, just before the war, 1859, 1860, I believe it was. We live there now. You see, with Father gone, we have no other family. We were born at sea, raised at sea, and always lived at sea. We hardly know what it is to come ashore, and we have no idea what it means to have relatives. Or even close friends," Miss China said.

"Our father, Captain Havener, always spoke highly of the Mitchell family," Miss Persia said. "I believe he had gammed with captains of Mitchell family ships in ports throughout the world."

"Yes," said Miss India, as Miss China and Miss Persia stopped to draw breath. "We talked it over, my sisters and I, and we decided that we must make an effort to . . . to get to know other ladies. It seemed to us that we might draw on our seafaring neighbors as a means to begin our acquaintance."

"We are quite shy, you see," said Miss Persia, "but we heard much of you and your husband while we were berthed in Hawaii, Mrs. Mitchell, and since we took it upon ourselves to crochet things for your baby, we thought introducing ourselves to you and your family might be the proper and prudent thing to do."

"I am deeply honored," I said. "And I know that all my family will be proud to make your acquaintance."

"Yes," Mother said. "We are most happy that you have called, and look forward to many more such afternoons."

The Havener sisters glanced at one another and smiled with pleasure.

"Perhaps," Grand Fan said, "you might consider staying here at Abbott's Reach next summer as my guests."

"And you must come to stay with us in September," China said warmly. "Our house is large and right near the beach."

"Yes," Miss India said. "It's a very large house. Six bedrooms upstairs and several more down, plus the parlor and the dining room and the library and the kitchen, and perhaps one or two other rooms. And a very commodious piazza, all very well done. Father wanted Mother to have the best. Mother loved beautiful things, though she was no snob, not in the least."

At that moment, Blythe stirred in her basket, where Mother had placed her after she had fallen asleep. I picked her up and deposited her in Miss India's arms. For a moment the lady seemed at a loss, but she quickly adjusted her hold on Blythe, and I saw her gaze lock onto that of my tiny daughter. After a few moments she passed Blythe to Miss China, who eventually passed her to Miss Persia. And Blythe, newborn and tiny as she is, gazed into their eyes as if she were enchanted.

Later, after the Misses Havener had boarded the steamer and returned to Cape Rosier, I told Mrs. Maude, Mother, and Grand Fan that it was as if the Three Graces had appeared, like fairy godmothers, to bless Blythe's life on Earth.

"It seems to me," Grand Fan said, very quietly, as if she too had been charmed in the sisters' presence, "they have blessed us all." I knew then that she and the Havener sisters would befriend each other in some lasting way.

*As for myself, there is something about motherhood that settles
me and makes me feel safe and confident of the future, no matter
what it brings. I had my adventure upon the seas of the world. Now
I have a new adventure upon the seas of matrimony and motherhood. I will captain those vessels as surely as Madras captained the
Boreas, as surely as Father captained the Fairmount.*

*And one last thing as I finish this entry—we have had word
that the Boreas has been sighted and will be berthed in Boston
harbor within the week. Madras travels there on the steamer tomorrow. Father and Sam will go with him.*

7.

More than a year had passed, and it was spring again.

Fanny gazed out the window of Abbott's Reach, assessing the
parameters of her world, watching the river flow and the osprey as
it wheeled over the water. It was early morning and the sun had
only just come up, spreading a soft pink glaze over the landscape.
Fanny sipped a cup of tea and wondered, not for the first time, if
she had taken leave of her senses or was merely turning the page
and moving on to another chapter in her life.

So much had changed. M and Madras lived happily in a house
on the Searsport Road where Blythe toddled, growing more
beautiful and charming each day. Madras worked in the family
shipping firm but still sailed a small boat around Searsport harbor
on fine summer days.

Elizabeth and Abner were settled in what once had been
Hannah Bailey's boardinghouse—and the first property Joshua
Stetson had owned when he first came to Bangor—and there they
took in boarders, respectable mariners and genteel ladies and gentlemen in town to attend court sessions. "I find satisfaction in

coming full circle," Abner said. He and Elizabeth made new friends and joined the Congregational church. Elizabeth involved herself in the work of the Bangor Children's Home.

Maude and Sam had sold their house and now lived with Fanny. They were still in good health, but knew the time would come when they would not be able to do for themselves. "You are our family," Maude had told Fanny.

All of them, upriver and down-, even the extended Mitchell family, including Augusta and Honoria, gathered frequently at Abbott's Reach for visits, especially during the warmer months. This day was no exception.

Fanny had not wanted any fuss, and for the most part she had gotten her way. Only M, Madras, Blythe, the Webbers, and Elizabeth and Abner would be there on this day. She had written the Havener sisters and the Misses Merrithew, telling them the news and inviting them to a Fourth of July gathering.

The house was quiet. Maude and Sam had not yet stirred.

Fanny felt oddly suspended in time, floating effortlessly between that long-ago day when she had run away with Robert Snow, thinking they'd marry and that she'd be happy forever, only to find herself shamed, alone and desperate. The river had been her road that night, and it had been her road when she had made her way to Bangor to find Joshua Stetson. It had been her road as she made her way back to Fort Point to establish herself, respectably this time, at Abbott's Reach.

And now, on this day, the river would take her away again. It seemed fitting.

She sat down at the kitchen table, her thoughts tethered to the past, catching here, snagging there—that day Mrs. Veazie had snubbed her as their carriages passed one another on State Street; the day Maude had come to help her give birth to Elizabeth at the rooming house in Portland; the day Elizabeth had stood before her, grown and begging for employment. And the night Pink Chimneys had burned, the mob's anger, how Abner had rescued her—the flame and smoke thrusting her out and away onto a new journey, which had led to this day and to yet another tributary of her life.

Ellis Harding had been gone nearly a year before he had come back to Abbott's Reach. He had spent a few months in Hawaii with his daughter, Nancy Davis. When he returned, he went back to New Hampshire to visit his daughter, Damaris, and her husband. And finally, he had gone to New York City where he had caught up with his son, Benjamin, who had risen to the rank of mate and was learning the intricacies of working a steamship. Then he came home to Fort Point where he lived alone for nearly a month before he called on Fanny.

She remembered that day clearly. When she went to the door to answer his knock, she did not know what to say to him. She had not heard from him in all that time, although she had word of him and knew that he was visiting his children. Her first impulse was to slam the door in his face, but too much had passed between them for her to dismiss him with such childish behavior.

"I'm back," he said.

"So I see," she answered, stepping out onto the piazza.

He hadn't changed, so far as she could see. His eyes still regarded her with that same calm admiration that always set her heart racing. His hair was as white, his stance as strong and solid.

"I've had a lot of time to think," he said.

"I should think so," she said, wanting to embrace him, but not daring to reach out to him for fear he would not take her hand, or worse, would take it and she would feel only distance and disconnection in his touch.

"Everyone is well, I hear."

"Yes, everyone is well and settled and happy, I'm glad to say."

"I didn't write."

"Maybe you didn't have anything to say."

"On the contrary, my dear, I have a great deal to say." And in that moment, he reached for her hand and led her off the piazza, across the grass, and down to the beach where the tide had just turned. She drew a deep breath and decided to say nothing. She was wise enough to know that whatever would come, would come, and nothing that she said or did had the power to alter some situations, and surely this was one of them.

"I talked to all three of my children, and I didn't leave anything out. I told them all of it, and I told them I'd be guided by what they thought," Ellis said.

Ah, here it comes, Fanny thought, withdrawing her hand from his and stepping away from him in order to brace herself for what she felt certain she would hear next.

"They weren't happy at first, but the more I talked, the more they came around to see what I was saying. And in the end, while they weren't over the moon about the idea, they felt that I should do what was right."

"And that would be?" Fanny asked icily, turning her face away from him. A breeze had sprung up, and it pulled strands of her hair out of its pins. She gazed out across the water, unable to look at him.

"A long time ago you gave me a piece of blue beach glass."

"Yes, I remember."

"Well, I've carried that glass in my pocket for years. When I was in New York to see my son, I finally decided to do something with it."

"And what was that?"

Ellis reached into his coat pocket.

"I had it set in silver and made into a ring." He closed the gap between them and took her hand. "I had it made for you with the idea that I might talk you into marrying me."

Fanny drew a sharp breath and turned her head quickly to look at him. His grin said it all, and when he opened his arms to her, she stepped into them as if he had never been away.

Now, it was late afternoon and everyone had gathered. Only the justice of the peace had yet to arrive. Fanny paced back and forth in her room, fretting.

"He'll be here, Fanny," Maude said. "He'll be here if I have to send Sam all the way to Searsport to get him."

The door opened and M stepped in. "I have something for you," she said. She held out the lace veil that she had worn at her wedding. "I know it's supposed to be the other way around—the older woman handing on her wedding finery to the younger woman. And I know you don't want to wear a veil—poetic justice, that—but I'm hoping that you will wear it as a shawl. And see, Mother added this little white satin square here in the corner and it's embroidered with your initials and Ellis's, and your wedding date, and below that, her initials and mine."

"Clever plot on your part, M. You know perfectly well I can't refuse, nor would I want to." Tears pricked Fanny's eyes, and she pulled M into her arms to embrace her. "Someday, it will be Blythe's turn to wear this."

Fanny turned to look at herself in the mirror. *Not bad for an old girl*, she thought. She was dressed in pale blue silk, a confection the Misses Merrithew had sewn from a length of silk the Havener sisters had brought from China on one of their voyages there. The lace shawl was the perfect accessory. On her head she had placed a small straw hat fixed with tiny yellow silk roses. She carried a nosegay of wild violets.

"A bride, Fanny, is always beautiful," Maude murmured, "no matter what her age."

"You wicked old lady," Fanny said. Her laughter rang out, and the smile that lit her face made tears prick Maude's and M's eyes.

"He's here!" Elizabeth said as she came into the room. "It's time."

And ten minutes later, Frances Abbott, also known all those years ago as Fanny Hogan, the notorious woman of Pink Chimneys, said, "I do," and became the second Mrs. Ellis Harding.

As Fanny and Ellis made their way down to the steamer that would take them to Boston where they would honeymoon for a week, Fanny handed her bouquet to Elizabeth. "Daughter," she said, "press this and send it to the Misses Havener. And tell them that I said there is such a thing as happily ever after."

Epilogue

M lived to be ninety years old. She died in 1942. She saw the end of the era of sailing ships and the advent of the steamship. She was shocked by the sinking of the *Titanic* and by the death of one of her grandsons in the trenches of France during World War I. She lived to see her granddaughter, Augusta, learn to fly a biplane, one of those wire-and-fabric contraptions that had no business leaving the earth. She also lived to see her great-granddaughter, Frances Maude, join the United States Navy as a registered nurse, serving in the Pacific during World War II. The logs M kept during her wedding voyage ended up in the library of a marine museum.

Madras lived to be eighty. He stayed alongshore even though he recovered fully from the injuries he had received in 1873. He worked in his father's various enterprises in shipbuilding and outfitting ships in Searsport. In summers, even after the age of sail was over, he, Abner, Sam, and Lex Nichols took parties out on the *Boreas*, sailing Penobscot Bay and making ports of call at Castine, Bar Harbor, and Belfast. Madras helped his family's shipping firm switch from sail to steam, accomplished with the help of his brother Gordon, who studied engineering and steamship navigation after he graduated from Hampden Academy. In his mature years, Gordon worked for the Cunard Lines in New York, captaining the great ocean liners back and forth across the Atlantic.

Blythe developed many interests. She learned embroidery from her grandmother, Elizabeth, sailing from her father and grandfathers, gardening from Maude, and how to run a business from Fanny. She especially adored her great-great-aunt Honoria, with whom she had a special relationship. She went to Castine Normal School and after graduation, taught school in Bucksport, Belfast, and Bangor. She met Jasper Cole, the love of her life, at a roller-skating rink in Bangor in 1895. When they married, she wore the lace veil her mother and great-grandmother had worn at their weddings. She and Jasper, a lawyer, lived in Bangor, but spent summers at Abbott's Reach and Cape Rosier.

Madras's Hawaiian son, Naihe, made several visits to Searsport while still a youth, and as a young man attended Bowdoin College, where he studied history. He returned to Hawaii and took a teaching position at Punahou school. His mother, Kapiolani, married a Japanese merchant and they were happy and prosperous.

Ellis died in 1900. Fanny died in 1902. She left Abbott's Reach to Abner and Elizabeth. Fanny and Ellis had, indeed, lived happily ever after.

Maude died in 1890 and Sam died later the same year. They were well into their nineties, living at Abbott's Reach, where they had spent their final years.

Elizabeth and Abner went, eventually, to live at Abbott's Reach in order to be near M and Madras and their family. Elizabeth wrote her memoirs, which were published as a series in a local newspaper. After that, she and Abner were in great demand as speakers at ladies' and gentlemen's clubs.

The Havener sisters became fast friends with everyone at Abbott's Reach, and with the Mitchell family. They wrote their memoirs, published by a Boston press, and became local celebrities. They never married. They became especially fond of Madras and M's children. When they died, they left all their worldly goods to Blythe, and her brothers, Lex Lancaster, Samuel Treat, and Isaiah Nichols, and her sister, Grace Frances.

The Misses Merrithew died on the same day in the same hour in their little house a few years after M's second child was born. They left their considerable estate to the town for the establishment of a marine museum, the same museum that would eventually house M's logs.

Lancaster Treat recovered and spent the rest of his days running a store in Old Town. After he and Matilda Drew married, she
continued to practice medicine. In her later years, she taught
classes in hygiene at the University of Maine. They had no children, but were frequent guests at Abbott's Reach, where they were
treated like family.

Augusta Mitchell's bad disposition improved considerably as
she was absorbed more and more by the liveliness of Madras and
M's family. She died in 1900, just as the century turned.

The rest of the Mitchell clan prospered, leaving behind them
vast troves of seafaring history, grand houses, memorabilia, and
memoirs.

About the Author

Ardeana Hamlin grew up in Bingham, Maine, in the 1950s and 1960s in the days of the river drives, the veneer mill and the woods operations. Now a newspaper journalist, she lives in Hamden, Maine, and is the author of two previous novels, *Pink Chimneys* and *A Dream of Paris*.